FIRST BLOOD

A few minutes before, the *Jaeger* had been one of Hitler's most feared U-boats, fresh from her latest devastation of Allied shipping. Now, her rudder smashed, her propellers shot off, her periscope destroyed, she was a helpless floating target despite her desperate attempts to slide below the surface.

All guns blazing, the *Wasp* moved closer to finish the job. For the *Wasp*'s orders were: Leave no traces, take no prisoners.

This was the Wasp's first testing—and the hard-bitten commander was following to the letter the motto of his mission:

"You cannot overkill."

THE SEA GUERRILLAS

From U-boats hunted in the depths of the ocean to the bloodstained decks of a U.S. fighting ship—this is the war at sea as it was, and action writing as it should be!

D1048738

The Best in Fiction from SIGNET

THE SEA GUERRILLAS

Dean W. Ballenger

A SIGNET BOOK

NEW AMERICAN LIBRARY

TIMES MIRROR

Publisher's Note

This novel is a work of fiction. Names, characters, places, and incidents are either the product of the author's imagination or are used fictitiously, and any resemblance to actual persons, living or dead, events, or locales is entirely coincidental.

Copyright © 1982 by Dean W. Ballenger

All rights reserved

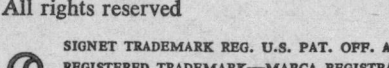

SIGNET TRADEMARK REG. U.S. PAT. OFF. AND FOREIGN COUNTRIES
REGISTERED TRADEMARK—MARCA REGISTRADA
HECHO EN CHICAGO, U.S.A.

SIGNET, SIGNET CLASSICS, MENTOR, PLUME, MERIDIAN AND NAL BOOKS are published by The New American Library, Inc., 1633 Broadway, New York, New York 10019

First Printing, March, 1982

1 2 3 4 5 6 7 8 9

PRINTED IN THE UNITED STATES OF AMERICA

Chapter One

The six-ship American convoy, zigzagging through the rolling green seas of the Atlantic between the Azores and the Strait of Gibraltar, was transporting troops and material to U. S. Forces in North Africa.

Two Fletcher Type destroyers flanked the convoy's three merchantmen and its troop transport, the former Caribbean cruise ship S. S. *Southern Star*.

For twenty-four hours, U-273, a 1,200-ton submarine of the Germans' dreaded U-Waffe, had been stalking the convoy, and now, in the impenetrable fog of dawn, she was going to torpedo the Americans.

The U-boat was the *Jager* ("Hunter"), an XX/K. unterseeboot that had sunk more than 90,000 American and British tons and killed hundreds of British and American sailors. She had a crew of fifty-one officers and men commanded by Kapitän Oskar Hasmueller, thirty-two, a wily practitioner of stealth and patience.

The destroyers' Adsic, an early and largely ineffective ultrasonic detector (known later in refined form as sonar), should have been able to detect the U-boat, as close as it was. But Hasmueller had pursued the convoy between its last and next-in-line tankers. The tumult of the hard-working screws of the heavily loaded tankers made the sound of the U-boat's propeller indiscernible.

So Hasmueller's U-boat went along with the convoy, right in the middle of it, and the Americans did not suspect it because no one but an idiot—or a fox—would put a submarine between two zigzagging ships less than 400 meters apart.

It was time to strike—before the sun burned off the morning fog which made a periscope difficult to detect, and before the convoy went through the strait into the Mediterranean, a British lake with Gibraltar at one end and Malta at the other. Sub-killing fighters and bombers were based at each of these great fortresses. They could drop their deadly depth charges on a hostile submarine before it could dive out of range.

Kapitän Hasmueller, six feet two, blond in the Teutonic tradition, his straw-colored hair cropped short, had been pacing the deck of the *Jager*'s periscope compartment. He looked at his watch again. "Up attack scope!" he barked to Seaman 1/K. Karl Schmidt, twenty-one, who was on periscope duty.

Hasmueller was biting his lips. If the fog had lifted—morning fog in the east Atlantic is capricious in March—the Americans would see the periscope. The *Jager* would have slight chance of surviving the destroyers' depth bombs.

This was a chancy game, but Hasmueller savored its risks, and its rewards. Maybe after I torpedo two or three of these *dummkopf* Americans, he reflected, Kriegsflotte will refer to me as the Sea Fox, as General Rommel has become known in North Africa as the Desert Fox.

It was a heady thought for Hasmueller, a handsome fellow except for his gray-green eyes, which were set too deeply in his Teutonic face. He shoved Schmidt aside and looked into the periscope. He saw nothing. The fog was swirling murk. He made a slight adjustment and swung the periscope 360 degrees. There was no break in the fog.

He went to the voice pipe on the bulkhead beside the navigation chart bench. He swooped up its tube and piped Torpedo Officer Edmund Reichert. "Are you ready?" he asked.

"*Jawohl!*" Reichert, who was always ready, said quickly.

"Stand by to fire," Hasmueller said.

He piped Helmsman Chief Petty Officer Martin Niemeyer. "Active position for the troop ship and any of the merchantmen."

Moments later Niemeyer came on the voice pipe. "Positioned, sir," he said.

Hasmueller piped the torpedo compartment. "Salvo six!"

Leutnant Reichert and his crew fired six torpedoes, all that were in the bow tubes of the big U-boat.

Immediately, Kapitän Hasmueller ordered flood to make up for the loss of the torpedoes' weight, then he ordered Helmsman Niemeyer to put the *Jager* into 30-degree dive. The big U-boat began its descent propelled by full power from its electro engines.

The U-boat tremored. Then again. "Were those depth bombs or our torpedoes," asked the navigation officer, Leutnant 2/K. Bodo Kessler, sitting on the stool at the navigation chart bench, his face showing concern.

"Christ, can't you tell the difference by now?" Hasmueller said. "Those were torpedoes. I was hoping for more than two hits from a six-salvo spread, but—"

The *Jager* tremored again, but not as much as the first times. "Another hit!" Hasmueller said excitedly. "*Wunderbar* . . . three ships!"

"That's certainly a major score, sir," Lt. Kessler said, "for an attack by just one U-boat. But it isn't really surprising with an officer of your capabilities planning the strategy."

You boot-licking peasant, Hasmueller reflected. Then he quit thinking about the ingratiating Leutnant. His lips became tight. The *Jager* was diving as fast as she could, but it seemed interminably slow. Not for several more minutes would the *Jager* be beyond the range of depth bombs. Hasmueller stood beside the navigation chart bench, his fists clenching and unclenching.

There were no depth bombs, and when the *Jager* was as deep as she could go without risking broken hull welds from the sea's increasing pressure, Hasmueller picked up the voice pipe's tube. "One six five degrees starboard true," he said to Helmsman Niemeyer, ". . . for 3,000 meters."

It would be dangerous to show a scope even 3,000 meters (1.86) miles from here. The destroyers' big guns and depth bombs would be a hazard of the first degree. So would aircraft from any English or American carrier that happened to be nearby.

Hasmueller had to take the chance. He had to know the damage the *Jager*'s torpedoes had done. He would need specific and confirmed information for his action report. Without it Kriegsflotte might not credit him with the sinking of the American ships.

"Bring me coffee," said Hasmueller, speaking into the voice pipe, to a rating in Commissary.

He would remain here, near the periscopes, until the *Jager* reached its destination. It would be a little while before he could assess the damage to the American convoy; in the meantime he might as well relax.

After his orderly brought the coffee he motioned Lt. Kessler, twenty-three and rosy-cheeked as a Sachsen peasant, off the navigation chart bench's stool. He sat on the stool and sipped the coffee. Whatever mischief he had done, he reflected, had been a positive contribution to the German cause. It was also another measure, perhaps the precipitating one, toward his acclaim as the Sea Fox, the ace of the U-Waffe!

"Three thousand meters, Herr Kapitän," Helmsman Niemeyer said through the voice pipe.

"Take her up!" Hasmueller said.

Soon Hasmueller was looking into the attack periscope. The fog had lifted. He could see the convoy, what was left of it, with amazing clarity. *"Wunderbar!"* he babbled, grinning. It was a *fait accompli* of the most daunting kind.

He darted over to the sky periscope, swung it 360 degrees and then back 360 degrees. No aircraft. He scooted back to the attack periscope and looked at the convoy. His grin broadened. What a score! A merchantman was missing. She had, of course, been sunk by the torpedo in her vitals. The troop ship was listing 40 degrees to port, her bow higher than her stern. Another merchantman was sinking. Her stern was already below the surface, and oil gurgled out of a great rent in her port flank.

The oil had spread over the seas surrounding the crippled convoy. Soldiers from the torpedoed troop ship, civilian seamen of the merchant marine, and Navy radiomen and gunners from the sunken merchantman were in the oil-blackened water. Some were on survival rafts, but most were sustained by life jackets.

One of the destroyers was gliding among these men, taking them aboard. The other destroyer was rescuing men from the weather deck of the rapidly sinking merchantman.

"Surface!" Kapitän Hasmueller piped to his helmsman.

The moment the *Jager* broke water, Hasmueller ordered his gunners to man their battle stations on the sea deck. They climbed the conning's aluminum ladder onto the seasplashed deck and ran to their guns; the conning tower platforms of XX/K U-boats had been extended and twin 2cm flak Vierlings, deadly four-barrel AA guns, had been mounted on forward and aft ends of the platform. Additionally a 6.5cm rifle had been mounted forward of the conning tower, between the tower and forward Vierlings.

Hasmueller climbed the conning's ladder followed by Executive Officer Ronstedt, Navigation Officer Kessler, and Chief Technical Petty Officer Kurt Schoeller. "I want each of you," Hasmueller had said to these men, "to witness the victory we have achieved for the Reich so that there will be no question about my action report."

Climbing the conning ladder behind the officers was little glasses-wearing Yeoman 1/K. Fritz Lowenbusch, who was very good with a camera. Hasmueller had told him he wanted "at least ten photos" of the torpedoed convoy.

Kapitän Hasmueller, standing on the sea deck with the officers, said, "Has each of you witnessed the damage we inflicted on the enemy?"

The officers said they had witnessed it.

Hasmueller turned to Lowenbusch. "Did you get photos? Of all of it?"

"*Jawohl*, sir," Lowenbusch said.

"Then get below!" Hasmueller ordered the officers and Lowenbusch.

He motioned for the Vierling gunners to begin fire.

His strategy was uncomplicated: Permit three officers of known reliability to witness, briefly but thoroughly, the damage to the convoy while Lowenbusch took photos, then order these men below and open fire from the Vierlings, all of this before the American destroyers could swing their guns toward the *Jager*.

The Vierlings' fire—every ninth bullet was a tracer— would ignite the oil spillage. The dense black smoke would obscure the *Jager*, which would submerge and be underway before the destroyers could get through the smoke with their deadly depth bombs. And of course their gunners would be unlikely to harm the *Jager*. They wouldn't be able to hit a target they couldn't see.

As for the Americans in the sea who would be burned to death by the flaming oil, they were ciphers in the greater drama. Hasmueller barely gave them thought.

It was a sound strategy. But the best of strategies sometimes develop cracks, and so it was with Kapitän Hasmueller's scheme.

One of the destroyers was in an area over which little oil had spread. The smoke barely reached its bridge. The destroyer came full speed toward the *Jager*, its 3-inch rifles and 40mm AA guns firing at the surfaced U-boat.

"Mein Gott!" Hasmueller croaked, staring at the approaching disaster.

Before a surfaced U-boat can dive, thirty seconds at minimum are needed to clear its deck of its gun crews, who must watertight their weapons and munitions boxes before they can run to the conning tower.

Hasmueller didn't wait the thirty seconds. He leaped onto the conning's ladder and slammed the conning's heavy steel hatch and began to secure it, at the same time bellowing for someone to order the helmsman to dive.

The *Jager* was in dive before Hasmueller put the final thrust on the conning's steel-arm lock. Too bad about those five gunners up there, all of them loyal and competent men with families back in Germany. But a U-boat captain has to consider the greater good, and in this case it's the verification and photos of the damage to the convoy.

What an impressive action report they would make!

Soon, Hasmueller reflected, smiling while he climbed off the ladder, I will be known throughout the Fatherland as the Sea Fox!

Chapter Two

At 1400 hours on 21 March 1943, eight hours after the *Jager*'s escape from the American destroyer, the big U-boat prepared to surface. She was approximately 900 kilometers southeast of the Azores' São Miguel Island, almost directly on latitude 36 north.

Kapitän Hasmueller would give his men a rest, permit them to go topside and breathe fresh spring Atlantic air. The stalking and attack on the American convoy and the flight from the destroyer had been harrowing for everyone.

The *Jager* would wait here, unless an Anglo-American plane showed up, until the submarine that serviced the *Unterseeboots* of U-Waffe Squadron 3 appeared from its secret cove on the west flank of Madeira Island with munitions, food, water, and torpedoes to replace the torpedoes that had been used in action against the convoy. The *Jager*, like other XX/K. U-boats, carried twenty-three torpedoes.

"Up sky scope!" Kapitän Hasmueller ordered his periscope watch, a grim-faced petty officer 2/K. who was embittered by the Kapitän's sacrifice of his friend Vierling Gunner Hans Koppenhauer. Hasmueller hadn't had to close that hatch so damn fast, the petty officer had said to his colleagues. Another few seconds wouldn't have made the *Jager* significantly more secure from the American destroyer. It was barbaric, dooming Koppenhauer and the other gunners to death, whirled into the diving submarine's vortex and drowning while they vainly struggled to overcome the U-boat's powerful suction.

Hasmueller was clenching and unclenching his hands, as he always did when he was apprehensive. Upping the sky scope was risky. It stirred up more white water than the attack periscope. It could be seen for miles by aircraft.

Hasmueller looked into the sky scope, swinging it over the sky, back again, then twice more. "No planes," he muttered. He motioned for the petty officer to up the attack scope, and soon Hasmueller was looking into this instrument.

Nothing on the sea's surface except a Portuguese fishing boat. *Ligia Mondego* her name was, painted in fading red letters below her starboard bow rail.

Kapitän Hasmueller strode to the electronic speaker on the bulkhead beside the voice pipe—no need of electronic silence now—and ordered the duty helmsman to surface the big U-boat.

"Gun repair crew, report to the sea deck!" Hasmueller said on the *Jager*'s PA system. The U-boat's gun repair crew consisted of Technician Mechanics 1/K. Hasso Schmitz and Karl Taggemeier, who were also the submarine's diesel tenders and ship's repairmen. They would dismantle, clean, and lubricate the deck's twin 2cm Vierling flak guns and the forward 6.5cm rifle, whose sea seals most likely had not been put into place by the abandoned gunners before the *Jager* began the dive that drowned them.

Hasmueller and his executive officer, Leutnant Ronstedt, followed the gun repair crew up the conning ladder and onto the sea-washed deck. "*Gott,* that air smells good!" Hasmueller said, breathing deeply. The air in the U-boat, though chemically washed, was fetid. It stank of human odors, the U-boat's batteries, the cooking, the heads, the diesel fuel. The combination, after hours under the sea's surface, churned stomachs and created irritabilities and shortened tempers.

Hasmueller again inhaled deeply of the pleasant spring sea air. Then he put his binoculars to his eyes. He looked at the skies, all around the surfaced U-boat, at the seas, finally focusing on the Portuguese fishing boat, which was about 200 meters, or a little more than an eighth of a mile, off the *Jager*'s starboard flank.

That floating pile of junk, Hasmueller reflected, is typical of Portuguese fishing boats. Untidy, unkempt. Not neat and orderly like German fishing craft in the Baltic. Hasmueller's lips curled with contempt. The Portuguese were a miserable species.

Hasmueller's binoculars swept over the men on the *Ligia Mondego*. Filthy, ragged *Schwein*. Stupid creatures, too; he could tell by the expressions on their dirty unshaven faces. Hell with them, they were no problem, no concern of his. He turned to Executive Officer Ronstedt. "Send the men up by sections. A half hour topside for each section. Then repeat the sequence until chow time."

During all of this, U.S. Navy Lieutenant Floyd Marlatt, twenty-eight, the boat's captain, was looking at the Germans with nonreflecting optic glasses from within the deck shack.

This was unbelievable! A U-boat popping up out of the sea practically right in front of the *Ligia Mondego*, which was really a U.S. Navy PT, a motor torpedo boat, that had been camouflaged to look like a Portuguese fishing boat.

Chief Quartermaster Steve Pollard, twenty-six, the PT's helmsman, was also in the deck shack. He was looking at the *Jager* through the 20mm Oerlikon's aperture in the shack's starboard bulkhead. "All I've got to say," he croaked, "is that looking at a real live U-boat is one hell of a lot different than talking about it up there at Gibraltar."

He looked over at Lt. Marlatt. "You know something? This cat-and-mouse the big boys dreamed up for us had better work."

"You know something else?" Marlatt said, taking the binoculars from his eyes. "We'll know damn soon if it does."

"Suppose it don't?"

"Think positive," Marlatt said.

"I can't," Pollard said. "I left my guts back home."

Marlatt handed the binoculars to Pollard. "Take a look at that Kraut captain. Then you'll realize what a service to humanity we are about to perform."

Pollard looked at Kapitän Hasmueller, at the German gun repair crew, and at the five crewmen who had come onto the seadeck. Then he looked back at Hasmueller. "Admiral Kraut," he said, grinning, "in two shakes of a lamb's tail you are not going to be such a big shot. In fact, you are not even going to be a little shot."

"That's the old spirit," Marlatt said. "Keep watching them. I'll get everybody ready."

Marlatt shuffled out of the deck house. He went to the stern, where Wally ("Cowboy") McLean, twenty-five, the PT's navigator, and Chief Petty Officer Art Schilling, thirty-one, both appearing to be ragtag Portuguese fishermen, were pretending to be preparing to lower a beam trawl—a long conical net, its mouth held open by X'd wooden beams, which is dragged along the sea's floor by a fishing vessel, scooping fish into the net.

"Get that sucker into the water," Lt. Marlatt said, "then mosey over to your battle stations. But play it cool . . . don't hurry. Act like you've got all day and that U-boat there doesn't mean a thing."

"All of a sudden," McLean said, with a wry grin, "I wish I'd joined the Army."

"You'd be in a foxhole," Marlatt said. "That's worse. Now hurry, you guys, but don't hurry."

Marlatt lit a cigarette, then sauntered to the bow, where Chief Petty Officer Russ Broughton, twenty-three, the PT's engineman and forward machine gunner, was ostensibly repairing a wooden bait box. The box was a four-wall shell that concealed the PT's forward twinned .50-caliber machine guns. "When the big gun goes," Marlatt said, "sweep that platform."

"OK. But we're going closer, aren't we?"

"You bet," Marlatt said. "Right after Haney blows their conning tower we're closing in."

"Who's driving?"

"Me," Marlatt said. "I'm taking us straight toward her middle to fifty yards."

"Then?"

"Then we'd better have the job done."

"You got something there," Broughton said grimly.

Marlatt picked up a purse seine, a cylindrical seine with a rope at the bottom which permits drawing the bottom together like the drawstring on a purse. He made a production of examining it, his cigarette between his lips, meanwhile observing the U-boat's activities. Then he carried the seine, which required both arms, to Gunner's Mate First Class Paul ("Guns") Haney, twenty-six, the PT's 3-inch rifleman, who had been leaning on the starboard rail looking at the Germans and waving to them whenever they looked his way, as though he were a friendly fisherman.

"Get at your station, Guns," Marlatt said, pretending to be showing Haney something about the purse seine, his cigarette bobbling while he talked.

"Gotcha," Haney said, taking the purse seine.

"Take your time," Marlatt said. "That conning's got to go with number one."

"Don't insult me," Haney said, with a wink. "I happen to be the best gunner in the United States Navy."

It wasn't braggadocio; Haney was scared, and so were the others. It would be their first attack in the masquerading PT and if they failed there would be no next time.

Joe Silva, twenty-eight, GM1/c, the PT's 20mm Oerlikon gunner, had already gone into the deck shack, carrying a wine bottle and staggering, which amused the Germans, who had been looking at the *Ligia Mondego* and its ragtag crew.

Immediately Silva went to the Oerlikon, quickly checked its load and firing mechanism, then sighted it on *Jager*'s conning tower through the aperture on the shack's starboard bulkhead.

Meanwhile, Pollard had been keeping his eyes on the surfaced U-boat. The Germans weren't showing any signs of action. It was, in fact, a laxity unusual for Germans.

Lt. Marlatt and Haney, carrying the purse seine, dropped it outside the deck shack's hatch and came inside, being leisurely about it, as though they had all the time in the world.

Haney went to the 3-inch rifle, made sure that it was loaded with an HE—high explosive—and that its breech mechanism was in order, and that four more HEs were on the deck beside the big rifle. "You've got it, naturally—we rehearsed it often enough," Haney said to Pollard, who would be his loader. "But just to be sure, the instant I eject, shove one of those babies into her, then immediately pull back your hands.

"Remember the hands," he repeated, "because I'm slamming that breech, and we don't need any pinkies in there."

"Don't worry," Pollard said, obviously nervous. "I want to keep my fingers."

"Everybody ready?" Marlatt asked.

"Ready as we'll ever be," Haney said.

"Let her go!" Marlatt said.

Haney pulled the big rifle's lanyard, and an instant later most of the *Jager*'s conning tower vanished in sheets and splinters of torn steel.

The firing of Haney's gun was the signal for the other Americans to open fire and for Marlatt to put the masquerading PT, which had been idling on one engine, into full speed forward with all three of her powerful twelve-cylinder Packard engines at maximum rpm.

The PT sped toward the *Jager* at an incredible 50 knots. Meanwhile Haney shot off the *Jager*'s rudder and screws with another HE, the twinned .50-caliber machine guns, mounted fore and aft, began to sweep the *Jager*'s platform, and Joe Silva's Oerlikon tore off what was left of the U-boat's conning tower, also lopping off the heads of two Germans with Schmeiser machine pistols who were coming up to aid their colleagues with whatever was going on up there on the sea deck.

Schilling and Broughton had begun firing their twinned .50s at opposite ends of the U-boat's platform, Schilling sweeping the platform from bow to stern, Broughton from stern to bow.

Kapitän Hasmueller was between the *Jager*'s forward Vierlings and the conning tower, which gave him a moment to realize that he had been tricked. *"Amerikanisch Schwein!"* he screamed, his eyes wide. *"Verdammt—"*

He never finished. The bullets from the Americans' machine guns converged just above his hips and swept on past, in opposite directions, slicing him into two grisly parts.

His torso slid off the port side of the doomed U-boat, his deep-set gray-green eyes staring as though he couldn't believe that for him the war was over.

Chapter Three

The Germans in the U-boat did not know who was attacking them. They had no way to find out. Joe Silva's Oerlikon had shot off the *Jager's* periscopes. The men who climbed the conning's ladder to see what was going on were decapitated by the Oerlikon's 20mm bullets the moments their heads rose above the shot-off conning tower's stubby base.

Helmsman Chief Petty Officer Niemeyer, proceeding without orders, tried to dive the big U-boat. The engines, their propellors shot off, raced uselessly.

The *Jager* also had no rudder. The American gunner Haney had shot it off with the masquerading PT's 3-inch rifle.

"By God, we can do something even if nobody else can!" Torpedo Officer Reichert screamed to the men of his crew.

He ordered them to salvo the torpedoes in the forward tubes, all six of them. Then he salvoed the six torpedoes in the stern tubes. "Maybe we got the bastards!" he screamed.

He ordered his men to reload; they would fire the torpedoes they had left.

One of the other officers told Reichert he was an idiot, that they were being attacked by aircraft. "It's an entire squadron . . . I can tell by the bombs they're dropping on us."

Chief Radioman Kurt Zeigler also thought the *Jager* was being bombed. He sent a message to Kriegsflotte in straight language. No time for code. After he identified his ship and gave its location he screamed, "We're being attacked by a squadron of enemy bombers. Our situation is desperate. Send help immediately. Please!"

Reichert's torpedoes sped fore and aft of the surfaced U-boat. They didn't come even close to the *Jager*'s attacker. The PT was off the starboard's midsection. She was firing all her guns at her helpless victim.

It was a savage attack. "You cannot overkill," Navy Captain John Langer had said to the PT's crew during indoctrination for their dangerous mission. "Keep in mind the proverb—I think it's Chinese—'A tiger uses all his might in attacking a rabbit.'

"Hit with everything you've got and keep it going. Don't terminate until you've deep-sixed the bastard. And then drop a couple DBs"—depth bombs—"to make sure."

The *Jager* had been no rabbit. The big heavily armed U-boat had been the tiger of the analogy. It was the PT that was the rabbit. The *Jager*—if she had known the PT wasn't what she pretended to be—could have torpedoed her to oblivion, shot her out of the water with deck guns, or dived out of range of her depth bombs.

But all that had been possible only before Gunner Haney's first go with his 3-inch rifle, with which he was a virtuoso. After that shot, which destroyed the *Jager*'s conning tower and its watertight hatch, the U-boat was doomed.

Lt. Marlatt, at the PT's helm, took his boat within fifty yards of the *Jager*'s flank before he brought the speeding craft to a stop. He ran into the deck shack and yelled to Haney, "Lay four into her waterline!"

Haney fired a 3-inch HE at the *Jager*'s battered starboard flank, at her waterline. Then he punctured her steel-plate skin three more times, going from port to starboard.

Each of the powerful shells, fired at point-blank range for such projectiles, exploded inside the *Jager*, killing her men and flooding compartments.

The *Jager* was sinking rapidly now. The sea was rushing into her through the rents in her flank. There weren't many men still alive, but Torpedo Officer Reichert was one of them. "I'm not going to drown!" he screamed.

He had always had a fear of drowning. He put the muzzle of a Walther pistol just under his left ear and pulled its trigger.

If he had waited a moment he could have died without either suicide or drowning. A torpedo in the forward torpedo compartment exploded, detonated by shrapnel from one of Haney's high-explosive shells.

The *Jager*'s steel skin bulged outward, popping rivets and welds and tearing an enormous jagged rent on the starboard flank. It was so wide that the Americans on the PT could see into her.

The sea rushed into the *Jager,* and moments later the big wounded U-boat sank with a swirling gurgle.

"We're supposed to depth-bomb her, too," Marlatt said. "To make sure."

"What for?" Gunner Haney said. "We totaled that baby. Christ, you could see right inside of her for a minute there, before she sank. Bodies and everything."

"That's right," Marlatt said, "but somebody at HQ, sure as hell, is going to say if we didn't depth-bomb that German U-boat how do we know for sure she was really deep-sixed?"

"OK, then let's depth-bomb her," Haney said. "Let's drop all our DBs on her—every one—so those chairwarmers at HQ won't worry. We don't want those jerks worrying. It tears me apart just thinking we might be the cause of some jerk's ulcer."

Marlatt didn't dig his rank into Haney. The big gunner had a case of GI nerves. Manning his gun, so much of which depended on his skill, had been a strain.

Marlatt turned to Pollard, the PT's helmsman, who was standing at his wheel, waiting for Marlatt's orders. "Take her forward," Marlatt said, "where the Krauts sank."

Pollard took the PT to the still-gurgling site of the U-boat's sinking. Bodies, fragments of bodies, and floatable debris were surfacing. "Belay the depth bomb!" Marlatt shouted to Schilling and Broughton, who had rolled one of the PT's twenty-one Torpex DBs onto the little boat's stern.

The lieutenant looked back at the U-boat's flotsam. "Bodies and junk don't float up from a functional submarine," he said to Pollard and Haney, who were looking at the *Jager*'s horrible debris.

"War is sure a beastly thing!" Pollard said, leaning on the port rail and staring at the body of Lt. 2/K. Bodo Kessler, which was floating on its back, the blue eyes open and seeming to stare at the sky.

"Take that Kraut there," Pollard said. "A handsome, intelligent-looking guy. In his middle twenties, I'd guess.

Now he's dead, and whatever he wanted to get out of life, whatever he wanted to be, it's all over for him."

"He would have killed us if we hadn't killed him," Haney said. "You have to look at it that way."

"I have to look at it that way," Pollard said, "and he had to look at it that way. Which adds up to both sides justifying killing each other . . . making it a noble, patriotic thing to do."

"Maybe my memory's slipped a gear," Haney said, "but aren't you the guy that kept that 3-incher loaded? Or did you think I was shooting seagulls for supper tonight?"

"I know what I did," Pollard said, his eyes still on the floating dead German, "and I know what that gun did to the U-boat and the guys inside of it, including this guy down there. I'll do it again, too, because the United States Navy has made me a trained, professional killer. And I don't want the Krauts to win this fucking war. But that doesn't make killing some young guy right."

"OK, OK!" Lt. Marlatt said. "Let's discuss the abstracts of the war some other time. Right now, somebody fish that book out of the water."

A large heavy-bound book had gurgled up out of the sea. Joe Silva reached out with a gaff and snagged the book. He gave it to Marlatt, who handed it to Art Schilling. "What is it?" Marlatt asked.

Schilling could read German. "It's their log," he said, turning its wet pages. "When we show this baby to the big shots at HQ there'll be no question that we . . . Jesus Keerist!" Schilling blurted.

"Jesus Christ what?" Marlatt said.

Schilling had come upon something important, no doubt of it. You could tell by the tense look on his face as he read the log's water-soaked entries.

Schilling looked over at Marlatt and the others. "Listen to this, fellas. . . . Yesterday the U-boat—its name was *Jager*, that means 'Hunter'—yesterday they torpedoed and sank a U.S. troop ship and two U.S. merchant ships."

He turned a page. "The sons of bitches!" he said, his face grim.

"What is it?" Marlatt demanded.

"The sea washed off part of their writing . . . they must've used some cheap ink . . . but . . . here's a clear part, and, man, this'll burn your ass."

Schilling began to read from the log, translating into English. " 'We ignited the oil spill with our Vierlings' tracers, which created a smoke screen. It was inadequate, and a destroyer began attack pursuit, coming through the flaming oil which was incinerating the Americans who had survived the troop ship. . . .' "

Schilling closed the log. "Can you imagine that, for God's sake . . . they set those helpless guys on fire!"

Haney turned to Pollard. "And you were feeling sorry we had to kill those bastards!"

"That's enough right there!" Marlatt said crisply. "Pollard was merely expressing a normal civilized man's revulsion toward war. We all feel the same way. It's a nasty, barbaric business. But we've got to do what we've got to do, and what we did today, according to that log, was one hell of a good thing. It has saved whatever convoys that sub would have attacked in the future . . . and the lives of a lot of men."

Lt. Marlatt looked over the rail at the flotsam that kept bobbing up out of the sea. "Let's get out of here," he said. "They might have got a radio message off, and if they did German planes could be showing up. Or a Kraut surface ship. Or another U-boat. They might wonder if we had anything to do with it, in which case we would have our balls on the barbed wire."

Pollard took a final look at Lt. Kessler's body, and at the floating fragments of bodies. Then, his face grim, he went toward the deck shack. It was a brutal thing he had helped do today. It was a brutal thing the Germans had done yesterday.

Whoever outbrutalizes the other will win this war, he reflected.

He went into the deck shack and over to the little boat's helm. Then he looked over at Marlatt, who had followed him into the deck shack. "Where we going?" he asked the lieutenant.

"Take her home," Marlatt said.

Home was Pico Cove on the eastern shore of São Miguel, largest of the nine islands of the Azores group. A volcanic overhang extended over the water. Once the masquerading PT glided under this ledge it would not be seen by Luftwaffe reconnaissance planes. Further, this retreat was sheltered from view of sea traffic by a parabolic promontory on which 7-foot wild grass grew.

17

Pollard took a feint course to the north, then coursed toward Pico Cove, but only on one engine, and that one had a muffler that made it sound like the engine on a Portuguese fishing boat that had seen better days.

Chapter Four

In the last light of dusk the disguised PT tied up at its hideout in Pico Cove on the eastern shore of the Azores' São Miguel island.

After a much-needed meal—Chief Helmsman Steve Pollard doubled as the outfit's cook—Lt. Marlatt said to the others, who were sitting around a fold-up table on the PT's bow, "I've been thinking about the fact that the U-boat we deep-sixed had surfaced and its captain was giving the crew a topside break, and that their log, which says yesterday they torpedoed one of our troop transports and two merchant ships.

"The way this comes together, at least the way I see it, they had surfaced to wait for supplies, including torpedoes, from some German ship, probably a tanker that services the U-boats around here.

"So tomorrow why don't we fish in the area of today's action, then follow the tanker home, meanwhile pretending to be dragging our beam trawl, hauling it up now and then to make everything look authentic—so it will appear to be just a coincidence that we're going in the same direction as the tanker. And then give the tanker and its depot the treatment."

This, Marlatt continued, would be a costly loss to the U-Waffe and an enormous victory for the Allies.

"I see a leak in that program," Guns Haney said. "What if the tanker identifies us and lays it on so fast we can't get into focus before we've had it? Or they pretend they don't recognize us, meanwhile radioing for a bunch of Kraut planes? It could happen, either way, because personally I think there's a chance the Krauts on the U-boat got off a yelp for help."

"I think you're wrong, Guns," Marlatt said. "I doubt like hell any of the U-boat bunch were able to send a message identifying us. The sea-deck Krauts got aced in

Act One. The crew in the U-boat, the men inside of it, never got a look at us. The ones who tried got their heads blown off."

"Maybe," Art Schilling said, "one of them got a peek and didn't get his head separated from the rest of him. He could have got a quick peek—that's all it would take—then ducked down and Silva's bullets just parted his hair. It could have happened. We don't know for sure that Silva got every one of them that tried to look over what was left of their conning. You can bet they tried. They must have been curious as hell who was attacking them."

"I'm pretty sure I got all of them," Silva said. "I concentrated on the conning after I took care of the periscopes. I don't see how any of them could have seen us and lived to talk about it. I was chopping that conning's stub down an inch at a time, back and forth, and if my 20s didn't give the guillotine treatment to anybody trying to peek, the pieces of steel from the conning would have done it."

"But still," Silva continued, "I won't one hundred percent guarantee nobody inside that U-boat saw us. I don't see how they could have, but it's possible, I suppose. Anything is always possible."

"If that's the case," Haney said, "Kraut planes or U-boats or surface craft could be waiting for us to stick our neck in the noose by going out there, in that same water. They wouldn't have to know for sure it was us that deep-sixed the U-boat, but they might figure here's a fishing boat in the area and we don't see any others around here so this one has to be the one."

"You've got a point there," Marlatt said. "But it's a chance we're going to take. This whole assignment is a risk. But we all knew what we were getting into, and each of us had a chance to turn it down. But we didn't. So now, when we've got the possibility of scoring real big we're going to take a crack at it."

Their mission was, indeed, a risk. It was one of World War II's most dangerous, most exciting, and least known adventures, and it had its inception in the U-Waffe's costly and frequent sinkings of Allied shipping in the east Atlantic.

Hitler had imposed upon the Deutschen Kriegsmarine, the German Navy, an order to blockade the United Kingdom and to prevent American and British convoys from carrying arms to British forces in North Africa.

The Germans' goal: 800,000 Allied tons per month. Added to the sinkings of this enormous tonnage would be the deaths of hundreds of skilled merchant-ship sailors and Navy men of the convoys' escorts.

The German Navy, long accustomed to a peripheral role in the German armed forces, saw an opportunity to excel in Hitler's orders. Admiral Karl Doenitz, Kriegsmarine's Chief of U-boat Operations, changed tactics of most of the U-Waffe (submarine) branch of the German Navy from independent free-hunt forays against Anglo-American shipping to teamwork attacks.

Convoys transporting civilian and military supplies to England and to the beleaguered British forces in Africa were torpedoed, with astounding success for the Germans and devastating losses for the Allies.

Attacks on U-boats by the destroyers that escorted the convoys were mere pinpricks. Improved escort methods did little good. The frightening facts were clear: The Germans were achieving a substantial victory.

As if the attacks by the U-Waffe's wolfpacks weren't bad enough, almost simultaneously Allied shipping suffered a double blow in the spring of 1942. The Americans virtually withdrew their escorts from Anglo-American convoys; American destroyers, frigates, gunboats, and other convoy escorts were needed for the war in Asiatic waters.

A greater blow, though unknown to the Anglo-Americans for costly months to come, was the fact that U-boats acted on intelligence messages after German cryptanalysts broke the British convoy cipher.

The tonnage of Allied shipping reaching Europe plummeted. At the same time the Germans improved their unterseeboots, making them faster, arming them more heavily, and giving them longer cruising capabilities.

It became clear to the Anglo-Americans that the war could not be won, and in fact might very well be lost, if the U-boat attacks continued undiminished.

This low ebb in the Anglo-Americans' fortunes was attributed not only to the Germans' prowess but in a big part to the determination of Portugal's dictator, Dr. Antonio Salazar, to continue his little nation's neutrality—a resolve which made a Nazi lake of the area of the North

Atlantic bounded by the Azores Islands, the Iberian Peninsula, and the northwest coast of Africa.

It was almost impossible for Anglo-American carrier planes—the only aircraft with access to the sanctuary—to bomb its surfaced U-boats. The Germans' Naxos gear gave warning of the approach of hostile planes so far in advance of their appearance that the U-boats had time to submerge beyond range of bombs and depth charges. Meanwhile the carriers were still in grave peril of Nazi torpedoes.

During this bloody era of U-boat supremacy, American technicians were trying frantically to develop a submarine detection device which, if it worked, would enable Allied ships to know if submarines were in the vicinity. This would end surprise attacks. The U-boats would no longer be the wolves of the sea. Allied ships would no longer be the rabbits of the sea.

But development of this device, which was to be known as sonar, was frustratingly slow. The concept was by no means an innovation. It had begun at the end of World War I in a joint effort between English and American technicians known as Adsic, an acronym for Allied Submarine Detection Investigation Committee.

Adsic was to be an ultrasonic impulse detector which could pick up echoes from impulses sent out by the apparatus. It did not achieve the results expected of it, and until the beginning of World War II it had been largely forgotten.

But now, with urgent need for such a device, American technicians were working around the clock to make it functional.

Meanwhile, while sonar was being developed into a dependable submarine detection system, something had to be done to neutralize the dreaded U-boat attacks on Allied shipping.

American war strategists came up with an audacious scheme, one of the war's true long shots—equip a Navy PT boat with special U-boat-killing weapons and disguise it to look like a Portuguese fishing boat right down to "the last little detail."

The crew of this boat—seven carefully selected U.S. Navy men—would pretend to be fishing in the U-boat's sanctuary. When the Germans' vaunted *Amselrudel* ("blackbird wolfpack") surfaced, they would attack and destroy it.

The wolfpack of nine U-boats was a predatory outfit commanded by Kapitän Gerhard von Seggern, ace of the U-Waffe. His flotilla was the dread of Allied shipping and the pride of the German Navy.

After the *Amselrudel* was destroyed, American planners reasoned, the Germans would be almost psychotically wary of each of the more than 10,000 Portuguese fishing boats in their sanctuary. This would present the Germans with the option of sinking every Portuguese fishing boat their ships and planes came upon, which would surely put Portugal on the Allied side of the war, close the U-boats' sanctuary, and establish Allied air strips in Portugal from where U.S. and British planes could patrol all of the Atlantic coastal waters.

Or, exercising another option, the Germans could attempt to intimidate the Portuguese government into withdrawing its fishing boats from all but immediate coastal waters, which would be a disaster for Portugal's economy and would most certainly be rejected by the Portuguese people.

It would not be a pleasant choice for the Germans, but somewhere out there would be an American U-boat killer which looked exactly like 10,000 legitimate fishing boats.

The American military and State Department strategists who had conceived this scheme calculated that U-Waffe's fear of the masquerading PT would cause the Germans to withdraw their U-boats from the sanctuary until the situation could be resolved with the Portuguese government. During this period of withdrawal and negotiation it was hoped that development of sonar would be completed.

A nice scheme—if everything fell into place.

U.S. Navy Captain John J. Langer, Deputy Commandant, Azores-Gibraltar (AG) Sea Frontier, headquartered at Gibraltar, was appointed field chief of the project, which was to be known as Operation Sting.

Captain Langer, forty-two, was a rough and wily strategist. "I want PT men who have been in action," he said. "One combat engagement teaches more lessons than a year of training.

"Each man will have his duty station in line with his specialty, but he must also be able to fill in for any of the others. So he's got to know gunnery, engine repair and op-

23

eration, basic navigation, helmsmanship . . . the whole program.

"And at least one of these guys has got to be able to speak fluent Portuguese."

While U.S. Navy's BuPers (Bureau of Personnel) was searching its files for such men, Captain Langer requisitioned a unit of PT Squadron 9, based in the Gulf of Tunis, for the masquerade.

The PT was a 66-Class 77-footer with a plywood hull. She was armed with four 21-inch tubes, twinned .50-caliber machine guns in turrets, a single 20mm Oerlikon, eight depth charges, and a smokescreen generator.

There was nothing like it in the German Navy. She was powered by three Packard-built twelve-cylinder engines capable of short bursts of 55 knots and a service speed of 40 knots.

"I want this baby rigged to be the fightin'est little devil there ever was," Langer said, "and I want her to look like a Portuguese fishing boat from every angle."

The deck and other externals of the PT were altered at the Gibraltar naval yard to duplicate the quaint, medieval style of Portuguese fishing boats, even to a baleful Eye of God on her bow.

A 3-inch rifle and an M6 Oerlikon were installed in the interior of the pilot house, which was enlarged and rebuilt to look like the jerry-made deck house of a typical Portuguese fishing boat.

The torpedoes and their tubes were removed. The .50-caliber machine gun turrets were concealed by false bait boxes. Provisions were made for the concealed storage and fast launch of twenty-one 500-pound Torpex depth charges. Everything was camouflaged to resemble the apparatus of a fishing boat.

Meanwhile, from PT flotillas in South Pacific coves and from Flotilla 2 at Tunis a crew of seven PT veterans were flown to Gibraltar. The altered PT's regular crew was nine; the gained space would be utilized for the Torpexes, other munitions, and fuel.

"I'll lay it out in cold-ass English," Captain Langer said to the recruits. "You're here for one purpose—to be trained to attack and destroy the German U-boat Navy's blood-eating *Amselrudel*, which is a Kraut word meaning 'blackbird wolfpack.'

"They're the biggest of the Germans' wolfpacks, which

means a bunch of U-boats under a single command that hunt and kill together. Those U-boats, the way they're sinking our ships, are going to win this war unless we can destroy them. Which is why you men are here."

Langer explained the masquerade. Then he said, "You must have resolution, coolness, and skill, in that order.

"When you get out there and you see a surfaced U-boat, hit her fast and hard. First, blow off her conning tower so she can't dive. That's a job for the 3-inch rifle. Meanwhile—this is for the Oerlikon—blow off her attack and air scopes, which will leave her blind.

"Then blow off her ass—her rudder—so all she can do is turn in small surface circles, and her screws so she can't move at all.

"Then finish her off, and after she sinks go right on top of her vortex and depth-bomb her.

"There must be no cessation in the intensity of your attack and no concern about survivors, because there will be no survivors.

"Your job will be to sink U-boats and kill their crews, and if your heart is going to bleed for some Kraut Navy man on a U-boat's sea deck—maybe some young guy who looks like your kid brother back home—speak up right now and we'll send you back where you were, because I want that German and all the rest of them deep-sixed!"

The masquerading PT's captain would be Lt. (jg) Floyd Marlatt, twenty-six, a tough little crewcut who had been a PT skipper in Squadron 6 at Port Salamaua in New Guinea.

Marlatt was five feet six and somewhat stocky. His nose had been broken in Golden Gloves, and it tilted to the left. His lips were full, and he had a square jaw. His hair was dark brown. His eyes were deep brown, almost black, and they penetrated.

His voice was authoritarian, but he was a fair man and his crews liked him. His language reflected the Mississippi riverfront background of his boyhood; he was the fourth son of an East St. Louis dragline operator who'd had a hard time supporting his large family.

Marlatt had been a tug captain when the draft caught him. Because of his occupation he was assigned to the Navy, and after boot camp he was sent to the PT training center at Melville, Rhode Island, and later for combat training to Miami, where he was commissioned.

"Captain Langer," he said, "are we going to be the only PT on this assignment?"

"The one and only," Langer said.

"Sir, since obviously one PT—no matter how much luck we have—can't do much more than give the U-boat fleet a kick in the balls, there's more to this mission than we've been told, isn't there?"

Captain Langer, hands on his hips, a cigarette bobbling from the corner of his mouth, said, "Your job, Marlatt, will be to kill U-boats. Not to ask questions. Got it?"

"Yes, sir," Marlatt said. "I've got it."

Marlatt and his men decided to call their boat *Wasp* because of the nature of her missions. Though this was the same name as the Navy's aircraft carrier CV7 (torpedoed while covering a convoy near Guadalcanal on September 15, 1942) and later CV18, an Essex Class carrier, there was little probability of confusion in Navy society. Few aside from Marlatt and his crew would know their boat had been named *Wasp*; officially she was PT-169 (66E).

In subsequent days, Marlatt and his crew were indoctrinated in the life-styles and procedures of Portuguese fishermen. "You've got to look like Portuguese fishermen, you've got to fish like them," Langer said, "because you'll be looked at by U-boat people with binoculars. And if they suspect you're phonies you won't even have time for one Hail Mary."

Marlatt and the others completed their preparations for the masquerade on March 7, 1942. "I have confidence in your ability and resolve to do this damn dangerous job," Langer said, "but there is one thing you must know. If all of you are lost—and this may happen—your loss will be the equivalent of one PT and its crew, a gnat in the scope of the U.S. Navy. But if you succeed, you will save many merchant ships and American and English lives. Your successes may very well change the course of the war and its duration."

To test the masquerade, the *Wasp* and its crew accompanied a bonafide Portuguese fishing flotilla in the Gulf of Cádiz for four days. During this time Joe Silva, twenty-four, the outfit's Portuguese-speaking member—a former San Diego tuna fisherman—masqueraded as the PT's captain, speaking the language of his history to men on the other boats, none of them suspecting that no one else on the disguised PT spoke Portuguese.

26

The shakedown masquerade was a success. "If you can fool real 24-karat Portuguese fishermen," Captain Langer said, "the Germans sure as hell won't catch on."

The crew was ready now to begin its deadly work. "I want you men to get some blood-and-bullets practice before you tackle the wolfpack," Langer said. "Go out there and kill three or four free-hunt U-boats. You'll get the feel of the business, besides doing some good while you're practicing.

"Then attack that wolfpack!"

Chapter Five

Six days after Lt. Marlatt and his doughty little crew sailed from Gibraltar on the masquerading PT, they attacked and sank the XX/K. U-boat *Jager*. The morning after this exhilarating first victory they glided out of their refuge in Pico Cove on São Miguel island in the Azores. They intended to stalk and kill the German tanker for which, they reasoned, the surfaced U-boat had been waiting.

A little after 1300 hours they came to the site of the U-boat's sinking. There was no debris on the cold March Atlantic's rolling surface. Winds during the night had drifted it away; fish had devoured the bodies of the dead Germans.

Cowboy McLean and the PT's Oerlikon gunner Joe Silva, both unshaven and wearing ragtag garments of Portuguese fishermen, began to lower a purse seine into the sea. Meanwhile Steve Pollard, the masquerading outfit's helmsman, who had the sharpest vision of all of them, swept the seas in methodical 360-degree scans with a non-reflecting optic glass while he stood in the deck shack, its camouflaged apertures permitting views in all directions.

Two hours elapsed. Marlatt had come into the deck shack to relieve Pollard. He held out his hands for the powerful glasses. "I think I saw something!" Pollard said, keeping the glasses at his eyes.

He kept looking at the sea's rolling green surface. "What is it?" Marlatt asked impatiently, a little apprehensively.

"I think I saw a sub's air scope," Pollard said, keeping the glasses at his eyes. "In fact, I'm sure it was an air scope. No fish in these waters that I ever heard of cuts a straight surface course."

"Let me look," Marlatt said, reaching again for the binoculars.

"Not right now, sir," Pollard said. "I don't want to lose my bearing."

He kept looking. Then he blurted, "An attack scope's coming up!"

"Jesus . . ." Marlatt said, his tongue flicking over his lips. In this water it would be a U-boat. Had its crew been alerted by the *Jager*? If it had, that unterseeboot out there was preparing to attack the PT. Maybe they wouldn't surface to attack. Maybe they'd torpedo the PT. Right now it was possible the German torpedo officer . . .

Marlatt came out of it. This was no time for reflection. "What's the bearing!" he demanded.

Still looking at the sub's scope, Pollard said, "About 160 . . . make it 170 . . . east northeast."

"Don't lose her!" Marlatt said. "We're going to attack!"

He darted out of the deck shack. "General quarters!" he yelled. "A Kraut sub's 170 off our starboard bow!

"Prepare to depth-bomb!"

Everybody knew what to do. They had practiced it often enough, and now, in a real situation, no one panicked.

McLean hurried to the PT's powerful engines—one was always kept on idle—and revved it and the other two engines to full speed. The little boat practically leaped out of the water while Pollard, at the helm now, sped her forward and then starboard in a great sea-slicing arc toward the U-boat's periscope.

Meanwhile Silva had sprinted into the deck shack and over to the 20mm Oerlikon. At his heels, Haney ran to the 3-inch rifle. Behind them was Marlatt. On the stern Schilling and Broughton were loading the depth charge's thrower.

The U-boat was the *Schwangerfrau* ("Pregnant Woman"), a bulbous S/K. supply submarine whose function was to bring fuel, munitions, water, food, and torpedoes to surfaced submarines of U-Waffe Squadron 3. She wasn't sleek and fast, as attack U-boats were. She was fat and slow and heavy.

She had received a message in Kriegsmarine code from the *Jager* after the U-boat's attack on the Anglo-American convoy. The *Jager* would surface here, on latitude 36 north, the message had said.

The *Schwangerfrau* had raised her air scope first to see if Allied aircraft were in the area. The big fat supply submarine was vulnerable to enemy aircraft. Her rate of dive was so slow that even a distant bomber could be on her before she could reach a safe depth.

Kapitän Werner Zimmerman, the *Schwangerfrau*'s CO, had personally examined the skies through his boat's air scope. He trusted no one but himself for this important duty. He had seen too many *unfahig* officers during his long career in the U-Waffe. *Verdammt* incompetents! This was no time, no craft, for incomplete observations. This was a time to know for sure that the skies were safe.

They were. Zimmerman waddled to the attack scope. He was grossly overweight. He looked like the *Schwangerfrau,* or the *Schwangerfrau* looked like him, the men at the secret cove where the supply sub was based said of him when he wasn't within hearing range.

He swept the scope 360 degrees, slowly reversed it, then did it twice more. He was a cautious man. No enemy ship was going to attack his command; before he surfaced he always made sure the seas were safe.

Nothing but a Portuguese fishing boat. No sign of the *Jager.* This perplexed Kapitän Zimmerman. If the *Jager* had been diverted to another mission, why hadn't she informed Squadron 3's HQ?

Zimmerman was thinking on this when suddenly and with incredible speed the fishing boat leaped up like a hungry herring, turned on a sea-cutting parabola, and sped toward the big U-boat.

"*Mein Gott!*" Kapitän Zimmerman screamed, sweat breaking out on his porcine face. That was no fish boat. That was some kind of enemy war boat. "Down scope!" he bellowed to the periscope watch, a youthful seaman 1/K. who had stood aside to permit the kapitan to use the scopes.

Zimmerman spun toward the glasses-wearing Leutnant at the navigation chart bench. "Tell Kreutzer to dive!" he bellowed. "Immediately! Full speed!"

On the *Wasp,* Joe Silva was firing his Oerlikon 20mm rifle at the *Schwangerfrau*'s receding scope. Meanwhile Haney lobbed two 3-inch high explosives aft of the scope, and below the sea's surface. His objective: to blast sea-drowning punctures in the U-boat's steel skin.

Both gunners missed their targets. The U-boat was submerging, the *Wasp* was on the arc of its parabola, the seas were rolling four-footers. The misses were understandable.

Then the *Wasp* was over the U-boat, on top of her.

Broughton and Schilling triggered the depth charge thrower and two 500-pound Torpex bombs arced into the sea.

The murderous bombs straddled the U-boat and sank beneath her before they exploded. The big U-boat rocked like a child's bathtub toy. Water seeped into her through broken welds and twisted seams.

"Damage repair crews . . . man your stations!" Kapitän Zimmerman bellowed, his fat face red from the terror of the situation, sweat oozing down from his face onto his duty uniform.

He swooped up the scope compartment's voice tube. "Dive faster, damn you!" he screamed to Helmsman Kreutzer.

"Sir, I'm diving as fast as I can!" Kreutzer replied.

Zimmerman slammed the voice tube's speaker into its cradle. His deep-set blue eyes sparked his fear. *Mein Gott,* he reflected, they'll be back with more of those depth charges and we're diving too slowly to be out of their way.

Meanwhile there wasn't a thing he could do. Just stand here and wait to be killed. Blown to bits by a depth charge, or blown out alive and drowned. Damn those sneaky Americans up there! They were Americans, no doubt of it. The British were too stupid to think of such trickery.

The *Wasp* was back now, right on top of the U-boat. Broughton and Schilling laid two big Torpex eggs onto her.

"Oh, Jesus . . ." Kapitän Zimmerman croaked. One of the depth charges had struck the conning tower. The other had hit the sea deck just above the scope compartment, only a few feet above Zimmerman's head.

The depth charge detonated, bursting great gaping holes in the *Schwangerfrau*'s steel flanks. The Torpex shrapnel hurtled into the *Schwangerfrau*'s interior, just ahead of the incoming sea, mangling men and equipment and ripping on through bulkheads into other compartments.

Kapitän Zimmerman died quickly, a plate-size shrapnel going through his chest, exiting between his shoulders, and tearing through the bulkhead back of the navigation chart bench.

A Torpex shrapnel struck the detonator of one of the *Schwangerfrau*'s forty-two torpedoes. She had no tubes herself; her torpedoes were replacements for combat U-boats.

The torpedo exploded, setting off the others. The *Schwangerfrau* disintegrated in a gigantic orange burst that fragmented its still-living men and blew out its flanks like a stick of dynamite in a tin can.

It was like an underwater volcano. The sea seemed to explode. Great torrents of water, bloodied by human gore and laced with slivers of the big U-boat, went skyward.

Great waves rippled out from the explosion's vortex. They swept over the *Wasp*, rolled her almost onto her port flank, and washed Russ Broughton off the stern.

"Jesus Keerist . . ." Pollard babbled, gripping the helm.

The welfare of the *Wasp* and the lives of its crew were in his hands now. "Gotta keep her out of a trough," he muttered, biting his lips. "If we get in a trough we're dead!"

Basic navigation . . . keep your ship out of a trough in rough seas or the sea may capsize her. Keep her at right angle to the waves! Watch those troughs!

Pollard was a skilled helmsman, and the *Wasp*'s engines were powerful. The combination saved the little PT from becoming a corollary victim of its attack.

The *Wasp* was out of danger now, but debris from the *Schwangerfrau* rained onto her, along with thousands of gallons of water that the U-boat's exploding torpedoes had blown skyward.

The horrible shower ended. Schilling, who had been on his knees beside the depth charge thrower, his arms around its steel shafts, leaped up and ran toward the deck house. "Broughton got washed overboard!" he screamed. "We gotta find him!"

No one else had known of the big engineman's disaster. "Start circling . . . a little more each time!" Marlatt shouted to Pollard.

Pollard began circles, using one engine, because more would make the *Wasp* go too fast. The other men leaned on the deck rails looking for Broughton.

"He could still be alive, couldn't he?" Schilling said, glancing at Marlatt and then back at the sea.

"I don't know how he could be," Marlatt said, his face grim.

"I wouldn't be so sure about that," Joe Silva said, his eyes scanning the sea. "I've been on boats in squalls where somebody got washed overboard three times. The guy was still alive. The next day they were up and at it like nothing had happened."

"God, I hope that's the way with Russ," Schilling said. He and Russ Broughton, who had been a Ford mechanic in Kansas City, had gone through boots together at the Great Lakes Naval Training Station, where they had become friends. They had been buddies afterward, wangling assignments on the same PT flotilla at Port Darwin in Australia.

Haney was the first to see the missing man. He was floating on his back. "I'll get him!" Silva said.

He didn't wait for Marlatt's approval. He kicked off his shoes and dived off the port bow. He swam to the floating man. Broughton didn't seem to be alive. He wasn't breathing, not, at least, as far as Silva could tell here in these rolling seas. But maybe he wasn't dead. Sometimes you couldn't tell for sure.

As fast as he could, Silva trundled Broughton back to the *Wasp*, being careful to keep the sea out of his mouth and nostrils.

Marlatt and Haney lifted Broughton onto the *Wasp* and laid him on its forward deck.

"For chrissake," Silva wheezed, climbing onto the deck, "don't just look at him! Start working on him!"

Immediately Haney rolled Broughton onto his belly, straddled him, and pressured his lower ribs.

An unbelievable quantity of water flowed from Broughton's mouth and nostrils. "That's all the water," Silva said, still breathing heavily. "Flip him over and start mouth-to-mouth!"

Haney rolled Broughton onto his back. He put his mouth over Broughton's mouth and closed his nostrils with a thumb and forefinger. He breathed into Broughton's mouth, raised Broughton's head, closed Broughton's mouth, opened Broughton's nostrils. Then he did it again, and again and again.

"It's no use," Schilling said. "He's dead."

"He might not be," Silva said. "Sometimes it takes a long time."

Haney kept it going. Broughton blinked his eyes. Then he began to breathe. "Better keep helping him," Silva said. "We quit too soon one time there in California."

A little later Broughton looked around at the others. He sat up. "What happened?" he croaked.

He didn't understand, for a little while, why everybody laughed so happily.

Moments later the *Wasp* was wallowing on a feint course to Pico Cove. Higher speed would surely cause a periscope-watching U-boat or Luftwaffe planes to become suspicious, because Portuguese fishing boats were notoriously slow.

Marlatt's lips were taut while he swept the sea with his binoculars. Several of the facades that had made the PT appear to be a fishing boat had been damaged by the waves that had washed over her, and by the drenching downpour of water and debris from the explosions of the *Schwangerfrau*'s torpedoes.

If an alert U-boat periscope watch carefully observed the *Wasp* he could not fail to see that she was a very strange fishing boat.

Marlatt's face was grim. It would be a raw-nerve run back to Pico Cove, but speed, as tempting as it was, would be an invitation to disaster.

Interminable hours elapsed. But no U-boat watch, if any observed the *Wasp*, and none of the crews of the eight-plane squadron of Luftwaffe Goering Z-6 fighter-bombers which flew over the *Wasp* at 2,000 feet saw anything about the wallowing little boat worth investigating, and, in the last light of dusk, the *Wasp* glided into its sanctuary at Pico Cove.

Marlatt and Silva rigged up deck lights, and Pollard began to prepare a meal. "God, I'm hungry," Haney said.

"Me, too," McLean said. "But fifty percent of it is nerves. Christ, I thought we'd never get here."

"I wouldn't have bet we'd make it," Marlatt said. "Because right now we don't look a whole hell of a lot like a Portuguese fishing boat. But apparently no Kraut scope watch saw us, or if they did they were so far away they didn't see what we didn't want them to see."

"We must have looked all right from the air," Silva said, "or those Nazi planes wouldn't have kept on going."

"You know how long we'd have lasted if they'd attacked us, eight of them coming at us from all sides?" McLean said.

"I thought about it," Marlatt said, his face grim. "I've been thinking about something else, too. The way that U-

34

boat exploded, it was no ordinary U-boat. Not even a fully loaded attack boat. It must have been a supply sub. It probably had enough torpedoes in it to restock three or four attack boats."

"That was some explosion, all right," Silva said. "It blew a hole in the ocean you could actually look into, for a minute, there."

"Such a fragmentation of the submarine and its crew," Marlatt continued, "is pretty conclusive proof that it was a supply submarine, it seems to me."

"Well, all I've got to say," Haney said, "is, it damn near got us, too."

"You can say that in spades," Silva said. "I thought for a minute me and Jesus were about to shake hands."

"Did you have any idea it was a Nazi supply boat?" Haney asked the *Wasp*'s tough little CO.

"Of course not!" Marlatt said, his near-black eyes boring into Haney's eyes. "How the hell would I have known what it was? All anybody saw was an attack scope."

The lieutenant's eyes narrowed. "What are you getting at, Haney? Are you trying to say something? Like I'm such a gung-ho son of a bitch I'd have ordered depth bombs even if we might get blown up in the package?"

"No, sir," Haney said, dropping his eyes. "That isn't what I meant. I was just wondering, is all, if you knew what it was."

"Christ, man," Marlatt said, "you must have left your brains in your sea bag."

He turned away. No point in pursuing this dialogue, he had decided. It was a stupid thing Haney had implied. Besides, it was time to eat. Pollard, who was a better helmsman than a cook, had prepared hamburger steaks, fried potatoes, bread and orange marmalade, and coffee, which he had spread onto a fold-up table on the little boat's bow.

"Now hear this!" Pollard said, a grin on his long bony face. "Lay down to the forward galley! On the double!"

Marlatt smiled. It was good, after so harrowing an experience, to hear this mockery of Navy protocol.

He and the others, including Pollard, sat around the table. "You could have cooked this thing a little longer," Haney said, looking at his meat, into which he had cut with his knife. "It looks like some of those hamburgered Krauts we washed off the deck."

"Sit down and quit thinking about it!" Marlatt said.

"I can't," Schilling said.

Marlatt turned to Pollard. "Give Schilling's meat another go on the fire. And while you're at it, cook mine some more, too."

"Mine, too," McLean said.

The rest of the meal was eaten in silence, and afterward, after Silva drank his third cup of Joe, he said, "I feel better now. My nerves aren't jumping all over the place."

Everyone felt better. "You guys that got a case of hard-mouth, how about shaking hands?" Marlatt said. "We've got a rocky road ahead of us, and, on this mission, everybody needs everybody else. If we've got to be P.O.'d at somebody, let's save it for the Nazis."

Hands were shaken and apologies were offered. "Fellas," Marlatt said, filling his cup with coffee, "if any of you want to kick my ass for not realizing that the Krauts might send a supply sub out there instead of a surface ship, and then ordering DBs on her, go ahead and kick it."

"None of us had it put together," Pollard said. "So don't lay it on yourself, Mr. Marlatt. Besides, like I read somewhere, 'All's well that ends well.' "

"That's the way to look at it," Haney said. "Everybody got back and nobody got hurt, so everybody's happy. Right, guys?"

"Right!" everyone said, all of them meaning it.

"Thanks, men," Marlatt said with deep sincerity. He had worried that his miscalculations might cost the cohesions, if not the loyalties, the *Wasp* would need for future hunts—most especially when their free hunts ended and the masquerading PT attacked the dreaded German U-boat wolfpack.

In that terribly uneven battle every man's utmost effort, coordinated with every other man's maximum skill—and a hell of a lot of luck—would be needed.

Surviving the attack would require even more luck. It would be like a feisty little terrier attacking a pack of fierce Dobermans. The outcome, most likely, would be the same, the lieutenant reflected, his lips tight.

Thinking on this while he sat at the fold-up table on the *Wasp*'s little bow, he said, "Pollard, under the emergency food rations is a rolled-up bait seine. And inside of this

36

rolled-up bait seine is a bottle of Ancient Age. Bring it here. With seven drinking glasses."

While his crew sat around the fold-up table, Marlatt poured the quart of bourbon whiskey into seven equal portions. "Not that I'm complaining," Schilling said, licking his lips while he watched Marlatt pour the whiskey, "but I thought drinking alcoholic beverages on a U.S. Navy craft was strictly against regs."

"Fuck regulations!" Lt. Marlatt said, lifting his glass.

"Fuck regulations!" everybody else said, raising their glasses.

Chapter Six

The morning after the *Wasp* returned to Pico Cove, an Algorma Class oceangoing tug, the *Dauntless* (43-B), 375 tons, chugged into the cove.

She was bringing provisions for the *Wasp*: Torpex depth bombs, HE and incendiary shells for the *Wasp*'s 3-inch rifle, cans of ammo for its 20mm Oerlikon and its four .50-caliber machine guns, gasoline for the three Packard-built twelve-cylinder engines, four 5-gallon containers of distilled seawater for drinking and cooking, food, cigarettes, and candy.

The *Dauntless* also brought matting, plywood, paint, and other material to repair the camouflages the violent seas caused by the incredible explosion of the *Schwangerfrau*'s torpedoes had damaged, or washed entirely off the masquerading PT.

All of these supplies were in response to Marlatt's report to Azores-Gibraltar Sea Frontier in GB Code by Chief Schilling, the *Wasp*'s radioman, at the beginning of the *Wasp*'s return from its sinking of the Nazi supply submarine.

"I don't suppose it's any of my business what you guys are doing with this PT jazzed up like a Portuguese fishing boat and armed like a DE," the tug's affable young captain, Lt. (jg) Warren Graham, twenty-four, asked Lt. Marlatt.

"We catch fish for the officers' mess," Marlatt said, grinning.

"That's what I thought," Graham said with an even bigger grin.

It was none of his business. He shouldn't have asked. But whatever it was, his duty as skipper of this wallowing little tug—the delivery boat for the Albemarle Naval Supply Base on the other side of São Miguel island—appeared to be a healthier if not as heroic a way to serve the U.S. Navy.

"Well, good luck," Graham said. "See you in Sunday school."

He motioned to the helmsman in the wheelhouse and the *Dauntless* began a parabolic exit out of the cove.

The *Wasp*'s crew spent the next two days refurbishing the PT's camouflages, Silva telling how they should be done, and being a perfectionist so that when they finished, the PT once more looked like an authentic Portuguese fishing boat.

Silva was an indispensable part of the masquerade, because he spoke Portuguese. If a German U-boat captain or someone on a Nazi surface ship hailed the *Wasp* in Portuguese it would further the masquerade if someone on the little boat could understand what was said and respond in the Portuguese language. It was important, also, to have a Portuguese-speaking crewman in the event that the masquerading PT encountered the crew of a bonafide fishing boat.

Silva was a small man, about five feet four. He "looked Portuguese," as indeed by heritage he was, though he had been born and reared in California. He was articulate, and he had been gifted with an affable and outgoing personality. His left cheek had been scarred by a gaff hook in a hassle on a tuna boat five years before, and this deep scar had become his most distinguishing physical feature.

He was one of the *Wasp*'s best men, Lt. Marlatt had decided early in the game. He was intensely patriotic, he despised Nazis, he got along well with the other men, and he was a virtuoso with the *Wasp*'s 20mm Oerlikon, a murderous weapon in the hands of so skilled a gunner.

Six days after the refurbished *Wasp* wallowed out of Pico Cove, she came upon a surfaced U-boat on an unruffled sea 120 miles north of Madeira, an island between the Azores and Morocco.

The Nazi submarine was U-515, the *Seetotschlager* ("Sea Killer"), a much-cited unit of the U-Waffe captained by twenty-eight-year-old Oberleutnant Erwin Kreissler.

Kreissler, six feet one, craggy-featured with piercing green eyes that were too close to his nose, a wide mouth, a chin that jutted, and crewcut hair the color of ripened hay, was the son of the police president in Hildesheim, a

39

medium-sized city in north-central Germany. From him he had learned the significance and importance of order and service to the government. "There must be rules and the rules must be enforced," Polizei Prasident Kreissler had impressed upon his son.

According to Kreissler senior, the world's ills, especially the Reich's, could be attributed to the sinister part played by Jews and Freemasons. "The American president, Roosevelt," he said, "is a Jew whose real name is Rosenfeldt."

Erwin Kreissler had become, like his father, a martinet and a fanatic for the Nazi cause. His father had been right; without order and discipline, nothing succeeds. As for the Anglo-Americans, they were the stupid, unwitting tools of international Jewry. The more he killed the better for the Reich.

Two days before the *Wasp* came upon Kreissler's surfaced U-boat, her periscope watch had seen a 2,000-ton APD transport off Portugal's Cape São Vicente. She was a Worthington Class auxiliary of the Royal British Navy. She was transporting surgical equipment, whole blood, medical supplies, and fourteen nurses of the Third Florence Nightingale unit of the Combined Royal Medical Corps to Philippeville, a seaport on Algeria's Gulf du Nord, from where they would be dispersed to Anglo-American field hospitals.

The periscope watch, Seaman 1/K. Hans Neidemeyer, summoned the officer of the day, Leutnant Martin Hegmann, to the periscope. After a brief look, Hegmann, who had been a Germanic languages instructor in a Hanover *Mittelschule* before the draft, went to the bulkhead voice tube and summoned Oberleutnant Kreissler.

Kreissler looked at the transport, at the seas in all directions, and at the sky. Then he looked back at the transport. She was painted white. She was flying flags of the Red Cross. She had no armaments.

Kreissler strode to the bulkhead speaker. "I want a tube check!" he said to Torpedo Officer Bodo Schulz, twenty-seven.

"All tubes rigged for firing, sir," Schulz replied immediately.

"Stand by to fire bow tubes," Kreissler said.

The firing order would be 1-3-2-4, he continued. He ordered his navigation officer, Kurt Seltzer, to give him the

Seetotschlager's bearing in relation to the English ship's position. Then he ordered his forty-one-man crew to action stations.

"But sir," Lt. Hegmann said while Kreissler went back toward the sea scope, "she's an unarmed mercy ship. According to the Geneva Convention—"

"Never mind the Geneva Convention," Kreissler said, grinning as he always did before a kill. "That was nothing but an international conspiracy to keep Germany weak and under the thumb of Jewry. Just keep in mind that any Anglo-American ship we sink, regardless of its class or mission, furthers the cause for the Fatherland."

Kreissler had come to the scope. He shoved Neidemeyer aside and looked into it. His grin broadened. He could see nurses on the port bow. "I hope some of those ladies survive," he said, his eyes on the scope's lens.

"Why?" Lt. Hegmann asked.

"Why the hell do you think why?" Kreissler said, bringing the scope's cross-wire sight on the mercy ship's stern, away from the nurses. "Have you been at sea so long you have forgotten what it's like to make love to a woman?"

"Of course not, sir. But raping a prisoner of war—"

"Who said they're going to be prisoners of war, donkey? After we solace ourselves with them we'll . . . uh . . . consign them to the deep."

"Jesus Christ, sir . . . you mean we'll kill them? In cold blood?"

"You do catch on," Kreissler said, swinging the scope slightly to starboard. "Now shut up!"

A moment later Kreissler said, "Fire one! Fire three!"

His face became tense. This business of waiting to see if his torpedoes had struck their target was always nerve-wracking. "Dammit!" he muttered, observing that torpedo one had missed its target. "Fire two!" he barked.

A smile creased his craggy face. Torpedo three had struck the mercy ship just aft of amidship. It exploded in a kind of bestial grandeur. Great fragments of decking, plating, and bulkheads flew skyward along with the bodies of suddenly killed crewmen, nurses, and corpsmen. Then great orange-red flames spewed up out of the horribly wounded ship.

Torpedo two made its murderous strike while the carnage of Torpedo three was still airborne. It had hit the

41

doomed ship 20 meters forward of the first torpedo's penetration.

Its explosion blew more plating, equipment, and bodies into the crisp morning air. Then its flames shot skyward, horribly burning the airborne bodies, and men and women on the ship who were in the vicinity of the penetration.

The ship lurched sharply to port. Quickly her stern began to sink. "Take us down 70 meters and forward 1,000 kilometers!" Kreissler shouted into the scope's voice tube.

He stepped back. "Down scope!" he said to Seaman Neidemeyer.

It had been a despicable attack and of no real consequence, a flouted violation even of basic humanity, but Kreissler was smiling happily. Another score for Germany! Another score for Oberleutnant Kreissler. No medal for this one, he reflected, lighting a cigarette. And only a Good Service medal for the last one, an American troop transport which the *Seetotschlager* had torpedoed in the Strait of Gibraltar right under the noses of its destroyer escorts.

More than 400 Americans had died. Four hundred damned Americans who had not lived to kill German soldiers!

When the diving U-boat reached a depth of 70 meters (230 feet), a level beyond which her hull could not with certainty withstand the hydrostatic pressure, Kreissler announced over the U-boat's PA tubes, "We'll coast here for a short while. Meanwhile, all hands and all officers, except Ensign Rustedt and the other men of hydrophone watch, will stand with bowed heads and repeat with me the Lord's Prayer."

Oberleutnant Kreissler, like his police president father, was convinced beyond the slightest doubt that God was on the Germans' side and that, in truth, Germany was God's country. Therefore, in his reasoning, it was fitting and proper to express gratitude for the victory he had just achieved for Germany.

He began to intone the prayer. Kreissler's a bloodeater, a religious fanatic and an all-around son of a bitch, Lt. Hegmann reflected while he mumbled the words of the venerable Christian prayer. How can that animal recite this beautiful prayer after murdering helpless men and women . . . and planning to rape the nurses who survive?

". . . forgive us our trespasses . . ." Kreissler said, his

eyes piously closed, his right hand gripping the voice tube's speaker.

You murdering, blasphemous *Schwein,* Leutnant Hegmann reflected, no longer saying the words of the prayer. How can you stand there, with a church-door look on your ugly face, and ask the Lord to forgive you for the premeditated slaughter you have just done, while up there on the sea's surface noncombatants are drowning and dying of injuries and burns that you have caused them to suffer?

The prayer ended. Kreissler looked at his watch. Twenty minutes since he had ordered dive. No depth bombs. No sounds of the propellors of American or British destroyers or other combat ships. He picked up the voice tube again. "Anything?" he asked Ensign Rustedt.

"Nothing at all," the hydrophone officer replied. "Except the sinking of the torpedoed ship. She went down 130 meters aft of us, as I calculate it. She broke up at 90 meters."

Kreissler put the tube's speaker onto its cradle. He took another cigarette from his shirt pocket. "We will wait twenty more minutes before we surface," he said to Lt. Hegmann.

A lascivious expression swept over his stern Teutonic face. "I hope at least one of those nurses is alive up there. And I hope she isn't some old hag."

I hope they're all dead, Lt. Hagmann reflected. I feel sympathy for those who might still be alive. After my saintly, heroic captain satisfies his lust he'll kill the poor devils.

"How do you intend to execute them, sir?" he asked Kreissler.

"Hell, I don't know. I haven't thought about that part. For chrissake, put it into perspective, Hegmann!"

"Jawohl," Hegmann said.

Chapter Seven

Oberleutnant Kreissler ordered his crew to surface the U-boat where the British ship had been when he torpedoed her.

He told Hydrophone Officer Rustedt to listen carefully for the slightest indication of a lurking American or British destroyer, a command that was unnecessary, because Ensign Rustedt was one of the U-Waffe's most competent hydrophone men.

Navigation Officer Seltzer began an ascent, taking the *Seetotschlager* in an 180-degree arc, then toward the surface site of the U-boat's latest victim.

Kreissler was tense. His lips were tight, which, with his long hook nose and his protruding chin, made him look like a Black Forest witch, Lt. Hegmann reflected.

This was a time of maximum peril. Enemy destroyers or other ships with depth bombs could be lurking up there, their engines shut off, their electrical facilities silent . . . no fans, no running motors, no radios, no phones, communications by whispered voice tube.

Kreissler took the speaker off the bulkhead beside the navigation chart. "Hear anything at all?" he asked Rustedt.

"No, sir. Nothing!" the hydrophone officer said.

"Any indication of planes up there?"

Kreissler worried that an enemy bomber, or even a squadron, might be circling overhead, waiting for the U-boat to come up out of the sea. "No sign of aircraft," Rustedt reported.

"You positive? God, man, if there's just one plane up there the son of a bitch could kill all of us. Just one bomb could do it."

"Sir," Rustedt pleaded, "I'm personally listening for even the slightest indication of the enemy. So are my men. Now please, Oberleutnant, let me resume without interruption. I'll inform you, if anything shows up."

Kreissler slammed the speaker into its cradle. "Goddam peasant!" he muttered, his teeth clenched. Commission one of those donkeys and they use every credible opportunity to be insubordinate, he thought.

"What's the word, sir?" ex-schoolteacher Hegmann asked.

"What the hell's it to you?" Kreissler snarled.

"Quite a hell of a lot, sir," Hegmann replied. "It could be said we're all pickles in the same jar."

He's right, Kreissler reflected, his ugly face grim. The intelligent little bookworm is always coming up with some smart parable you can't refute because of its logic. "No sign of anything," Kreissler said.

"I hope not," Hegmann said.

"What do you mean, you hope not? All at once do you think you know more than the best hydrophone officer in the whole U-Waffe?"

"No, sir, of course not," Hegmann replied. "I was merely expressing the thought that the Anglo-Americans, the Americans especially, are ingenious rascals. They may have invented some way of circumventing our detection devices."

"I suppose you think I didn't think of that!"

"No, sir. I know you thought of it," Hegmann said, wishing he hadn't brought up the subject. Kreissler was a mean bastard at his best. When he was apprehensive, as he was right now, he was insufferable.

Soon Kreissler was looking through his attack scope. He swung it 360 degrees, then back, and once more. "Nothing," he said, "except the survivors and some flotsam."

"Any nurses among the survivors?" Hegmann asked, hoping there were not.

"Shut up! You're making me nervous with your stupid questions!" he barked, darting over to the air scope. He scanned the skies, 360 degrees, back and around again. Then he picked up the electronic speaker. No need now for the less efficient voice tube. "Surface!" he said. "All hands surface stations! Deck gunners, prepare to man your weapons!"

The *Seetotschlager* surfaced, the Atlantic's green waters breaking off its conning and deck platform. Chief Gunner Karl Scheidt, waiting on the conning's ladder, swung open the hatch lock and pushed the heavy steel hatch open, and he and the big U-boat's six other deck gunners ran to their weapons—two twinned four-barrel 2cm flak Vierlings, a 6.5cm rifle, and two twinned Kluge machine guns.

With precision teamwork they removed the watertights from the guns and ammo boxes and loaded the weapons. Meanwhile, behind the gunners, Oberleutnant Kreissler, followed by two burly seamen 1/K.s with Schmeiser machine pistols, had run out onto the platform.

Kreissler's eyes glided over the sky, then the sea, turning 360 degrees on his heels while he looked, his face showing his apprehension. Then his tautness vanished. He had seen nothing indicating the enemy's presence.

He took his first comprehensive look at the transport's survivors. Eleven floating dead bodies, four face-up, the others with their stupid English faces in the water. Seven warm bodies, three of them females. The women, sustained by vest-style life jackets, were clutching the bed of a surgical table whose padding kept it afloat. The men wore life jackets. Two were clasping hands. The other two floated alone, but all of them were within 20 meters of each other.

The survivors looked with terror at the Nazis on the U-boat's platform. The aft machine gunners had swung their terrible weapons toward them. "They're going to kill us!" quaked Nurse Lydia Cathcart, twenty-two.

"They won't kill us. They'll rescue us," said Anesthesiologist Laura Thomas, thirty. "The Geneva Convention forbids the killing of prisoners of war. Besides, the Germans aren't barbarians. That's all just propaganda."

"I'm scared," babbled General Nurse Irene Carroll, twenty-four. "Germans are so cruel."

"I would venture they are no more cruel than our own fighting forces given the same circumstances," Nurse Thomas said. "War is a brutal endeavor. But quit worrying, Irene. Germans are civilized. We'll merely be taken prisoner and, no doubt, transported to the nearest prisoner-of-war camp."

Kreissler looked at the women through binoculars. Three of them. Just right! One for him, one for the other officers, one for the enlisted men. I'll take the blonde with the pushy mammaries, he decided. She's got a pretty face, too, though that is of small consequence.

The lecherous Nazi turned to the seamen who had accompanied him onto the platform. "I want those women brought back here unharmed."

"Yes, sir," beefy, ruddy-faced Seaman Max Scheier said. "But what about the others?"

He indicated the male floaters. "Don't worry about them," Kreissler said. "Just carry out your orders! And hurry it up. This is enemy water, and the quicker we submerge the better!"

"Yes, sir," Scheier said, crisply saluting.

Stupid peasants, Kreissler reflected, watching the seamen begin to remove the deck gig, a small paddle boat, from the hasps which secured it, keel upward, paddles underneath, to the platform aft of the forward Vierling.

Kreissler went to the forward Kluge gunner, Otto Buchmeister, a burly, square-shouldered former Solingen cutlery factory foreman. "Shoot everybody except the women around that floater," he said. "I don't want them just dead. I want them in pieces so small that small fish can eat them."

The recovered body of an obviously executed survivor would create problems, he reasoned. The English and the Americans were addicted to abstracts that had no place in war. The provisions of the Geneva Convention concerning prisoners of war, for example. A German warrior took a realistic point of view: Prisoners of war, like wounded men, were a liability.

"What are you waiting for?" Kreissler demanded, glaring at the Kluge gunner.

"Sir," Buchmeister said, "I can kill a thousand men in combat and not blink an eye. But those men, Oberleutnant, are totally helpless. Killing them will not be an act of war, but an act of savagery. Can't we take them prisoner, sir?"

"If you aren't a poor excuse of a German fighting man!" Kreissler bellowed. "Get out of my way, you weak-livered bastard!"

He shoved Buchmeister so violently the gunner nearly fell off the platform. He sighted the twinned machine guns on one of the floating men and pulled its trigger, swinging the Kluge's muzzles back and forth across the doomed man's chest.

"Mein Gott!" Buchmeister croaked.

The terrible fusillade of bullets had severed the Englishman into two hideous parts. The lower part sank into the sea. The upper part fell backward on the water, held afloat by the life jacket. Kreissler fired at it, lacing it with the twinned machine gun's bullets until nothing remained but a horrid red blob on the rolling green sea.

"Now do the same to the others!" Kreissler said, turning to Buchmeister. "Shoot them until only tiny fragments remain!"

"Yes, sir," Buchmeister said, his face grim and ashen.

It would be an atrocity of the first degree, but what could an enlisted man do when an officer issued a direct order? He would be executed if the order was given under war conditions and he refused.

Buchmeister aimed the Kluge at another floating man. At least, he reflected in the instant before he pulled the trigger, the poor guy won't live long enough to suffer.

The British nurse, Lydia Cathcart, witnessing the atrocities, shrieked, "They're going to kill us! Oh, God . . . !"

"No . . . they want us alive!" Nurse Carroll said, pointing toward the approaching paddlers.

"I don't understand it . . . I don't understand it at all," Nurse Thomas said, looking at the Kluge's third victim, and then at the men in the *Seetotschlager*'s little gig.

The last of the male survivors had been fragmented before the seamen came to the nurses. "Get the boat in," Seaman Scheier said in understandable English.

"No!" Miss Cathcart babbled. "No! I won't!"

"What are you going to do to us?" Miss Carroll quaked.

Thomas said nothing. It was all too shocking, too unbelievable. Germans were civilized. They wouldn't slaughter helpless men. But they had, and it was all too much for her.

"It looks as if there's going to be a little more to this project than old Horseface figured on," Scheier said, speaking German to the other seaman, Luther Kestel.

"Well, we've got to bring them back or he'll blow his fuse," Kestel said.

"*Ja*," Scheier said, glancing back at the U-boat and observing that Kreissler was on the platform looking at them. "We'd better hurry it up, too, or the bastard will piss in his pants."

He held out a hand to Cathcart. "Get the boat in," he said, "or I will schlagen you the paddle mit!"

The terrified nurse held out her hand. Scheier lifted her into the little boat. Carroll, sobbing uncontrollably, extended a hand, and the big seaman lifted her out of the water. Then Scheier reached out for Thomas. She grabbed his hand, and he pulled her into the boat. "I demand to talk to your commanding officer," she said. "Take me to him at once!"

"What did she say?" Kestel asked the other seaman.

"I didn't get all of it. I only had two years of English in *Oberschule* there in Eisenstadt, and I wasn't the best student there ever was. But I think she said she wants to see our lovable commandant, Oberleutnant Kreissler."

"I hope she kicks him in the balls," Kestel said, paddling toward the U-boat.

"The one with the straw hair is a real nicely put-to-gether woman," Scheier said, looking at Surgical Nurse Cathcart. "Especially in a wet dress."

"I've noticed. But I wouldn't push the other one out of my bunk," Kestel said. "She's got bumps in all the right places, too."

Both men glanced at Nurse Thomas. "I've seen sexier-looking beanpoles," Kestel said.

"Sometimes that kind are the best lovers," Scheier replied.

"That's what I've heard," Kestel said. "But I have often wondered why the beanpole types always have ugly faces. Like this one here, for example."

Scheier said he had wondered about that, too. "There must be some connection between a pretty face and a pretty body."

"What are you two talking about?" Nurse Thomas demanded. "I think it's about us, the way you keep looking at us."

"Nicht verstehen sie Englisch," Scheier said.

"You're lying! You spoke it a moment ago . . . as atrocious as it was!"

"Shut your mouth up!" Scheier said.

"She reminds me of my mother-in-law," Kestel said.

He looked over his shoulder. "Well, here we are. At the end of our heroic rescue mission."

The paddlers had come to the U-boat. "Get up!" Scheier said to Nurse Cathcart, indicating that the frightened little nurse should climb onto the U-boat.

Soon the other women were on the platform. The seamen pulled the boat onto it and began to secure it to its hasps. Meanwhile the gunners put the watertights on their weapons and their munition boxes, and in less than a minute everybody was off the platform, Scheier had secured the conning's hatch, and the big U-boat had begun to submerge.

"Frauleins," Kreissler said to the nurses, "you have nothing to fear. You will merely be interrogated. I will interrogate you." He indicated Lydia Cathcart. "And you"—he pointed to Irene Carroll—"will be interrogated by the other officers. And you"—he nodded toward Thomas—"will be interrogated by the enlisted men."

"What kind of interrogations?" Nurse Thomas demanded.

The biological kind, Oberleutnant Kreissler explained, winking at the officers and enlisted men.

Chapter Eight

Two days after Oberleutnant Kreissler and the other men of the *Seetotschlager* began their interrogation of the English nurses who had survived the U-boat's torpedoing of their unarmed mercy ship, the U-boat surfaced on a calm sea between the Azores and Morocco's west coast.

This was where they would execute the English women, Kreissler had decided. This part of the Atlantic was deep and far from the nearest land; a properly weighted body would not surface and drift ashore.

The interrogations of the pretty blond surgical nurse, Lydia Cathcart, had taken place, frequently and with great zeal, on the bunk in Kreissler's private compartment.

The other officers, except Leutnant Hegmann and Oberleutnant Alex Stoermer, had drawn cards for the raping order of the other pretty young nurse, Irene Carroll. The enlisted men, except four who were repulsed by such bestial mistreatment of prisoners of war, shared anesthesiologist Laura Thomas's charms, drawing cards in order of rank—chief petty officers first, 1/K.s second, and so on, so that Apprentice Machinist's Mate Willie Hausner, the *Seetotschlager*'s only nonrated man, was the last to rape the unpretty, flat-chested English woman.

"I want nothing to do with these atrocities," Lt. Hegmann had said. "It's not that I'm a prude, or wouldn't take advantage of an opportunity to screw such a pretty girl under other circumstances, but this is a blatant violation of even basic human decency."

The former schoolteacher particularly resented Kreissler's use of the word "interrogation" when, indeed, he meant "rape." "Such a euphemism, a shallow pretense that indicates innate guilt, appalls me," he confided to his friend Alex Stoermer, the U-boat's executive officer. "It denigrates the German Navy's Officer Corps."

"You're taking a higher-flown look at it than I am,"

said Stoermer, thirty-two, a former Dresden architect. "I keep thinking about my pregnant wife, Ilse, and our three kids. I couldn't do that to Ilse. I think too much of her."

The rapes had ended with fat, unwashed Willie Hausner, taking advantage of his last opportunity with Nurse Thomas on the enlisted men's mess table, while the others stood around and cheered and made wagers about how long he would last.

The U-boat had surfaced. The nurses, naked, their hands lashed behind their backs, had been brought onto the *Seetotschlager*'s platform.

"Lash a 6.5cm shell to the legs of each of them," Kreissler said to Seaman Max Scheier.

"For God's sake!" Lt. Hegmann said, having come topside out of morbid curiosity. "Why don't you shoot them first? *Mein Gott,* drowning them is the ultimate atrocity!"

"Either keep silent or go below," Kreissler said, his lips curled in contempt. He could not understand why Hegmann hadn't shared in the raping of the officers' nurse. "How did such a freak ever get into the Navy?" he had asked another officer.

"Maybe he left his balls at home," the officer said.

This had provoked guffaws from Kreissler and the other officers.

"I will say no more," Hegmann said, his lips tight.

He didn't want to go below. For some reason he couldn't define, he wanted to watch how his bestial commandant disposed of the English nurses.

Scheier, aided by another seaman, wrapped a copper wire around a 6.5cm shell, just below the flange of its casing, then wrapped the wire around Thomas's legs. "You animals," she sobbed. "You insufferable, bestial animals!"

It is a son of a bitching thing I'm doing, Scheier reflected. I hope she drowns quickly. He got to his feet. "This one is ready, sir," he said to Kreissler.

"Well, then throw her overboard! Don't just stand there telling me she's ready!"

"Yes, sir," Scheier said, his lips tight.

It would be an act of decency, a gift to humanity, if he were throwing his sadistic commandant overboard instead of this unfortunate woman, he reflected.

Very quickly, because he couldn't bear to look into her eyes, Scheier darted behind the doomed nurse, swept her up, and flung her out into the sea.

She sank immediately. "Prepare the next one!" Kreissler said.

"Which one, sir?"

"I don't care. Just get on with it!"

Irene Carroll, so confused she didn't know what was going on, was next. Then Lydia Cathcart, the pretty young woman whom Kreissler had interrogated so often, and exclusively. Tears streamed down her face. She was mumbling a prayer. "God be with you," muttered Scheier, who had not participated in the rapes, just before he flung her off the U-boat's platform.

"Well, that is that," Kreissler said, leaning on the platform's rail. "God, this fresh morning air smells good." He lit a cigarette. "I'm hungry. Bring me a couple sandwiches."

Such constant screwing, he said, had been debilitating.

"Of course," he continued, looking over at Lt. Hegmann, "it wasn't screwing. It was interrogation. That's what I wrote in the log, and I would take a most unpleasant view of your future, if indeed you had a future, if you were to tell anyone at Kriegsflotte, or anywhere else, that our interrogations of the English prisoners were . . . uh . . . somewhat unconventional."

"I have no intention of mentioning the affair," Hegmann said grimly. "I prefer to forget it, to pretend that it didn't happen, that it was a nightmarish dream. But I am curious, Herr Oberleutnant—how did you enter their departures in the log?"

"According to the log, which entry I made preceding the recent incidents—right after breakfast, in fact—I, in my charity, surfaced so that the nurses might breathe a little fresh air, the fetid stink of a submarine nauseating them. But then, suddenly and totally unexpectedly, they leaped overboard and tried to swim away."

"You should have been a writer of commercial fiction," Hegmann said drily.

"You haven't heard all of it, Leutnant. Before we could lower our gig to recapture them the poor creatures were attacked by sharks. And devoured."

"And naturally you felt bad about it," Hegmann said, "and reproached yourself for having brought them onto the platform, not suspecting for even one moment that they would try to escape, because they had no reason, having been treated with the utmost kindness. And so forth ad nauseam."

The oberleutnant glared at the little officer. "Hegmann, you revolt me."

Hegmann didn't tell Kreissler what he would liked to have told him. Men had faced a firing squad for less.

Kreissler was leaning on the platform's starboard rail eating a braunschweiger-and-cheese sandwich, watching his deck gunners lubricate the 6.5cm rifle's hydraulic apparatus, when the *Wasp* came over the horizon.

He had known of its approach. Ensign Rustedt, the *Seetotschlager*'s hydrophone officer, had reported the proximity of a Portuguese fishing boat. The sounds of its engine had been easily identified. It was nothing to worry about. The waters between the Azores and the coast of Africa teemed with the decrepit little boats.

"It's a lucky thing for those Portuguese," Kreissler commented to his gunnery officer, "that they didn't show up while the English nurses were . . . uh . . . escaping."

He would have ordered the total destruction of the fishing boat and its crew, he continued. "Under no circumstances would I have permitted the witnessing of the escapes."

As befitted a Nazi who considered himself a "pure Ayran," his blood unpolluted by that of inferior species, he looked upon Portuguese as lowly in the ranks of mankind. "They are the mongrel products of sexual relations between the Caucasian inhabitants of the Iberian Peninsula and the Moors who invaded the peninsula, the Moors themselves being a species of Negro. As a result, the Portuguese are a miserable race."

He looked at the approaching *Wasp* with binoculars. His lips curled. "Untidy, stupid *Schwein*," he said, the binoculars sweeping over the masquerading PT's littered deck and its ragtag crew, and the Eye of God on its bow. "Superstitious fools," he muttered.

He lowered the binoculars and resumed his attack on the sandwich. Nothing to worry about. Not from that bunch of slothful Portuguese fishermen.

He could hardly have been more mistaken. Lt. Marlatt, wearing a tattered turtleneck sweater, obviously well-worn denim pants, and cheap canvas shoes, was looking at the

54

Seetotschlager with nonreflecting optic glasses through the cabin's 20mm rifle aperture.

Marlatt sauntered onto the deck, a cigarette dangling from his lips. "We're easing up real close," he said to the other Americans. "Keep right on pretending, and act nonchalant. But stay on top of your stations, because when we cut loose we're giving those Krauts the whole program."

"Gotcha," Chief Russ Broughton, the *Wasp*'s engineman and forward machine gunner, said, lolling beside the bait box that was actually a wooden shell concealing the boat's forward twinned .50-caliber machine guns. "How close we getting?"

"Right up where we can smell their sauerkraut," Marlatt said.

He looked over at Art Schilling, the aft machine gunner, who was pretending to be repairing a beam trawl. "Ready?" he asked.

"Ready and waiting," Schilling replied, his face tense.

"The first go from Haney's gun and you guys go," Marlatt said, the cigarette bobbling. "And lay it on good."

"Gotcha," Broughton replied.

"Yeah," Schilling said, his lips tight.

Marlatt stretched his arms over his head, yawned, and sauntered back into the cabin.

"Those simpletons don't even know a war's going on," Oberleutnant Kreissler said to his executive officer, Leutnant Stoermer, who had come up onto the platform.

"Who's better off?" Stoermer said drily.

"Aren't you philosophical all at once!" Kreissler said. "You've been associating too much with Hegmann!"

"I have nothing to say, sir," Stoermer said.

"You make me sick," Kreissler said. He looked back at the *Wasp*. She was very close now. So close that Kreissler waved to its crew before he resumed his assault on the sandwich.

"How are you fellas?" Silva said in Portuguese, waving at Kreissler and the others on the platform.

"What did he say?" Stoermer asked.

"Well, how the hell would I know? Do I look like I spoke that mongrel's language?"

"No, sir," Stoermer said dispiritedly. He wondered, as he had wondered many times in the past seven months, what he had done to deserve assignment to this lout's command.

"How we doing?" Lt. Marlatt, inside the cabin now, asked Guns Haney, who was sighting the *Wasp*'s 3-inch rifle on the *Seetotschlager*'s conning, and Joe Silva, who had gone into the cabin and was at the PT's Oerlikon rifle.

"Any time," Haney said, his face grim.

"I'm set!" Silva added tensely.

Marlatt looked out at the surfaced U-boat. "Go!" he said.

Haney pulled the big rifle's lanyard. Its high-explosive projectile tore into the U-boat's conning; its explosion, inside the conning, blew fragments of steel onto the men on the platform and down into the compartment below the conning, killing four of the U-boat's crew.

The shrapnel that flew out onto the platform, part of it from the powerful shell, part from the conning's splintered wall, killed five Germans. One was Oberleutnant Kreissler. A huge splinter of the U-boat's conning ripped through his chest. His suddenly dead body fell over onto the rail, head and arms hanging toward the sea, blood and gore from his ghastly wound dripping down onto them, and on into the sea.

At the same instant that Haney fired the 3-incher, Silva shot off the U-boat's air and attack scopes with a burst from the *Wasp*'s Oerlikon, blinding the attacked submarine, continuing his gun's murderous sweep over to the conning, sawing back and forth, effectively keeping anyone from climbing up to see what was going on, at the same time reducing the conning to a splinter-edged stub above whose level any German would suffer the sudden loss of his head.

Swiftly and with practiced efficiency, Haney, the 3-incher reloaded, had mangled the *Seetotschlager*'s rudder, making it totally useless. On his third go he put a projectile through the U-boat's skin at waterline, then another and another.

Meanwhile, Silva kept swinging the Oerlikon's muzzle across the conning. Fragments and ricocheting projectiles danced around in the compartment below the conning, mangling the already dead bodies of the first-killed Germans, killing others who entered the compartment, destroying its periscopes, communications equipment, and chart bench.

During these attacks, Broughton and Schilling were sweeping the U-boat's platform with bursts from their twinned .50-caliber machine guns. Executive Officer Alex Stoermer, standing beside Kreissler, was one of their victims. He lived long enough to see Kreissler's sudden and gory death, and then the *Wasp*'s gunners began their sweeps. In his last brief moment he realized the truth of the Portuguese fishing boat, that it was not a fishing boat but an artfully camouflaged and heavily armed enemy attack boat. Probably an American PT boat, was his last thought before the crossfire machine gun bullets laced his chest.

Lt. Hegmann, pouring himself coffee in the officers' wardroom, thought an aerial bomb had struck the *Seetotschlager,* followed by an attack from American or English fighter planes. "Dive!" he shouted into the speaker he swooped off a bulkhead.

There was no response. The electronic communication system had been destroyed. "I'll use the voice tube!" he said aloud.

They were his last words. A 3-inch projectile ripped through the U-boat's hull and exploded in the officers' wardroom. Hegmann was mangled.

Seaman Scheier lived a little longer. He was chief of the starboard aft damage control party. Aided by another man, he was reaching up to secure an overhead fissure between riveted platings when the sea burst into the compartment, quickly drowning him and other seamen.

There were no living Germans on the platform, only mangled bodies. The conning had vanished. The big U-boat was listing to starboard and rapidly going down by her stern.

"Cease fire!" Marlatt signaled the gunners in the deck shack, running outside to signal the machine gunners.

"Think we need to Torpex her?" Broughton asked, getting up from his twinned machine guns.

"Well, we're supposed to," Marlatt said, looking at the U-boat, whose bow was sticking up almost vertically from the sea's gentle but bloodied surface. "So let's drop a four-spread."

This time he said, they wouldn't be as stupid as the last time, when their depth-bombing of the Nazi supply sub had almost destroyed them in the explosion of the U-boat's torpedoes. "This time we'll drop them on the run, then get the hell out!"

The *Seetotschlager*'s bow had vanished. Great gurgles

came up, spewing debris and bodies. "Belay the depth bombs," Marlatt said. "We couldn't kill that U-boat any deader with a hundred Torpexes!"

"For chrissake, Marlatt," Silva shouted, "one of 'em's still alive!"

Everybody looked in the direction of Silva's pointing arm. A German was flailing the sea. "Go over to him!" Marlatt said to Helmsman Pollard.

Moments later the *Wasp* was beside the German. He was moaning. He had no eyes, only empty burned-out sockets. Most of his nose was gone. His moans were piteous. "Shoot the poor bastard!" Marlatt said, turning to Silva.

"No, sir, I can't!" Silva said. "I'm sorry, sir, I just can't!"

A strange thing from a gunner whose murderous weapon had just killed an indefinite number of the U-boat's crew. But that had been a legitimate operation against an enemy. This would be murder of a helpless and grievously wounded man.

Marlatt ran into the deck shack and came back with a .45-caliber Colt service semi-automatic pistol. He leaned over the rail and fired twice at the agonized German.

He turned back to his men. "It was an act of mercy," he said.

"Nobody said it wasn't," Pollard said, his face grim.

Chapter Nine

Lt. Marlatt looked over the rail of the masquerading PT at the body of the German Navy man he had just killed.

"He wouldn't have made it," Pollard said, his face grim. "You did the right thing, ending the poor devil's agony."

"I'll put your gun away," Schilling said, taking the .45 pistol from the lieutenant's dangling right hand.

He went toward the cabin with the .45, intending to replace the bullets that had killed the Nazi, then put the gun back into Marlatt's belt holster, which was suspended from a nail on the bulkhead just inside the hatch.

"Don't beat yourself," Haney said. "It was an act of humanity. That guy wouldn't have made it anyway, and he was suffering terribly. Jesus . . . you could look right into his head where his eyes used to be. Imagine how it must have hurt with seawater in there. Not to mention his other hurts. You did the right thing, Mr. Marlatt."

Marlatt turned toward his men. He looked at the camouflaged deck shack and at the little boat's other deceptions. Nothing had been damaged during the sudden and fierce attack. "How's our ammo?" he asked.

"I've got plenty of big bangers," Haney said. "Enough for another go."

"I only used a third of the Oerlikons," Silva said.

"We're OK," machine gunner Broughton said. "In real good shape. We've got way over half. I'd say close to two-thirds."

"Well, then," Marlatt said, "let's find us another of Mr. Hitler's big iron fish and . . ."

He hesitated before he continued. "Maybe you guys would feel better with some other skipper. I chickened out there for a minute."

"You didn't chicken out," Haney said. "You just showed us you're a decent guy." Haney looked around at the others. "Right, everybody?"

"Right!" all of them said, each man meaning it.

Marlatt took a Camel from a pack in his pants pocket and made a production of putting a match to it so no one would see the tears that had misted in his eyes, although he fooled no one, then said, the cigarette bobbing between his lips, "First, we'd better get the hell away from here."

He looked over the sea, and at the sky. "Do you suppose there was any chance they got something out on their radio?"

"I would sure doubt it," Silva said. "I got their scopes the first thing. Nobody from the platform got inside. Nobody inside got out. So I don't know how the ones inside could possibly know what was going on."

"But the radioman might have lived long enough to report some kind of attack," Marlatt speculated.

"He might have," said Schilling, the *Wasp's* radioman, who had returned from the deck shack. "It wouldn't take but a couple seconds to get a May Day on the air and identify with position."

"Right," Silva said. "But the important thing is, they wouldn't be able to say what had attacked them. So even if planes or surface ships or whatever come, they won't suspect us."

"We hope," Lt. Marlatt said, a grin on his affable face for the first time since the *Wasp* had begun to stalk the *Seetotschlager*.

"Tell me which way you think we ought to go, and we're on our way," said Pollard, the little boat's helmsman, who was as skilled at the wheel as any quartermaster in the U.S. Navy.

Marlatt said it didn't make much difference where they went as long as they didn't deplete their powerful engine's gasoline tanks, allowing sufficient fuel for a feint course back to Pico Cove, and zigzag escape runs if they should be attacked.

Pollard took a half-dollar from a pocket, tossed it, caught it with his right hand, and plopped it onto the back of his left hand. He looked at it. "We go east," he said.

The day after the sinking of the *Seetotschlager*, the *Wasp* came upon a Doenitz Klasse U-boat, the *Ich Dien* ("I Serve"), U-DK7.

It was not surprising that the masqueraders had come upon another surfaced U-boat so soon after the *Seetot-*

schlager. This part of the Atlantic was a Nazi lake, a sanctuary for U-boats of the German Navy's mighty U-Waffe.

Allied destroyers and other warships feared to enter it. It would be suicidal for Anglo-American submarines to penetrate its waters. Allied seaplanes, bombers, and fighter planes avoided this area too. They would be too far from their bases and extremely vulnerable to Nazi air squadrons from Ellsenborn, El Haik'n, and Kleinmeerbusen (Little Bay).

U-boat commanders had few qualms about surfacing here, even in daylight hours. No Allied aircraft or ships were likely to molest them. And of course the Portuguese fishermen, who looked upon this prime fishing ground as an ancestral claim, were of no concern to the Nazis.

"That U-boat looks like a real fancy job," Silva said, looking at the *Ich Dien* along with everybody else on the *Wasp*.

The *Ich Dien* was indeed a fancy submarine. She was one of Germany's fastest and most modern U-boats. She was equipped with the newly developed Snorkel apparatus. She had a streamlined hull which gave her the sleek appearance of a shark. She had an enlarged battery capacity and an innovative system for rapid reloading of her torpedo tubes.

"We're going to do a number on that baby," Lt. Marlatt said. "But we're going to fish up close and look her over before we start being heroes."

Silva turned up the volume of the *Wasp*'s radio, which was tuned to state-owned GOZA in Lisbon, a station which specialized in information and music of interest to the men of Portugal's 10,000-boat fishing fleet—weather reports, fishing news, and Portuguese folk music.

It was so loud it could be heard by the Nazis on the *Ich Dien*'s platform. It was part of the masquerade. A Portuguese fishing boat without blaring music from GOZA would be unusual and might make the Germans suspicious.

"God, I hate that stupid music," Schilling said, gritting his teeth.

"It doesn't do anything for me, either," Broughton said, "but if it keeps us in business it's worth it."

The *Wasp* trawled its nets closer to the *Ich Dien*, its crew appearing to be engrossed in the business of fishing. The Germans on the *Ich Dien*'s platform, and its periscope watch, looked at them, then ignored them. Portuguese fishing boats were everywhere. They were nothing.

The *Wasp* had almost reached attack range. "The Fuehrer's going to miss this big pretty boat," Schilling said to Marlatt, both of them on the port stern, pretending to be mending a trawl net.

"We'll send him a sympathy card," Marlatt said.

The tough little officer, a cigarette dangling from his lips, glanced over at the *Ich Dien* again. "We need to be a little closer, and angled a little better," he said. "That baby is big, and she looks tough."

He turned from the trawl net to saunter over to Helmsman Pollard and tell him to close in at about 45 degrees, a position from which the *Wasp* could make itself a fast and elusive target if the U-boat's periscope watch or platform people saw anything about the *Wasp* that would make them suddenly try to destroy the little boat.

There was always the chance, he worried, that a really alert German would see something suspicious about the masquerading PT. Though the camouflage had been artfully and carefully done, maybe some little thing had been overlooked. Or perhaps a German would get a glimpse, somehow, of one of the *Wasp*'s guns, or even just a part of a gun.

Marlatt's face was taut while he conferred with Pollard. "Take us in another 100 feet," he said, "then put us at our usual action angle."

"Hold everything, boss man!" Pollard replied, looking past Marlatt's shoulder. "We've got company! Kraut company!"

Marlatt turned in the direction of Pollard's stare. A seaplane was coming toward the *Ich Dien*. She was a gull-winged two-engine Siebel, her pontoons at the angle of her wings. She was, obviously, intending to land on the sea beside the U-boat.

"It's a good thing we hadn't declared war," Marlatt said. "Or we would have been stuck."

"Want me to mosey on away from here?" Pollard asked.

"Not right now," Marlatt said. "Let's see what's going on."

"Maybe we can zap both of them," Pollard said. "It won't take much to lay a crunch on that plane."

Before Marlatt could reply, two Nazi seamen came out

of the conning carrying a litter to which the body of a uniformed German U-boat officer had been lashed.

"For chrissake!" Pollard said. "A dead Kraut!"

The dead man was Kapitän Frederick Wolfgang von Maelzer, a haughty Prussian, a member of the wealthy Maelzer industrial family, owners of a sprawling industrial complex.

Kapitän Maelzer was forty-seven. He was six feet in height and a chilling figure. His left cheek had been scarred by a saber in a duel at prestigious Heidelberg University.

His hair was thinning, fading to gray from its former straw color. His eyes, wide-spaced and piercing green, seemed to bore into an adversary. His voice was harsh and guttural. He was the epitome of a Prussian aristocrat in both appearance and demeanor, looking upon most Germans, and all non-Germans, as inferiors.

He was reading *Sonderfahndungsliste GB* ("Special Search List") at the desk in his cabin on the *Ich Dien* when he suddenly slumped over his desk.

Seaman 2/K. Otto Wassenhaur was bringing coffee to his commandant when he discovered the slumped body. "*Mein Gott!*" the young seaman croaked. He ran outside and babbled to Navigation Officer Karl Gault, the first officer he came upon, that something had happened to Kapitän Maelzer. "I think he's dead!" Wassenhaur said excitedly. "He looks just like my *grossvater* Schmidt after he had a heart attack. *Grossvater* Schmidt was only fifty-one and . . ."

He didn't say the rest of it. Leutnant Gault had swooped up the bulkhead phone and moved its toggle to public address. "Medizinisch Offizier Thiesen, lay down to Kapitän Maelzer's cabin on the double! Korvettenkapitän Genscheimer, please come at once to Kapitän Maelzer's cabin!"

Thiesen, twenty-three, the *Ich Dien*'s medical officer, wasn't really an officer. He was a medical corpsman 1/K. Skilled and competent, he had a fair knowledge of medical practice, including surgery. He had been a second-year student at the Munich Medical and Surgical College before he had been conscripted into the U-Waffe.

He examined Kapitän Maelzer quickly and efficiently. Then he took the stethoscope's tubes from his ears. "He is dead, sir," he said, looking at the big U-boat's executive officer, Korvettenkapitän Heinrich Genscheimer.

"You are absolutely sure?" Genscheimer asked.

"There is no doubt of it. It was either a massive coronary attack or a cerebral hemorrhage. There is no way, without autopsy, we can know with certainty."

"Jesus Christ," croaked Genscheimer, thirty-seven, a short overweight man. "That's something nobody had figured on!"

He turned toward the other officers who were standing in the hatch, looking at the activity in their captain's cabin. "Well, now I am in command!" Genscheimer said, as though the thought had just occurred to him, which it had.

Nobody said you weren't, you blowhard tub of lard, reflected Ensign Franz Gartner, the U-boat's radioman.

"What do you want me to do with the body?" Thiesen asked his new commandant. "I can give it a cursory embalmment, which I would advise if you intend to have someone come for it. Or I can prepare it for burial at sea, which merely involves tying off the penis, plugging the anus and other body openings, and—"

"Goddam, Thiesen, I don't want the technical details!" Genscheimer said, his fat face blanched, cheek muscles tremoring.

This ghoulish medical man was making him sick to his stomach. It was bad enough just looking at this dead man, right here in front of him, without thinking about the macabre preparations for his burial.

Genscheimer's tongue flicked over his blubbery lips as he turned to ask the officers at the hatch what they thought he ought to do with the body. Then it occurred to him that as the *Ich Dien*'s new captain, he didn't have to ask anything of anybody.

He and he alone would make the decisions. "Radio Africa Naval Command," he said to Ensign Gartner, "and ask them to send a seaplane for Kapitän Maelzer's body, naturally explaining that he died without warning of a heart attack, and request arrival as quickly as possible."

Gartner left to carry out his orders, and Thiesen said, "Sir, shall I proceed with embalmment or shall I merely—"

"Embalm!" Genscheimer barked. He didn't really know which procedure would be best, but he didn't want to hear the rest of whatever the garrulous little officer was going to say.

It didn't disturb him to torpedo an English or American ship, causing the ghastly deaths of hundreds of men, if it was a troop ship—but exposure to a corpse, especially the corpse of a man with whom he had lived in the confined quarters of a submarine, was most unpleasant.

"Do you want him laid out in his dress uniform after we prepare the body?" Thiesen asked.

"*Ja! Ja!* Now everybody out!" Genscheimer said.

He went out, too, and closed the hatch. That *verdammt* little medical man was making him a mental case.

Radio Officer Gartner had contacted Africa Naval Command at Port Risner in GR code. They reported that they would send a seaplane for Kapitän Maelzer's body the next morning sometime between 0900 and 1100.

It was 0900 when the *Ich Dien* surfaced and almost an hour later before the *Wasp* maneuvered into attack position, the German seaplane appearing at the same time.

The Americans watched the seamen carry the body onto the big U-boat's platform. "Doesn't he look natural, sir?" Medizinisch Offizier Thiesen said proudly. "I had to improvise the eye caps out of thin plastic. And some glue from the chart bench. But they're keeping his eyes closed."

"*Wunderbar!*" Kapitän Genscheimer said drily, glancing at the corpse and observing that it did, indeed, look "natural."

"I could have done better if I'd had a trocar such as morticians use," Thiesen said, pushing his glasses up on his nose, a habitual gesture. "That's a sharp-pointed instrument used for withdrawing fluids from the abdominal cavity. However, since they will probably fly him to Germany right away—"

"Silence!" Genscheimer snapped. "The headquarters officer is coming aboard!"

According to the protocol of the German Navy's U-Waffe, the headquarters officer, a Kapitän, merited no special civilities in this type of mission. But that medical ghoul had to be silenced.

He was making Genscheimer sick to his stomach, talking about jabbing a trocar or whatever it was into Maelzer's guts and drawing out their fluids.

Chapter Ten

Lt. Marlatt and the other Americans, still pretending to be fishing, kept watching the strange events on the *Ich Dien*'s platform.

"One of the Krauts has kicked off and the plane came for the body," Silva speculated. "He must have been a big shot or they would have buried him in the blue."

"Right now, while they're fooling around with that dead guy, might be the time to give them the treatment," Haney said. "If I put my number two on the plane and then swing back to the rudder, we wouldn't miss a stroke."

"Christ, man," Silva said, "you don't need a 3-inch rifle to zap that little bitty plane. One little go from my Oerlikon and that baby's bye-bye."

The plane would burst into flames, he continued, which would do the Germans on the platform no good. "Not to mention cooking that corpse."

"That's just it," Lt. Marlatt said. "The plane will explode, and the water all around the sub, at least on this side where we've got to do our thing, will be covered with flames. That might obscure what we're doing. We can't afford a sloppy job. Or we may end up on the wrong side of this little game."

The subs, he added, would not be easy to sink. "I wouldn't be surprised if even destroying that conning might take a hell of a lot more than we think."

The whole damn U-boat, he said, appeared formidable. "Her skin's got a different color, or texture, or something. It might be some kind of metal a 3-incher would need repeats to puncture. German technicians are ingenious bastards. In that case, with fire from the plane obscuring what we're doing, we might blow Operation Sting and its seagoing personnel, which, in case nobody remembers, is us."

"So what do we do?" Haney asked.

Before Marlatt could reply, Wally McLean, who had been in the deck shack, came to the hatch. He had been watching the U-boat and the plane with the *Wasp*'s nonreflecting optic glasses through the Oerlikon aperture, which appeared to be a small open-air window. "Mr. Marlatt!" he said. "A guy in the plane's watching us with binoculars!"

"Jesus," Broughton said uneasily.

"Don't anybody panic!" Marlatt said quickly. "And don't look over there. Everybody keep doing just what you're doing!"

He turned toward McLean. "Do you think he's suspicious, or just curious?"

"That's something I can't tell. He's had that glass on every one of you guys, and all over the boat. Whatever that means."

"Get back in there and watch him. Let me know right away if he says anything to the men on the platform."

Marlatt, seeming to be working on a torn seine, maneuvered himself and the net so that he could watch the action on the U-boat's platform and observe the man with the binoculars without being obvious.

"Suppose he catches we're not what we want them to think?" Silva said worriedly.

"In that case, wipe him out with the Oerlikon's first go. Then get the scopes. Haney, shoot the biggest damn hole you can in that conning. Right where it fastens on. Put three in the same place. I want that bucket unable to dive."

"How about the rudder?"

"Get it with number four. If you've got time. Which you might not have, because we're taking off like the fastest tomcat in town!"

"What about us?" Broughton asked.

"You and Schilling lace that platform and then the conning's hatch. I don't want anybody getting to those guns while we're leaving."

"There won't be any conning's hatch to lace," Haney said. "I'm shaving that baby off. You want to remember, from here to there with a 3-inracher, with steel-jacketed HE projectiles, is not good for conning towers."

"OK—we hope it works," Marlatt said. "But just in case that conning is as tough as I think it might be, stay with

67

its base until it's got a hole too big for any damage control party to glue together."

"I read you," Haney said, piqued. Marlatt was overrating the big U-boat, he reflected, his lips tight. It would be just like the other one, as Marlatt would see for himself after he saw what just one 3-incher did to that conning.

McLean came to the hatch again. "The Kraut—I think he's the pilot—quit looking at us. Then he started picking his nose. Right now he's screwing around with his fingernails."

Marlatt and the others were relieved by this news. The pilot had apparently just been curious about them.

"Now what's the program?" Silva worried.

"We'll let the plane go and zombie the U-boat as soon as she submerges."

"For chrissake," Haney said, "why let it submerge?"

"Because some of its men have seen us. You know that. You saw them looking at us. If we start to hit them they just might be able to get a message on the air that a fishing boat which ain't no fishing boat is biting their ass."

"It's our turn to be the heroes, anyway," Schilling said, grinning. "Besides which, our little old Torpex depth bombs do a much tidier job of fragmenting Nazis than that crude, primitive weapon you've been trying to scare them with."

"Up yours, flapjaw," Haney said. "When it comes to making fishbait out of Nazis, nothing beats a 3-inch rifle laying its eggs inside a U-boat."

There was no horseplay on the *Ich Dien*'s platform. It was all very serious and, for Korvettenkapitän Heinrich Genscheimer, most disheartening.

Genscheimer, the executive officer, had automatically succeeded to captaincy of the U-boat after Kapitän Maelzer's fatal heart attack. He had had the *Ich Dien*'s gig removed from its platform securities after the arrival of the Siebel seaplane from Africa Naval Command and had ordered two seamen to paddle the gig to the seaplane, which bobbled on the sea's gently rolling surface about 30 feet from the U-boat. "You will bring back the officer who has come for Kapitän Maelzer's body, and possibly someone else. Maybe two others. There are four men in the plane. One, at least, will stay in it, of course. Then, after certain protocols here on the platform, you will
68

return those men to the plane along with Kapitän Maelzer's body."

"Yes, sir," Seaman 1/K. Klaus Bergmann, twenty-four, said, saluting his overweight new captain.

Bergmann and the other seaman, Wilhelm Gisch, twenty, who had been rated 3/K. just prior to the beginning of the *Ich Dien*'s latest cruise, joining its ship's company at that time, lowered the little rubberized gig off the platform and paddled it over to the seaplane.

Leutnant Werner Stein, thirty-three, climbed down into the gig, followed by Seaman 1/K. Hans Schaffner. "Hold the gig steady!" Stein said to the gig's seamen. Then he and Schaffner reached up and helped Kapitän Ritter von Oberfelder, fifty-one, into the gig.

Soon the gig came to the U-boat. Several seamen helped the Leutnant and Schaffner aboard. Genscheimer, observing that the officer was a Kapitän, personally helped him out of the gig.

After von Oberfelder was on the platform, Genscheimer and the other men of the *Ich Dien* saluted him. Then Genscheimer said, "It is with the deepest regret—"

"Forget the formalities!" von Oberfelder cut in. He looked at the skies, and the sea. "This is going to be brief and right to the point. I feel uneasy here. God knows when the enemy might appear, and neither this surfaced U-boat nor that little seaplane are any match for a sudden attack."

"Yes, sir," Genscheimer said, his tongue flicking over his blubbery lips. "There is no reason for any but minimal time, sir. The body, as you can see, is here on the platform. I will have my men take it and your party back to the seaplane immediately."

"Slow down, Genscheimer!" von Oberfelder said. "I will issue the orders, and in their priorities."

The big German naval officer—he was six feet four, and towered above fat little Genscheimer—removed an envelope from an inner pocket of his jacket. "First, Genscheimer, it will be you, not I, who will fly back with von Maelzer's body. As of this moment, by order of Africa Naval Command, I am the *Ich Dien*'s captain. And you, relieved of your duties, will be reassigned." Von Oberfelder presented the envelope to Genscheimer, whose corpulent face had been swept with dismay. "Here is the transfer. And your orders."

"Ja . . ." Genscheimer said miserably, staring up at von Oberfelder's stern Prussian face.

I just had the shortest command of any officer in the German Navy, he reflected, taking the papers from their envelope. Less than one day. Then they send this big overgrown high and mighty Prussian to succeed me. Why didn't they let me continue as the *Ich Dien*'s new captain? I am no boy just out of officers' training school. I am an experienced . . .

Von Oberfelder terminated the fat officer's unhappy reflections. "Don't take time to read those papers now!" he said crisply. "Accompany the body to the seaplane! I am impatient to get this boat under the surface!"

"Ja . . . sir," Genscheimer said, saluting.

He turned to the deck hands. "Lower the body into the gig!"

Seaman Bermann, waiting in the gig, had overheard the dialogue between von Oberfelder and Genscheimer, as had everyone on the platform. "I don't feel sorry for old Fat Ass," he muttered to Seaman Gisch. "He'd have been a mean captain. But we might be worse off. That big Prussian looks to me like a total disaster."

"He's a mean looker, all right," Gisch said.

He wasn't greatly concerned, though. As low as he was in the pecking order of the *Ich Dien*'s crew, somebody was always bellowing at him. The big Prussian officer might as well be one of them.

"What the hell are you waiting for?" von Oberfelder shouted to the seamen who had picked up the litter.

"I wish now I'd dumped that son of a bitch while we were paddling back here," Bermann muttered.

"They'd have court-martialed you."

"I would have made it look like an accident. Then I'd have taken plenty of time pulling him back in. Meanwhile a shark might have grabbed him. In which case . . ."

He didn't finish. "Watch it, Gisch," he said, reaching up for the litter with the corpse. "If we drop old Maelzer in the drink our lovable new CO will execute us."

While the seamen on the platform lowered von Maelzer's body into the gig, the men in the gig reaching up and helping, the big U-boat's new captain bellowed at the gunners. "Secure! On the double!"

"Go to hell," Gunner 1/K. Johann Heschner said under his breath.

Already, he reflected, he didn't like his new captain.

Kapitän Ritter von Oberfelder, a career naval officer, was an easy man to dislike. Son of a prosperous Wasselburen fish cannery owner, he had grown up in boats of his father's fishing fleet on the North Sea. For the last two years, since his promotion to Kapitän, he had been on the staff of the Inspectorate of U-Waffe field operations.

He had been a competent officer. But he was a worrier, a perfectionist, and a martinet. U-boat commanders despised him. And now, because the *Ich Dien*'s CO had suddenly died, and because Africa Naval Command did not think that Heinrich Genscheimer had sufficient rank for so important a craft, he was about to assume his first command as captain of a U-boat.

The Americans on the masquerading PT, some pretending to be fishing, others appearing to be repairing nets and seines, continued to watch the activities on the *Ich Dien*'s platform.

"They're taking the dead guy over to the seaplane," Silva said. "Like I said, he must've been an important Nazi or they'd drop him in the blue."

A little later Silva said, "They're taking fatso over to the plane now. It looks like the big dude who came in the plane is going to be the new skipper. He's telling the gunners to secure. At least I think that's what he's telling them, because he's saying something and that's what they're doing."

After Korvettenkapitän Genscheimer and the Leutnant and seaman who had come with the plane were aboard the plane, its pilot began a takeoff. The wash from the Siebel seaplane's two propellors very nearly capsized the gig. "The bastard could have waited until we got back," Seaman Bermann said, maneuvering his paddle to keep the little fabric boat from going awash.

He and Gisch paddled back to the U-boat. "Hurry it up!" von Oberfelder bellowed, glaring down from the platform. "I want that gig secured in thirty seconds!"

"Yes, sir!" Bermann said, climbing up onto the platform.

His lips were tight. He wished von Maelzer hadn't died. Von Maelzer had been a martinet, but he was endurable. This new Kapitän was something else.

The Americans watched the German seamen hurriedly pull the gig out of the water, overturn it, and hasp it to the platform just ahead of the forward deck rifle, a 30mm AA. Then the seamen practically dived into the conning, their new Kapitän going into it immediately behind them.

Von Oberfelder, standing on the conning's aluminum ladder, quickly secured the conning's hatch. Then, looking around, he bellowed, "Where the hell's the pull for the diving horn?"

"Sir," Navigation Officer Gault said, looking up at the officer on the aluminum ladder, "the diving horn is not sounded unless it is an emergency dive."

"I didn't ask when it is used, I asked where it is!" von Oberfelder bellowed.

"Starboard of your shoulder, sir," Gault said. "The button with the blue light."

Von Oberfelder pushed the button. The diving horn sounded its raucous siren-type noise.

The big Prussian officer came down off the ladder. "I feel better with everyone at diving station," he said to Gault and the other officers, who had come to see what was going on. "Even though there is no emergency."

He did not know that the greatest emergency of his life was in the making on the deck of the decrepit little floater which he had thought to be a Portuguese fishing boat.

Chapter Eleven

The German seaplane's two powerful Heinkel eight-cylinder engines quickly sped it away from the submerging U-boat. The Americans on the masquerading PT, no longer pretending to be fishing, watched both activities.

They were a grim bunch. It was absolutely vital to refrain from attack on the U-boat until they could no longer be seen by the seaplane's occupants. On the other hand, if they waited too long to attack the *Ich Dien* they might lose its location.

The big U-boat was swift and agile. It would be hard to determine her direction after she had been submerged for more than a few minutes. "We might," Lt. Marlatt had said, "bomb a dozen wrong damn places."

What he wanted to do was to get right on top of the *Ich Dien* and then pattern her with six depth bombs. "I want a sure kill on that big fancy U-boat!"

He put his binoculars on the seaplane. "You guys keep watching the sub's wash," he said tensely.

The U-boat's new commandant, Kapitän Ritter von Oberfelder, had ordered down scopes immediately after he had pushed the diving button's horn. He was afraid of attack from an Allied destroyer or perhaps a submarine, though there was no sign of either on the *Ich Dien*'s hydrophone. The fact that this part of the Atlantic was a U-boat sanctuary made no difference. "I'll feel better with this submarine below the surface. A surfaced sub makes slow response to helm and rudder."

Now there was only the turbulence of the sea's surface caused by the rapidly diving U-boat to indicate its location. "If we lose that we can kiss that baby goodbye," Lt. Marlatt had said.

"I can still see where she is," said Silva, who had appointed himself chief wash watcher. "But just barely. We better not wait much longer."

"Well, goddamn, I've got to be sure that plane's too far gone to see us," Marlatt said, impatience blended with irritability in his crisp Midwestern voice.

He lowered the binoculars. "OK . . . let's go!" he said, his jaw squared.

The strategy had been discussed. No orders had to be given. The launcher on the little boat's stern was loaded with two powerful Torpex depth bombs. Four other Torpexes were in load position. "We'll only have time for six," Marlatt had said, "because we've got to be out of there before they blow or guess who'll get included."

Right on top of them when they exploded, everyone understood, was no place to be. "The bastards blow up as well as down," DB launcher Russ Broughton had commented.

Silva, who had kept his eyes on the U-boat's diminishing wash, pointed it out, standing on the *Wasp*'s bow, his right arm extended toward the wash.

Steve Pollard revved up all three of the Wasp's twelve-cylinder Packard-built engines, then turned the wheel toward the direction of Silva's pointing arm. But he didn't go too fast. A U.S. Navy destroyer would not be able to approach its victim as swiftly as a full-speed PT, and Lt. Marlatt wanted the Nazis to think a destroyer was attacking them.

"Those three engines will bug the soup out of their hydrophone people," Marlatt had said. "They won't think it's us. No fishing boat's engine can make ripples like these big babies. They won't know what it is. It'll just sound like the engines of some big ship."

Soon the *Wasp* was over the almost invisible surface turbulence of the diving U-boat. "Go!" Marlatt shouted to Schilling and Broughton, whose Torpex launcher was loaded and waiting.

Kapitän von Oberfelder had been addressing the officers in the compartment below the conning, beginning his little speech after the diving horn's raucous whoops ended. "You officers of the *Ich Dien*," he said, "have done gallant work. I have read the records of this U-boat's valiant service. You have surpassed the highest traditions of the U-Waffe. But under my command we will do even more. Beginning tomorrow—"

He didn't say the rest of it. Hdyrophone Officer Kurt Hafner had burst into the compartment. "Sir!" he said, his voice shrill. "Some kind of major enemy ship is approaching! It's damn near on top of us!"

"How could it be?" von Oberfelder said. "We have been submerged only a couple of minutes. No enemy ships were anywhere in sight. Further, when did you first notice these sounds?"

"Just an instant before I ran in here, sir!" said Hafner, twenty-four, tall, blue-eyed and handsome. His tongue darted over his lips.

"Why didn't you detect it earlier? You know why, hydrophone officer? I'll tell you why! I'll tell you on the basis of experience in the U-Waffe! What you heard was fish! An enormous school of fish. Probably—"

"No, sir! It wasn't fish! I know the sounds of fish, sir. This was the sound of a ship's engines!"

"A warship doesn't just suddenly appear out of nowhere," von Oberfelder said. "I want your name! Now! The *Ich Dien* is damn soon going to have a hydrophone officer who knows—"

Again he didn't finish. Two objects had struck the big U-boat, one on each side, aft of the conning. "What the hell was that?" von Oberfelder said, apprehension sweeping over his stern Prussian features.

"Depth bombs!" one of the officers said tensely.

"Impossible!" von Oberfelder snapped. "Absolutely impossible!"

Then von Oberfelder and the others heard the *click, click* that depth bomb detonators make.

"Mein Gott!" von Oberfelder croaked.

His eyes swept over the compartment. "Where the fuck's the voice tube?" he bellowed.

An officer pointed to a speaker on the bulkhead. The big Prussian ran to it. "Damage control parties!" he shouted. "Man your stations!"

He turned toward the officers. His face was ashen. *"Mein Gott . . ."* where did they come from!"

Broughton and Schilling had triggered the *Wasp*'s depth bomb thrower. "Two on the U-boat's stern, two in the middle, two on her bow. All straddles. One on each side," Lt. Marlatt had said. "Then we take off like we've got the devil on our tail, and we won't have all day to do it or we'll be finding out from firsthand experience just how effective our famous Torpex depth bombs are."

"Right on target," Schilling said while, very quickly and

75

very efficiently, he and Broughton rolled two more 500-pound Torpex depth charges into their murderous apparatus.

He was wrong. They hadn't been right on target. They had straddled the *Ich Dien* forward of her stern, just aft of the conning, which was approximately where the *Wasp* had intended to drop numbers three and four.

While the *Wasp*, its three engines revved up, sped over the submerging U-boat, Schilling and Broughton launched two more Torpexes. "Those last two ought to take care of the main showroom," Schilling said, helping Broughton reload.

The first two Torpexes exploded. The concussion in the U-boat was horrendous. The officers, including the *Ich Dien*'s haughty new CO, were knocked off their feet. But no great rents were blown in the U-boat's skin, only a few small leaks.

The officers got to their feet. Relief came to von Oberfelder and the others. The U-boat had withstood two depth bomb explosions right on her flanks. The damage control parties would quickly secure those little leaks. Meanwhile the *Ich Dien* was diving swiftly, and every meter would make subsequent depth bombs less effective.

Click! Click! This time forward of the conning. "Damn!" von Oberfelder said, his teeth clenched. Two more of those *verdammt* bombs. And there wasn't a thing he could do about them. Nothing anyone could do. The *Ich Dien* was diving as fast as she could. That was all that could be done.

The *Ich Dien*'s special alloyed-steel skin wouldn't break, though. It hadn't been broken by those first two bombs. These two wouldn't break it either.

They exploded with deafening violence. They rocked the big U-boat like a toy boat in a bathtub. The voice speaker fell from its bulkhead supports. Papers, slide rules, and other paraphernalia slid off the chart bench. Its chair hurtled across the compartment, striking Ensign Hasso Wuhrm, twenty-two, Navigation Officer 2/K., on his head, a leg of the steel chair breaking his glasses.

Sprawled on the tilting deck, which was rolling port, then starboard, he shrieked his agony, a large piece of glass sticking out of his left eye, its fluids dribbling down his cheek.

All over the big U-boat, everything that wasn't welded

to the decks or bulkheads hurtled about, damaging itself and injuring men—some severely. But still the outer seams' welds and rivets held, except for minor fissures and rents.

Kapitän von Oberfelder, on his hands and knees, looked over his shoulder at the port bulkhead, then the starboard bulkhead. No big leaks. He got up. "By God, they didn't kill us!" he said.

No one heard him. Ensign Wuhrm's shrieks overwhelmed his voice. He looked at the agonized young German. *"Mein Gott . . ."* he croaked, staring at the injured man's mutilated eye.

He looked at the other officers. "Get our medical officer immediately!"

Above the big U-boat, on the sea's surface, and slightly forward and starboard, Schilling and Broughton had triggered the depth bomb thrower for the third time. Its two big silvery Torpex bombs hurtled off the *Wasp*'s stern in a small arc and plopped into the sea. "That ought to take care of that!" Schilling said. "Two on her bow ought to deep-six her for keeps!"

No one responded. No one could hear him. Lt. Marlatt had signaled full speed forward. The three engines turned the PT's screws so fast the little boat practically leaped up out of the water, then proceeded with her bow above the surface, her stern low and shipping water, her screws churning a great white wake.

Meanwhile the men on the *Wasp* crouched behind shelters. They had learned their lesson: Don't be standing around like commuters on a ferry when a U-boat's torpedoes are detonated practically within spitting range. Each man had an arm wrapped around a support; each man kept thinking about the time Broughton had been swept off the *Wasp*'s deck and very nearly drowned.

One of the U-boat's officers, carrying out von Oberfelder's order to summon the U-boat's medical officer for Ensign Wuhrm, picked up the speaker that had fallen from the bulkhead. He switched its toggle to electronic communication—no need to try to conceal their location from whatever was depth-bombing them—and shouted over the *Ich Dien*'s public address: "Medizinisch Offizier Thiesen—"

Then the third drop of the *Wasp*'s depth bombs exploded. This time their effect on the *Ich Dien* was minimal. The DBs had been dropped forward of the bow, and starboard. They were not in contact with the big U-boat's tough metal skin.

Hydrophone Officer Hafner's voice came over a speaker—during the attack he had returned to his station. "Kapitän von Oberfelder, the enemy has withdrawn. He is now 140 meters west by northwest off our bow and continuing true."

"He'll circle back, the son of a bitch," von Oberfelder said, his lips tight. "But we'll be deep enough by the time he gets here to withstand another batch of his bombs."

He turned toward Ensign Wuhrm, whose shrieks were horrible. Wuhrm was leaning against a bulkhead, sitting on the littered deck, his mouth gaping and drooling, the glass still sticking out of his eye. "Where's that damn medical officer?" von Oberfelder bellowed.

Another officer he'd get rid of, he decided. He looked at the damage control men who were securing the leaks on the port bulkhead. They were doing an excellent job of it, working quickly, calmly, and with great skill. Their officer, von Oberfelder reflected, whoever he is, is one I'll keep.

The other officers, except Wuhrm, whom two enlisted men were taking out of the compartment, one on each side, had regained their composures. "We made it," one of them said happily. "By God, we made it . . . they were right on top of us!"

Von Oberfelder smiled. For a while there he had thought he was the same as dead. He decided he would report to Kriegsflotte that the new Doenitz Klasse U-boats were terrific war machines. Practically unsinkable. There was no doubt of it—the men who had designed the DK had thought of everything. It was incredible that a U-boat could survive depth bombs of such proximity.

"I wonder who hit us," he said to the other officers. "And where it came from!"

Before anyone could reply he began to cough. Suddenly, he couldn't breathe. His hands clasped his throat. His eyes distended. He looked at the other officers. They were choking, too.

The *Wasp* reduced its speed. Its bow settled onto the sea. Lt. Marlatt looked aft through binoculars. The other Americans were looking, too. There had been no explosions except the Torpex bombs. No torpedoes exploding and blowing a great hole in the sea.

"Anybody see anything?" Marlatt said, lowering the binoculars. "I don't see a thing."

"Me either," Silva said.

"Christ," Haney said.

No debris from a destroyed U-boat had surfaced. No great blotches of oil. Nothing.

"We must have missed the bastard," Silva said. "But we couldn't have. We were on her like a rooster on a hen."

"That's not a very nautical expression," Schilling said, "but I get the meaning."

"You know what I think?" Silva said. "I think we got her. But not a whole bunch of stuff came up. Sometimes hardly anything comes up."

"Why don't we go back and take a look?" Broughton said. "I hate to think I'm no longer the Navy's best depth bomb dropper."

Marlatt raised the binoculars again. He looked for a long while. Then he said, "Nothing's there. The sea's calm enough to see if there was. So we're not going back. We'll scratch this one. I don't know how those Krauts made it, but they did. So let's get out of here before they raise a periscope and put everything together."

The *Ich Dien*'s crew hadn't, as Lt. Marlatt had said, "made it." They were dying. The U-boat's designers, ingenious in so many ways, had made a horrendous miscalculation. They had not adequately cushioned the battery banks.

The shock of the depth bomb explosions had cracked several of the batteries, which were in the *Ich Dien*'s bow. Seawater from split welds had seeped into the batteries' fissures. Lethal chlorine gas emerged, permeating every compartment, every passageway.

There was no escape. No place to go. No way to stop the terrible, choking, invisible fumes. The men on the *Ich Dien* began their dying with coughs, then strangling, suffering agonizing searing of their nasal passages, the linings of their gaping mouths, their lungs.

They died in anguish, flailing on the decks of the compartments in which they happened to be, their mouths open, tongues sticking out, eyes bulging and blinded by the terrible searing gas.

For Kapitän von Oberfelder it was the shortest command in the history of the modern German Navy. In less than an hour from the time he assumed command of the *Ich Dien* he was dead.

So were all the others.

But the big U-boat kept going.

Chapter Twelve

Unaware that their depth bombs had fissured the U-boat's batteries and that lethal gas from the batteries had asphyxiated everyone aboard the U-boat, the Americans on the masquerading PT were a disgusted, frustrated outfit.

They did not know that 90 fathoms under them and 400 meters off their starboard stern the *Ich Dien* glided along like a silent underwater ghoul, its officers and men sprawled dead on the decks of its gas-filled compartments. They had died in writhing contortions, their blinded eyes distended, their mouths gaping, blood oozing from their mouths and noses.

After her full-speed burst away from the depth-bombed U-boat the *Wasp* was now wallowing on the gently rolling green sea at little more than trolling speed on just one of its three powerful engines. "How's our go-juice?" Lt. Marlatt said, lighting a Camel and looking over at Russ Broughton, who had been adjusting the air-intake screw on the *Wasp*'s running engine.

"I looked just a minute ago," Broughton said. "I'd say to be on the safe side, we'd better head for home."

"OK," Marlatt said. He turned to Steve Pollard, the little boat's helmsman. "Anchors aweigh, boy," he said with a grin on his handsome, affable face.

"I can't function without a cigarette dangling between my ruby lips," Pollard said.

Marlatt tossed him a Camel. "Some people buy their own butts."

"There's one like me in every ship's company," Pollard said, putting a match to the cigarette.

There was truth in what the big helmsman had said, Lt. Marlatt reflected. Everywhere he had been there had been a man who mooched cigarettes. Pollard was the man on the *Wasp*. At fifty cents a carton, five cents a pack in any overseas ships' service store, Marlatt reflected, you'd think they'd buy their own smokes.

Oh, well, his reflections continued, this was the smallest of matters. He picked up his binoculars and began to sweep the seas in all directions from the wallowing little masquerader.

"I'll be goddamned," he said a little later. He had seen a surfaced U-boat.

He lowered the binoculars. "We got gas enough to fish our way a mile or so off course?" He asked Broughton. "There's a nice big Nazi duck over there just askin'."

"Hell, yes, we've got plenty of juice," Broughton said, a grin spreading over his grease-smeared face. "A little while ago when I said we'd better head for home, I didn't mean we were scraping the bottom. You know me, man. I like to have enough stand-by juice in case something like that Nazi duck shows up and we have to do a little extra screwing around."

It would be a heartbreaking situation, he continued, if they came upon a U-boat just waiting to be deep-sixed and had to pass it up because they had only gas enough to get back to Pico Cove. "If that happened I believe I'd just sit down and cry."

The U-boat was the *Grossdeutschland,* 870 tons, all welded construction, six 21-inch torpedo tubes, four bow and two stern. Her class letters were ZI, and her platform was armed with four 30mm AA guns, two twinned Kluge machine guns, and a forward 6.5cm rifle.

She was a unit of the Sea Rats Group, a free-hunt outfit based at the U-Waffe's Atlantic Submarine Basin two miles up the Loire River. Her CO was Kapitän Wilhelm Wassermann, thirty-seven, a short stocky Swabian from Bavaria. Unlike the Teutonic types of northern Germany, who are characterized by blond hair, tall stature, blue eyes, and fair complexion, the Swabians are of moderate stature, darker complexion, and brown eyes.

Kapitän Wassermann was a round-faced man of jovial personality. He was a competent officer and a moderate disciplinarian. The *Grossdeutschland* was known throughout U-boat society as a happy ship. Assignment to Wassermann's boat was looked upon as good fortune.

Like other U-boat captains in the great "Nazi lake," Wassermann had no qualms about surfacing. No enemy aircraft or ships would be likely to attack, or were even within strike range. If they were, Africa Naval Command's radios would warn them in plenty of time to dive beyond range of Allied aerial or depth bombs.

"To make it look good," Lt. Marlatt said to his men, "we'll fish right up to doomsday range of that U-boat. Then we'll give it the treatment."

This, he said, would compensate for the frustrations and disappointments of their attack on the *Ich Dien*. "It burns my ass every time I think of those Krauts getting away."

"We can't win 'em all," Guns Haney said. "I still think we should have zombied her while she was on the surface. And shot down that plane at the same time."

"We couldn't have done it before either the plane or the sub got a message on the air telling the Kraut brass who was attacking," Marlatt replied. "And then there wouldn't be a U-boat in the German Navy that would let a Portuguese fishing boat get anywhere close. Which would put this caper out of business."

"I'll tell you guys what else we should have done," Silva said. "We should have—"

"Drop it right there!" Lt. Marlatt said. "The world is full of should-have-dones. Talking about it will do no good. That U-boat got away. I'm disgusted about it just as much as you guys. But we can't do anything about it now. What we'd better concentrate on is that U-boat up ahead, there."

"You got something there, boss man," Silva said. "We're spinning our wheels worrying about how we loused up that other job. What's important is what we do to the next customer."

Heads were nodded in agreement with this thinking. "Can I complain about something?" Pollard said with a wink.

"Don't tell me. I already know," Marlatt said, grinning. "You're out of cigarettes."

"No, sir, that wasn't it. But since you mentioned it, I can use one. Make it two and I won't have to ask so soon. What I was complaining about is, we're catching too many fish. We must be in some kind of school or something. Right now, with action coming up, we don't need fish all over the place. If somebody slips on one of them when he ought to be pulling a trigger we might bust out with a whole big bunch of regrets."

"Throw them overboard," Broughton said. "Or else quit catching so many."

Silva, who had been a professional fisherman, said, "For chrissake, you stupids don't have any problem at all. Let me show you how to screw that trawl so the fish swim right on out."

He showed them. Then, wisely, he said, "We want a bunch of fish showing, so we'd better keep the ones we already got. Those Krauts will look at us with binoculars, and the more we look like a legit fishing boat the better off we're going to be."

About an hour later the *Wasp* was in attack position off the *Grossdeutschland*'s port flank. Marlatt and the others pretended to be fishing, meanwhile observing the activities on the U-boat's platform. "It looks like payday," Marlatt said.

It did, indeed, appear that it would be an attack that could swiftly sink the U-boat. No one was manning its deck guns. Instead, eight enlisted men, standing at opposite ends of the platform and on its corners, were tossing a handball in a kind of X pattern over and between the platform's guns.

"That's something I never saw before," Silva said. "I didn't know a Kraut U-boat captain would hold still for anybody enjoying himself."

"That one looks like a halfway decent guy . . . for a Nazi, I mean," Marlatt said. "I was looking at him with glasses from inside the deck shack. He doesn't seem to have that 'Me and God' attitude the others had. Especially that one that got off the plane and took over on the U-boat with the dead body. That guy looked like an eighteen-karat jerk. A typical arrogant Prussian officer."

"Too bad he got away," Silva said.

"Well, this one won't," Marlatt said.

Haney had been looking off the starboard bow with Marlatt's binoculars. "I wouldn't be too sure about that," he said. "Take a look, chief."

Marlatt, his lips tight, snatched the binoculars from Haney's hands and looked out off the starboard bow. "Hell!" he said. "Just plain hell!"

He took the binoculars from his eyes. "That's just what we need . . . a fishing boat!"

"Christ," Silva said, taking the binoculars and looking.

"With ten thousand Portuguese fishing boats on the job it was bound to happen," Marlatt said. "But why did it have to happen right now when we've practically got that U-boat in the bag?"

"We've just been lucky up to now is all I can say," Haney said.

The *Wasp*'s little crew had seen many another Portuguese fishing boat since the beginning of their mission, but none had been in the areas of their attacks. None had any reason to suspect that the disguised PT wasn't just another fishing boat.

"What do we do now?" Pollard worried.

"A big fat nothing," Marlatt said. "If we make the hit, guess how long before every Portuguese fishing boat in the business will know about our little game! A day later the Nazis will know; you can bet some money-hungry Portuguese will sell the information. Then where are we?"

"Up the creek," Broughton said.

"We could zombie the fishing boat, too," Haney said. "Time I lay two—make it three—HEs onto that boat, halfway between the deck and their waterline, and if I spread those three HEs—one in the middle, one toward each end—that fishing boat and everybody on it will suddenly become nothing."

Rage swept over Silva's olive face. "You bloodeating pig! You talk like a Nazi! Those guys in that boat are trying to make a living for their wives and kids. They're not mixed up in this stupid damn war, and we've got no right to kill them!"

"Cool it, Silva!" Lt. Marlatt said, his face grim. "We're not going to do anything to that fishing boat!"

He turned toward Haney. "That was an asshole idea, Haney! We're not barbarians who'll butcher innocent men to cover an action. We'll pass it before we'll do a thing like that!"

Haney looked around. He saw sympathy in no one's face. "I guess I should have kept my mouth shut," he mumbled.

"It would have been a real good idea," Pollard said.

"OK, fellas," Haney said. "I said something I shouldn't have. I didn't mean it. For chrissake, I'm not a bloodeater. I just wasn't thinking. I was P.O.'d because that fishing boat is showing up at this particular time and screwing us out of a score."

Silva held out a hand. "I can forget it if you can," he said.

Haney grasped his hand. "I don't even remember what it was," he said with a wink.

The tensions ended as quickly as they had begun. "What we're going to do," Marlatt said, "is fish and watch those Krauts play ball. And hope that Portuguese boat goes away before the Krauts submerge."

"Which will probably be before night," Pollard said.

He looked over at the U-boat. "We couldn't ask for a nicer target," he said dispiritedly. "So what do we do? We sit here and catch a bunch of stupid fish."

Someone on the U-boat's platform blew a whistle. The Americans looked over at it, the sound of the whistle coming clearly over the 80 yards separating the Nazi submarine and the disguised American PT. Eight enlisted men had come out of the conning. The eight who had been playing ball went into the conning. "They're doing it by sections," Wally McLean said. "I'll bet it feels great to those guys after being cooped up in a submarine."

He could not have endured submarine duty, he said. "I'd actually rather be in the infantry than in one of those overgrown sardine cans."

The fishing boat had come within half a mile of the *Wasp*. "Put the big glasses on it from inside the shack," Marlatt said to Silva. "Then let me know what you see."

Silva would know what he was looking at, he reflected. The others wouldn't.

Silva looked for several moments at the approaching boat. Then he came out of the deck shack. "As far as I can tell they're just an ordinary fishing crew. One of those deals where the captain owns the boat and gets half the take from their catches, the rest of them dividing the other half."

McLean said that sounded to him like a lopsided deal. "I'd tell that captain to stick it. Seven guys dividing half and just one guy getting the other half! Christ!"

Silva said it wasn't as profitable for the captain as it might seem. "He furnishes the boat, which he's probably making payments on, and the gasoline for the engine. Also the food. If fishing is bad he stands to lose. If it's just fair he breaks even. But the crew always get their share of half of the proceeds, whatever they are. Which is on top of their meals. So every time they go home with at least some money."

"Did you work on that kind of deal back there in San Diego?"

"Uh huh. On both sides of it. Toward the last, before I was drafted, I had my own boat."

McLean said he was glad that Silva was part of the *Wasp*'s crew. "It makes me feel like we're not a hundred percent out in the woods, you speaking Portuguese and knowing the fishing business."

This was a sentiment that had been expressed by the others. It just wasn't such a harrowing undertaking with a man who knew what Portuguese fishermen were supposed to do, and who spoke the language.

Haney had been watching the Germans on the U-boat's platform while he gutted fish, throwing their entrails into a bucket. "Mr. Marlatt," he said, "I've been thinking. If they don't submerge when night comes, why can't two or three of us paddle over there in our dinghy and lay a crunch on that U-boat?"

"You're talking like a Section 8," Lt. Marlatt said, "but keep talking."

"OK . . . We paddle over there real quiet. I mean with absolutely no noise. We crawl up onto the platform, also with the quiets, and give the sentries some steel in their rear guts. Then we fast-pour two cans of gasoline down the conning and toss a torch into it. After which we get back in the dinghy and get the hell out."

This scheme, he said, would enable them to destroy the U-boat practically right under the other boat's nose. "We'll have it all done and wrapped up before those Portuguese dudes even wake up."

Chapter Thirteen

Haney's scheme to destroy the surfaced U-boat appealed to the other men on the masquerading PT.

"We've got to be Section 8's even to think about it," Lt. Marlatt said, looking over at the U-boat and the German enlisted men who were tossing a handball on its platform. "There's a hundred things that could go wrong. But those hundred things could go right, too."

"There you go," Wally McLean said, grinning in anticipation of the attack.

None of the Americans was more eager than tough little Joe Silva. "I can't hardly wait," he said. "I'm a tiger with a knife. Which several gooks at Guadalcanal could tell you, if they were in shape to tell.

"You easy up behind the guy and suddenly wrap your left arm around his throat, and at the same time, with your right hand, you shove your knife to its hilt just under his ribs. You don't stick it straight in. You angle it up at 45 degrees so you get his heart and lungs.

"The guy dies without a squeak, which is what the throat hold is for. If we can get on that sub tonight without spooking the sentries the rest of it will be downhill."

None of the Americans had listened more attentively than Guns Haney. "You're talking about Japanese soldiers," he said. "A little guy like you can handle them like you said. But how are you going to put a choking arm around a Kraut who's head and shoulders taller than you are, which might be the case tonight? A big percentage of the Krauts we've seen on that boat are big bastards. You ought to think about that."

Lt. Marlatt said the dimensions of Silva and the German sentries was academic. "You're not going, Silva . . . and it hasn't got a damn thing to do with your height. We've got to keep somebody on this boat who speaks Portuguese. The men on that fishing boat are going to ask what's going on, or say something about it, after we start the action. If there's no one here who can respond, they're going to be suspicious. And we don't want them to know we had anything to do with it."

Silva's black eyes flared. "So what do I do except talk to the guys in that fucking fishing boat! Big damn deal! While you guys are giving the treatment to that U-boat I'm sitting here with a bunch of dead fish for company. What about what I said about giving the Kraut sentries the gate with a knife? Tonight's not going to be the time for somebody to learn the business!"

"Mr. Silva," Wally McLean said, blowing a Lucky Strike's smoke through his nostrils, "I'll bet a month's pay that I have personally given the bleeds to more gooks than you have. Five times there at Leyte while we were evacuating our guys after the Japs took over the Philippines."

He had been in a U.S. Navy submarine's attack force at the time, he said. "I wasn't in ship's company—I hate sub duty like you wouldn't believe. I was one of the six special-duty guys who paddled ashore at different places and picked up our guys. So tell me about laying the quiets on enemy sentries, Silva."

"Five gooks!" Silva said. "Christ, I was just learning the business when I stuck my fifth gook. You're talking to a man who—"

"Knock it off, you guys!" Lt. Marlatt said. "You're both good at it. I've read headquarters' reports on both of you, and I wish you both could go tonight. But for the reasons I mentioned, Silva can better serve us by staying here."

He turned toward Silva. "Besides assuring the men in that fishing boat that you don't have the slightest idea what's going on, I want you to tell them—you'll be pretending to be this boat's captain, of course—that you're going to get the hell out of here.

"You drive over to the other side of the U-boat, pick us up, and we sail happily home."

Silva said this put a different face on things. "It would burn me just to sit here and do nothing."

An unpleasant thought occurred to the elated little gunner. "What if things don't work out like we know they will? Sometimes things happen nobody figures on. What do you want me to do? Lay it on the Krauts with my Oerlikon? I could give them a 3-incher from Haney's gun, too, if it was loaded and ready to go."

Lt. Marlatt said, "Silva, if things go badly for us—I'll lay it out cold. If the Krauts kill us on the platform or maybe see us sneaking up in the dinghy, if that happens, start moseying back toward Pico. Don't fly. Just normal fish-boat speed. I don't want the Germans to catch on where we came from. I want them to think we're a U.S. sub's boarding party. Go back to Pico, Silva, and help Captain Langer put another crew together."

"You telling me to just run away and leave you guys? Maybe some of you would just be wounded."

"I'm telling you not to be a hero! You'll be a dead one who died for nothing. You'll do as I said. That's an order, Silva. A direct order! Tell me you heard it!"

"I heard it," Silva said morosely.

Haney had been watching the activities on the *Grossdeutschland* while he listened to the dialogue between Lt. Marlatt and the tough little Portuguese-American. "Now that we got that settled," he said, turning back to the ohters, "let's get tonight's party put together."

The first thing to do, he said, would be to cut the tops—at least half the tops—from two 5-gallon gasoline cans. "We can't just pour it out of their spouts. It's got to go down that conning like it's got the GI trots, because the name of this game is going to be get that gas down there and on fire before the Krauts figure out what's going on."

The Americans began preparations for the attack on the *Grossdeutschland,* which remained surfaced, its handball games continuing, each group of enlisted men being replaced at twenty-minute intervals by other enlisted men, a procedure which offered every man an opportunity to breathe the sea's fresh clean air and to get exercise that is impossible in the confined quarters of a submarine.

The ship's officers, meanwhile, loitered in groups of three, on the U-boat's platform, leaning on its rails smoking cigarettes and talking to each other. Like the enlisted men, at intervals they were replaced by other officers.

"Some of those guys have been out there twice before," Silva said, watching a German Navy man dive off the platform to retrieve a ball that someone had failed to catch. "I remember that big one with the fat gut. I'll bet he's the cook."

"Maybe they'll submerge when it gets dark," Broughton said. "Jesus, I hope they don't."

This was a thought that had occurred to everyone.

There was nothing they could do to preclude it, no way to anticipate it, so preparations for the attack continued. Again and again Marlatt put the men through their paces, each man having a specific first thing to do, then another. "It's got to be 100 percent teamwork," he said.

They speculated on the events that could go wrong, each man coming up with one or more things. They talked about them, working out plans and stand-by plans for these contingencies.

The last light of dusk found the *Grossdeutschland* still on the sea's almost placid surface. The ball players and loitering officers were replaced by two Germans armed with Schmeiser machine pistols, fast-firing 9mm grease guns that had no counterpart in Allied arsenals.

The German sentries were Bruno Schwartzger, twenty-four, a Sieburg plumber's apprentice before the war, and Adolph Krupper, twenty-three, a Mulhausen *Mittelschule* student before he joined the Hitler Youth Movement, becoming its local Leitartikel.

Schwartzger, six-feet-two, pimple-faced and slow in speech, despised the U-Waffe. A shy personality, he dreamed of returning to his hometown, finishing his apprenticeship, and marrying his sweetheart, Ilse Rothberg, whose father was the local postman.

Krupper, short and stocky, with a wide mouth and liver lips, was an opposite type. He was an aggressive zealot for the Nazi cause. He liked the war. "It is the duty of German youth to free the world from Jewry," he said when he could find anybody on the *Grossdeutschland* who would listen. "Torpedoing American and British ships and killing their crews and troops is a service to the Reich!"

"You take that end of the platform," he said to Schwartzger, indicating the platform's aft end. "I'll take the forward end."

"All right," Schwartzger said. It angered him that Krupper was always telling him what to do, like right now. Krupper didn't outrate him, both men being Seamen 1/K. Someday he was going to tell Krupper to stick it, but he didn't want to do it tonight. It would start something. Maybe it would be better to put up with it. The war wouldn't last forever.

He leaned against the platform's aft AA rifle and looked up at the stars. This wasn't bad duty. In fact, it was better than anything inside. The night air was fresh and crisp. It was just boring as hell. Four hours of just standing here watching for . . . what were they watching for? They couldn't see anything at night. Besides, the hydrophone people down below would be the men who could detect if an enemy warship was trying to sneak up on the *Grossdeutschland.*

"It's nice and cool up here," he said to Krupper, because he thought he ought to say something.

"Shut up!" Krupper snapped. "We're not supposed to talk up here! Voices can carry halfway to the horizon at night!"

Schwartzger didn't say anything. It burned him, that little flag-waver shooting off his mouth as if he were an officer. Someday, Schwartzger decided, I'm going to bust him right on his mouth. Sometime when they were on the beach and there weren't any officers around.

He looked over at Krupper. He was sitting on an ammo box. This was a violation of regulations. Platform sentries were supposed to be on their feet at all times. Krupper would get away with it, though. If he, Schwartzger, sat on an ammo box some officer would come up the conning and see him. He wouldn't be on the box five minutes before he'd be in trouble.

He looked up at the moon. He liked to look at the moon. He and Ilse had liked to stroll down the Lindenstrasse back home in Siegburg and look at the moon and talk about their love for each other.

He was looking at the moon and thinking about Ilse Rothberg when Guns Haney suddenly flung his left arm around his throat. Before the startled young German could begin to free himself, or even to wonder what was happening, Haney shoved the 14-inch blade of a U.S. Marine field knife under his lower ribs, just to the right of his spine, and thrust it upward to its hilt.

Schwartzger died instantly. Haney grabbed his Schmeiser machine pistol and let his body fall to the platform.

Meanwhile Wally McLean, who had climbed onto the U-boat's platform at the same time Haney had crawled up out of the *Wasp*'s little rubber dinghy, had thrown his left arm around Krupper's throat. Krupper thrust his elbows back into McLean's belly. The American grunted and loosed his hold.

Krupper spun around. Before he could lower the Schmeiser, which he had been cradling in his left arm, McLean

92

shoved the knife into his throat, then swung it down on his right arm.

The Schmeiser and Krupper's arm, severed between his wrist and elbow, fell to the platform. McLean swung the knife in a hard and very fast left-to-right. It sliced off Krupper's head like a headsman's ax.

"You sure fucked that up. I thought you were so good," Haney said, picking up Krupper's Schmeiser.

McLean didn't reply. This was no time to talk about what had gone wrong. He and Haney darted over to the dinghy, which Pollard and Lt. Marlatt had paddled against the U-boat's port flank. "How'd it go?" Lt. Marlatt asked, handing up a 5-gallon can of gasoline.

"Nothing to it," Haney said, taking the gasoline can. McLean put the other 5-gallon can on the platform. Then he and Haney gripped the upreached hands of Lt. Marlatt and Art Schilling and pulled them onto the platform, Russ Broughton climbing up by himself.

Steve Pollard remained in the dinghy. He would stay on it. It would be hazardous to leave it unattended. If it drifted off, the Americans on the platform would be doomed. "The platform of an enemy submarine is sure as hell no place to be when you have no way to escape," Lt. Marlatt had said.

"Watch you don't slip," Haney warned Schilling and Broughton, who had picked up the cans of gasoline. "One of the Krauts lost his juice."

The Americans, Haney and McLean going first, the Schmeisers in their hands, crept toward the conning. "Jesus," Schilling muttered when he passed Krupper's body, a ghastly sight in the moonlight.

They came to the conning. Its hatch was open. Kapitän Wassermann had said, "Leave it open. We can all stand some nice cool night air."

There would be plenty of time to secure it if a dive became necessary. There were two sentries up on the platform and, more important, two experienced hydrophone men at their stations listening to the sea's sounds. There was no way an Allied warship could approach the *Grossdeutschland* without the U-boat's awareness.

Lt. Marlatt, gripping a Very flare pistol, looked quickly at his men. Everyone was at the ready. "Let her go!" he whispered.

Schilling and Broughton began to dump gasoline down

the conning's open hatch. It poured from the cans in great drenches; the Americans had sawed off most of the cans' tops, which had been a sweaty, slow task with the *Wasp*'s little hacksaw.

"That's enough!" Marlatt said. There might be some gasoline still in the cans, but enough was down there.

"Stand back . . . goddammit, stand back!" Marlatt shouted.

No need for silence now. He fired the Very's flare down the conning. Instantly a great whoosh exploded up out of the conning, its orange flames tinged with red from the Very's flare.

The Americans ran toward the dinghy. They lowered themselves into it one at a time. Two at a time would capsize the little rubber boat.

To Haney who was standing last with the Schmeiser, they seemed unnecessarily slow. "Get going, you bastards!" he said, uncaring that Lt. Marlatt was one of the men he had called a bastard. "If this baby blows we're going to the moon!"

Chapter Fourteen

Fritz Wiers, twenty-three, Seaman 1/K., Atlantic U-boat Fleet, German Navy, was polishing the sea scope's lens when the Americans who had crept up onto the *Grossdeutschland*'s platform knifed its night sentries.

"That ought to be clean enough," Wiers said to Ensign Konrad Rutters, twenty-seven, the officer of the watch. Wiers put his polishing rag into a hip pocket.

"I thought I heard something topside," Ensign Rutters said. "Like people walking on the platform. You hear anything?"

Wiers said he hadn't heard anything. "But I wasn't listening. I was concentrating on this lens. You know how the Kapitän is. One little tiny bit of dust and he raises hell."

"Maybe it was just my imagination," Rutters said.

Navigation Leutnant Heinrich Schalling was sitting on the chart bench stool plotting the *Grossdeutschland*'s course to the Madeira Channel, where the big U-boat would stalk an American troop convoy en route from New York to Portsmouth, a port city in south-central England.

"Shut up, you too!" Schalling said. "I can't concentrate with that stupid damn conversation."

What he was doing, he said, was of the utmost importance. "If we can torpedo a couple of American troop ships on our next mission, there will be a thousand American soldiers, at least, who will never kill Germans."

"I wish the Americans had stayed out of the war," Rutters said. "We had it made until—"

Rutters's eyes widened. "What the hell is that?" he said, staring at the conning tower's ladder.

Some kind of liquid was pouring down from the conning's hatch in great drenches.

Lt. Schalling looked up from the chart bench. *"Mein Gott!"* he croaked.

"What the hell happened?" Wiers babbled, staring, eyes distended, at the gasoline that the Americans on the U-boat's platform were pouring down its conning's hatch.

"Never mind what happened, *dummkopf*!" Schalling bellowed. "Get up that ladder and close that hatch!"

He didn't wait to see if Wiers carried out his order. He leaped up from the chart bench stool and sprinted toward the passageway that led to the forward compartments. It was gasoline that was being poured down the conning. He could tell from its smell. He wanted to get out of this compartment and close its hatch before the gasoline exploded.

It would doom Rutters and that enlisted man, who would be trapped, but in a situation like this a man had to look out for himself.

He hadn't taken more than two steps when Lt. Marlatt, up on the platform, fired a red flare from a Very pistol down the conning.

The gasoline was several inches deep on the deck near the base of the ladder and rapidly flowing over the rest of the compartment's deck. It exploded with a horrendous whooosh that shot flames up the conning and into the sky, totally enveloped the scope compartment, and sent flames down the passageway the full length of the big U-boat, and into the compartments whose hatches to the passageway were open.

Lt. Schalling, Rutters, and Wiers instantly became human torches, their bodies drenched with flaming gasoline. *"Mein Gott!"* Wiers croaked.

Those were his last words. Flames shot into his opened mouth. He collapsed and writhed in the deck's flaming gasoline in the moments before he died.

Ensign Rutters, his eyes melted by the flames, hands distended and burning, groped for a moment before he collapsed and died. Lt. Schalling remained on his feet the longest of any of them, staggering toward the hatch through which he had hoped to escape. He tried to brush the flames from his face. He kept moaning in an eerie, high-pitched way. Then he fell to his knees, remaining there, his entire body aflame, for a moment before he fell over onto the deck, writhed horribly, then lay still.

Chief Petty Officers Bruno Siebert, Karl Wandel, and Johann Kiger were lolling in their bunks in Compartment VI, the chiefs' quarters, when the gasoline exploded.

Siebert and Wandel were talking about the softball games on the U-boat's platform, and laughing about Wandel's diving into the sea three times to recover the ball that Siebert had tossed to him and Wandel had missed. Kiger was reading the editorial page of *Volkischer Beobachter.* A fourth man, Anton Busch, the U-boat's gunnery chief, was sleeping.

Flames from the terrible explosion swept through the hatch of the chiefs' quarters, which had been left open "to get some of the night air" from the conning's open hatch.

The chief petty officers leaped off their bunks, brushing and clawing at the flames that were blinding them and searing their flesh. "Oh, *Mein Gott!*" Kiger shrieked. Already blinded, his agony was indescribable.

It was no better for Siebert and Wandel. They screamed and clawed at the flames, and Wandel tried to wrap a blanket around his body to extinguish them. Both men, and Kiger, collapsed onto the deck and writhed and shrieked in the few moments that were left of their lives.

Chief Petty Officer Busch, who had also been sleeping when his compartment was suddenly filled with flames, leaped up in perplexed agony. In the moment before his eyes were melted he saw the agonies of the other chiefs. Then he leaped off his bunk and staggered toward the hatch that led to the passageway.

He didn't reach it. He fell and flailed on the deck, dying flat on his back with his arms sticking up, their fingers already burned.

It was the same sheer, raw horror in enlisted men's compartments II, IV, and VII. Suddenly and without warning the compartments were solid masses of flames, cremating their shrieking occupants.

The flames seared the U-boat's little sick bay, its intense heat igniting its medicaments and adding their flames and fumes to the disaster.

Mediziner Chief Petty Officer Adolf Schumann's final awareness was the shriek of someone screaming for the U-boat's medical officer. But Schumann could help no one, not even himself.

Kapitän Wilhelm Wassermann was in his cabin, its hatch closed. It denigrated the dignity and privacy of a ship's captain to be exposed to the view of every man who walked past. Besides, he didn't need the air that wafted down from the open conning. A fan on a bulkhead shelf, beside the photos of his wife and daughters, blew a refreshing breeze onto his cot.

He was sitting at the desk in his tiny quarters—everything on a submarine is designed for maximum utility of space. He was reading a secret message the *Grossduetschland*'s signals transmitter officer had just received in code from flotilla headquarters at St. Nazaire.

He was in good spirits. It had been refreshing being up on the platform this afternoon, breathing the clean air. The message from headquarters was pleasing. A good life, this captaincy of a free-hunt U-boat, he reflected. But then, he had done well for Germany. An espouser of stealth and ruse, he had sunk more than 27,000 tons of Allied shipping, destroying, in addition to weapons and supplies, hundreds of American soldiers.

Headquarters had not ignored his accomplishments. When he returned to St. Nazaire he would be awarded the Long Service Medal. After that, if he kept up his good work, it would be the Iron Cross, and then, perhaps, the highest honor awarded to anyone in the German Navy, the diamond-studded Victory Medal.

Of course, the Nazis had not yet achieved victory, but it was just a matter of time. The U-Waffe was winning the war for Germany. Actually, Kapitän Wassermann reflected, looking in the mirror above his bunk and twirling his long black mustache in upward sweeps like Kaiser Wilhelm's famed mustache, it is the few competent U-boat captains like myself who are winning the war. All we have to do is continue to sink the ships that are bringing supplies to England and American troops to aid their British cousins.

Stupid Anglo-Americans . . . they have no way to detect our submarines, even when we're close enough to see the barnacles on their keels. Their technicians have been unable to invent an impulse-detection device even remotely as efficient as our hydrophone equipment.

Wassermann smiled as he conjured up a vision of himself as *Gauleiter* in some big American city after the Fuehrer laid down the terms of surrender. It would be an appropriate reward for so competent and valuable a U-boat captain.

The explosion of the gasoline in the scope compartment and the immediate shrieks and screams of the men who were being burned by the explosion's flames jarred Wassermann out of his reveries. "For God's sake!" he babbled.

He leaped up and ran to the hatch that led onto the passageway. He took his hand from its locking lever. To step out of this compartment into whatever was going on out there without knowing what it was would be indiscreet. He swooped the phone off the bulkhead above his desk. "What the hell's going on?" he bellowed on the big submarine's public address. No one responded. "Executive Officer Hennig, report to the captain's office!" Wassermann shouted.

Korvettenkapitän Hennig did not report. He was dying, flesh falling from his face.

"Damage control parties, man your stations!" Wassermann bellowed into the PA speaker. "Fire control parties, man your stations!"

He hung up the speaker. "Jesus Christ . . ." he croaked, his tongue flicking over his lips. He wondered what had happened. Something terrible, that was obvious.

He could hear the crackle of flames and the shrieks of horribly burned men. "I've got to know what's going on . . . and assume command of the situation," he said aloud. "It is my duty as Kapitän."

Kapitän Wassermann may have been a glory seeker and a ruthless antagonist of Allied shipping, but he had personal courage and a sincere feel for his men. He cracked the hatch and looked out. The flames had burned themselves out in the passageway, but it was filled with the stench of burning flesh and smoke.

He went out into the corridor. Then he went back into his compartment and hurriedly soaked a towel in the sink of his private head, put it over his face, just below his eyes, and went back out into the passageway.

He went aft, toward the conning, stepping over charred, smoking bodies and around blinded still-living men whose screams were difficult for this crew-oriented officer to ignore.

He met his torpedo officer, Lt. Johann Triebelhorn, just before he came to the scope compartment. "What the hell happened?" he demanded, choking despite the towel.

"I don't know." Triebelhorn, an intense young officer with blue eyes and crewcut yellow hair, said, terror in his voice, "God, all I know is there was a hell of an explosion and it came from up this way, I think."

"How about the torpedoes? If they blow we're dead. Every one of us!"

"They're secure. Flames licked the paint off the port rack, but they're OK. That's the first thing I checked."

"Any word from hydrophone?"

"Those men are dead. Both of them. And their equipment is burned. It's gone, sir. Totally."

"How about communications?"

"They're dead, too. Their radios practically melted. You can't even tell who those men are. Just charred bodies."

Wassermann told Triebelhorn to keep the fire and damage control parties functioning. "I'm going topside. I've got to know what's going on!"

"Here, take my Walther, Kapitän. You shouldn't go up there unarmed."

He pulled the Walther semi-automatic 9mm pistol from its holster and extended it to Kapitän Wassermann.

Moments later Wassermann was on the *Grossdeutschland*'s platform. *"Mein Gott . . ."* he muttered, looking at Krupper's decapitated body, involuntarily looking around to see if he could spot its head.

He bent over Bruno Schwartzger's body and turned it onto its belly. "Stabbed," he muttered.

He went back to Krupper's headless body and turned it over with his shoe. "Uh huh," he said aloud.

He got up and looked around. Then he saw the gasoline can that Schilling had flung away but that had become lodged between a Kluge twin machine gun and its platform-welded metal ammo box. He picked it up. "USN" was stenciled on it in large white letters.

He flung the can back onto the platform. "Goddam Americans!" he said, his face twisted with rage. "The bastards got up here, knifed my sentries, and poured gasoline down the conning!"

And then, he reflected, they paddled their *verdammt* little boat back to their submarine. Or destroyer, or whatever it was.

But why hadn't the hydrophone watch become aware of the proximity of their ship?

He would never know, he reflected, climbing down the conning's ladder. They were dead. Cremated alive, Lt. Triebelhorn had said.

"Get some fans up here and blow this stinking air up

100

the conning!" he bellowed to two men he could see through the murk in the scope compartment.

One of them was Ensign Franz Holbuch, the *Grossdeutschland*'s deputy navigation officer. "I want a damage report, Holbuch. Right away!"

"Yes, sir," Holbuch said. "As fast as I can get it!"

He went down the passageway, holding a kerchief over his nose. "You!" Wassermann said to the man who had been with Holbuch, Apprentice Seaman Werner Kohrs, nineteen. "Find another man and start bringing the dead bodies here to this compartment!"

"Sir," the short blond youth said shakily, "I don't think I can do it. I already got sick two times just looking at them. I just know I won't be able—"

"Goddammit, shove off and carry out your orders!"

"Yes, sir!" Kohrs squeaked.

He saluted the captain and went down the passageway to find some other enlisted man to help him with his ghoulish task. He'd get sick again, he knew he would. In fact, just thinking about it was making him sick. He leaned against the bulkhead and vomited.

Chapter Fifteen

For several uncertain moments, Kapitän Wassermann remained in the scope room, the wet towel over his mouth and nose, deciding what he ought to do. The U-boat had been badly damaged. Many of its crew had been killed by the explosion's concussion or by its horrendous sheets of flames. Some, still alive, suffered ghastly and excruciatingly painful burns. "Damn those tricky American devils!" Wassermann said bitterly.

He hadn't particularly disliked Americans before tonight's disaster, looking upon them as fair game in the gory business of war. But now, after what they had done to his command—and what this disaster would do to his chances of winning an Iron Cross and the Victory Medal—he hated them with the fervor of a fanatic.

"I could cut the throats of the *Schwein* who did this to me," he said, not caring if anyone was within hearing, "and laugh while the sons of pigs bled to death."

We will still win this war, he reflected, going down the passageway toward his cabin. And afterward—if I can persuade the government to assign me as *Gauleiter* or police president in an American city, I will make those American *Schwein* dance to Germany's tune.

He jerked his phone off its hook. "This is your captain!" he said on the U-boat's public address. "All officers lay up to the platform immediately!"

Up there, where the air didn't stink like burning human flesh, and where the officers would be removed as far as possible from the screams and pleas of men who had been burned, he would assess the *Grossdeutschland*'s plight and decide what course to take.

Three officers reported to the platform: Torpedo Officer Johann Triebelhorn, Ensign Franz Holbuch, and Kapitänleutnant Hans Witters, the *Grossdeutschland*'s engineering officer. Triebelhorn and Holbuch, along with

102

Kapitän Wassermann, had escaped injury in the terrible explosion. Witters had third-degree burns on his back, buttocks, and legs. His crewcut straw-colored hair had been singed from the back of his head. His scalp in this area had been burned and blistered.

"Don't ask me if it hurts, you dumb idiots," he said to the other officers, not caring if Kapitän Wassermann thought he was included. "Of course it hurts, especially the backs of my ears. God, they're raw."

Triebelhorn said Witters was lucky he had had his back to the flames when they flared into the engineering room. "I'm lucky, all right," Witters said drily. "I'd have been a damn sight luckier if I'd stayed in my compartment with the hatch closed. But, being dedicated, I had to check things in engineering."

The burned officer's teeth were clenched. His agony was obvious. "There isn't a fucking thing left in the sick bay. That burn ointment Schumann kept on a ledge where anybody could get it in an emergency is gone. Even the tubes melted."

"I've heard that plain ordinary bearing grease is good for burns," Holbuch said. "I'll put some on your burns, if you want me to."

"*Ja* . . . anything. Jesus Christ, I'll try anything," Witters said, his face twisted in anguish.

"There's a can of grease in that box aft of the AA rifle," Kapitän Wassermann said, turning to the helpful young ensign. "Get some of it. You can put it on Witters while we're talking."

While the officers appraised the situation, Holbuch gently applied grease intended to lubricate the antiaircraft rifle's hydraulic mechanism on the burned engineering officer. "At least your balls didn't get burned. Some of the men, the ones wearing just their shorts, got their whole bag of tricks burned off."

"We didn't come up here to talk about incinerated genitals!" Kapitän Wassermann snapped. "It seems to me we have several more important items to discuss!"

"Yes, sir! Sorry, sir!" Holbuch said. He was just trying to make Witters feel better, he reflected.

Kapitän Wassermann said, "See the bodies of our deck sentries over there in the shadows? Look especially at the one who was decapitated. They weren't killed by the cool night air or flying fish. They were killed by an American

Navy boarding party. These same Americans poured gasoline down our conning's open hatch—there's a gasoline can with USN on it right over there. Then, of course, they returned to their submarine or surface ship.

"That is what happened, and don't ask why hydrophone didn't discover the approach of their ship. We'll never know. The hydrophone men and their equipment were destroyed. So now that we know the reason for our disaster we will proceed with what we must do, and what we have available to do it with."

He turned to Holbuch, who was continuing to apply grease to Witters's burns. "Let's have your damage report. You don't have to stop what you're doing."

Ensign Holbuch made his report. Then the other officers told what they knew about the damage. "Well, gentlemen," Kapitän Wassermann said, "summing it up, we're in one hell of a situation. We have burned men and no medicines and no medical officer. Only a third of the crew is able to function. We have no operable radio. We cannot ask for help.

"On the positive side, the *Grossdeutschland* is apparently operable. We have adequate fuel to return us easily to the nearest U-boat base, the one in Porto Santo. We have an engineering officer, a navigation officer, and a torpedo officer, who, for the duration, I am appointing as my executive officer.

"We will get underway at 0700. We will have to cruise on the surface. We have no functional periscopes. In the meantime I want the bodies of the dead brought up here for disposition. Which will be the first function of my new executive officer."

The screams of the wounded could be heard with nerve-jangling clarity, their anguished sounds coming up the conning. "What about them?" Triebelhorn asked.

"It would be an act of mercy to shoot them. But we Germans are not barbarians. I want all of them put into one compartment. One whose noises we can pretty much shut off. No one can function with them all over the boat. They'll drive the rest of us *Verruckt*.

"Right now," Wassermann went on, "we'll send up a distress flare, and repeat at half-hour intervals. With luck another U-boat will see it, or one of our patrol planes."

Ensign Holbuch, still putting grease on the engineering officer's burns, said, "Kapitän, sir, we have no flares. The flare locker must have been left open, or at least it wasn't secured. The fire ignited them "

Wassermann's lips became tight. "Damn those Americans!" he said bitterly.

With night-lens optics Joe Silva had watched the other Americans paddle the *Wasp*'s little rubber dinghy across the gently rolling sea toward the surfaced U-boat.

"Good luck, you guys," he said aloud. "You're gonna need it."

He couldn't see them crawl up onto the U-boat's platform. They were on the U-boat's far flank But he was able to watch them sneak up on the Nazi sentries, and when Wally McLean fumbled the knifing of the U-boat sentry, he said, deeply concerned, "You dumb ass! I told you you had to do it quick or you just might be the one that gets the—"

He didn't finish. McLean, swinging his knife like a machete, had killed the German. "Well, that's one way to do it," Silva said, unaware that he was talking aloud and not thinking that there was no one else on the disguised PT.

He watched his colleagues dump their two 5-gallon cans of gasoline—from the *Wasp*'s fuel tank—down the U-boat's conning, and Lt. Marlatt fire a Very pistol's red flare into it.

"Jesus H. Keerist," he said, grinning, watching the orange and red flames from the explosion of the gasoline shoot up out of the conning.

He put the glasses on his colleagues. They were lowering themselves into the dinghy. He looked back at the conning Obviously no one could come out of it with weapons with which to annihilate the Americans. But he felt better, making sure.

He looked over at the Portuguese fishing boat. Several of its lights had come on. "What the hell's going on?" someone on the boat yelled in Portuguese.

"How the hell would I know?" Silva shouted to the fishing boat. "I'm getting out of here!"

"Me, too!" the Portuguese shouted.

He's the fishing boat's captain, Silva realized. A crewman wouldn't be making the decision. Get going, cousin, he reflected. I don't want you to see me picking up our guys.

Silva turned toward the U-boat, looking at it and the waters off its port stern with the night optics. He saw the dinghy. Schilling and Broughton were paddling as fast as they could. The others were looking back at the U-boat. Silva turned the glasses toward the U-boat. Flames were still jutting up out of its conning's hatch. "If that sumbitch blows," he muttered, "we're all going bye-bye."

He looked over at the Portuguese fishing boat. It was underway south by southwest. That was great. The U-boat would conceal the rescue of the *Wasp*'s crew. Everything was working like four aces in a payday game. Silva began to take the camouflaged PT on a parabolic course toward the dinghy.

A little later he pulled up beside the dinghy. In less than a minute the pirates were on the *Wasp* and the dinghy was secured. "Let's go home!" Marlatt said, looking at the flames jutting from the hatch of the U-boat's conning, apprehension on his face.

The *Grossdeutschland*'s torpedoes did not explode, and soon the *Wasp* was wallowing on a feint course for Pico Cove. "That was what I would call quite an experience," Marlatt said after the *Wasp* was beyond peril of an explosion of the U-boat's torpedoes.

"It's the stuff from which heroes are made," Pollard said. "My kids will be proud of me."

"You don't have any kids," Schilling said.

"It's the poet in me," Pollard explained.

About four miles from the *Grossdeutschland*, Lt. Marlatt ordered his crew to secure for night anchor. "We'd better get some sleep. Tomorrow we wallow home. And it could be quite a day if Nazi aircraft get the word from the U-boat and start looking for scamps with arson in their souls."

"That's us, the famous Torch Brigade of the United States Navy," Silva said.

"You weren't even there, Frogface," Haney said. "You were playing nice-and-safe while the rest of us risked our lives for God and country."

"The rabble we have to associate with in the service," Silva said, shaking his head sadly. "My mother warned me there would be rascals like Haney."

Haney said if he wasn't so tired he'd bust Silva's ass.

"Excuses, excuses," Silva said, taking a cigarette from

the pack in Haney's shirt pocket and adding, "I need a match, too, Ugly."

Haney gave his friend a match. "Sure one butt will do it?"

"I doubt it," Silva said, taking two more cigarettes from the pack.

"Take the whole pack!" Haney said, not entirely joking about it.

"Thanks," Silva said, pulling the pack out of Haney's pocket.

"Well, Jesus Christ," Haney said, astounded by Silva's temerity. "Listen, man, I've only got that one pack. It's got to last until we get to Pico."

"If you feel the need for a cigarette," Silva said, "I'll lend you one, though I hate moochers."

Haney clenched his fists. "Uh uh!" Lt. Marlatt said, grinning. "According to the Articles of War you can't bust anybody's ass on a U.S. Navy ship while it is on assignment in hostile waters."

The next morning, at dawn, the *Wasp* continued toward Pico Cove. It would have to be refueled and reprovisioned before it made another foray into the Nazis' U-boat sanctuary.

Joe Silva and Guns Haney had emerged as the outstanding personalities of the crew of the masquerading PT.

Silva, twenty-four, Gunner's Mate First Class, was a very short man. "The first one of you freaks that calls me Shorty gets a kick in the balls," he had said. "After which I'll start getting mean."

He had black hair, a heavy black mustache, and wide-spaced dark eyes which reflected his intelligence and mischievousness. He was an affable man with a charismatic personality. "You can't help liking the cocky little bastard," Art Schilling, the *Wasp*'s radioman and depth bomb thrower had said.

Silva, who liked to say he was "pure Portuguese," was intensely patriotic. He was courageous. He was also a very tough little man. He had lived in southern California all of his life until joining the U.S. Navy in 1941. "The day after Pearl Harbor I signed up."

Paul Haney, twenty-six, wanted to be known as Guns. He was expert with the *Wasp*'s 3-inch rifle and proud of his skill with the big deadly weapon. He was six feet one.

He had unruly sandy hair, blue-gray eyes, a firm jaw, a nose that was too big, and ears that seemed to protrude straight out from his head.

He had a wife and two small children in Kansas City, where he had been an assembly-line supervisor in the General Motors Chevrolet plant.

He had an outgoing personality and a warm, friendly smile. But he could be tough when the occasion demanded toughness. He despised Nazis. "If it wasn't for those sons of bitches I'd be home with my wife and kids."

The more he killed, and the quicker he killed them, he reasoned, the earlier he would be able to rejoin his family. "When I lay a 3-incher into one of those U-boats it's a personal kiss from me," he liked to say.

The *Wasp* wallowed, at no greater speed than an authentic Portuguese fishing boat, toward its sanctuary at Pico Cove on the eastern shore of São Miguel. It seemed frustratingly slow. "I could swim faster than we're going," Haney complained, leaning on the starboard rail and looking out over the sea.

"I know how you feel," Lt. Marlatt said, "but we can't risk blowing the masquerade by going any faster than a legit fishing boat."

Haney turned toward Marlatt. "You know what I think? I think we got the shaft when they gave us this assignment. It's got to be the most dangerous work in the whole Navy. It's Russian roulette every time we tackle one of those U-boats. What's it all about, Mr. Marlatt? Without the bull, what are we doing this for?"

"There's some kind of big plan in it," Marlatt said. "That's all I know, and that's the foursquare truth. You heard Captain Langer give me the brush when I tried to learn the purpose of our work. He said, 'Your job, Marlatt, will be to kill U-boats. Not to ask why.'

"So I didn't ask why. A jg doesn't squeeze a Navy captain. So I don't know a damn bit more about it than you do."

He was telling the truth, and Haney and the others who were listening knew it. They had been right there when Captain Langer had given Marlatt the button.

"Like I said," Marlatt continued, "it's part of some kind of strategy that's got to be big. Nobody has told me this. I've noodled it myself. But common sense will tell us that even if we sank one U-boat per day, a ridiculous thing even to think of, it would take us a year and a half, working seven days a week, to destroy the German's U-boat Fleet."

"That wouldn't even do it," Silva said, a cigarette bobbling between his lips. "I read somewhere where the Krauts are grinding out ten U-boats a week. At one a day we wouldn't even be keeping even. So what's HQ's big deal of which we are a small, expendable, none-of-our-business part?"

Marlatt said he wished he knew. "I guess we just do and die, ours not to reason why."

"Forget that noise!" Haney said, his face grim. "This sailor boy's going home someday!"

"Maybe you will," Silva said, "and maybe you won't. We're supposed to keep killing every U-boat we see until we get good enough to tackle their famous wolfpack.

"You know what our chances are going to be then? One U-boat at a time we can handle, we've found that out. But take eight or nine and how the hell are we going to do it? We can't shoot off all their rudders and blast their periscopes and put holes in their connings then say 'We gotcha, you dumb Krauts.' "

Silva flung his cigarette into the sea. "You know what I'm going to do? The next time we see old blood-and-guts Langer—he'll have to see us to give us the green light on the wolfpack—I'm going to say, 'Captain Langer, you big fancy gold-braid mother, I demand to know for what reason you expect us to tackle a U-boat wolfpack all by ourselves, the chances of us living to tell our grandchildren being like A-zero.' "

"He will burn your ass," Haney said.

Silva ignored this counsel. "I will then tell him if he wants us to go on the same as a suicide mission we have got a constitutional right to know what we're going to be heroes for. Then I'm going to tell him it is illegal, immoral, and pure crap to expect us to get scragged and not even know what we got scragged for."

"He will still burn your ass," Haney said.

Chapter Sixteen

Captain John J. Langer, Deputy Commandant, Azores-Gibraltar Sea Frontier, field chief of Operation Sting, flew his Kingfisher Vought-Sikorsky VOS, a rigid-wing Navy-built single-engine seaplane, to the placid Atlantic waters off the eastern shore of São Miguel Island.

Skillfully, Langer, the Kingfisher's pilot and only occupant, taxied the little seaplane into the *Wasp*'s hideout in Pico Cove.

He had flown to the Azores from Gibraltar, 1,150 miles to the east, a decision he had made after he received the latest action report from the *Wasp*, radioed in code, while the disguised PT was returning to Pico after its crew's daring attack on the Nazi U-boat *Grossdeutschland*.

"I wonder what he wants?" Lt. Marlatt said, leaning on the starboard rail, watching Pollard and McLean paddle the *Wasp*'s little rubber dinghy toward the seaplane.

"I'll bet it's not to award any Big Hero medals," Joe Silva said, popping a cigarette into his mouth. "He either came here to bitch about something or else to give us the go on the wolfpack."

"You got it wrong," Guns Haney said, grinning. "He came here up replace you with somebody intelligent."

"Up yours," Silva said.

Lt. Marlatt turned toward Silva. "Joe," he said, "play it cool while the captain's aboard, will you? And watch your language."

"You will watch your language, won't you, Joseph?" Haney said, his grin broadening.

"Keep it going," Silva said. "Just keep it going."

Haney looked over at Marlatt. "Mr. Silva wants to tell the captain that if he doesn't cut us in on the reason for our little anti-U-boat campaign Mr. Silva is going to tell him we got constitutional rights."

"If I had a brig I'd bury both you idiots," Marlatt said.

"Seriously—pay attention, you guys—don't wise-ass while the captain's here. Now help him aboard, and put some class into it."

They helped Captain Langer out of the dinghy, and after the usual amenities he said, "The *Wasp* has made more kills than we had anticipated, which brings to mind a basic fact of war: 'Repeated tactics almost always end in disaster.' Therefore we see peril in continuing your assaults until we are ready for the attack upon the wolfpack, which is the reason for your operation. Your free-hunt attacks on individual units of the Germans' U-boat fleets have been, in our strategy, actually training preparations for the attack on the wolfpack. So we are putting a temporary hold on your forays."

"May I ask," Lt. Marlatt inquired, "what is the purpose of our forthcoming attack on the U-boats' principal wolfpack? Obviously, the results, even if we are totally successful, cannot be, from the Germans' points of view, a disaster greater than reasonable normal attrition in the hazardous game of U-boat warfare."

Captain Langer's stern face became taut. "Marlatt, I told you back at Gibraltar, when you asked a related question, if not the identical question, that we at Azores-Gibraltar Sea Frontier are sole custodians of the strategy."

"Sorry, sir," Marlatt said, his lips tight.

"The bastard," Silva muttered to Haney, who stood beside him, both of them being aft of the officers.

"Now's the time to tell him we've got a constitutional right to know what's going on," Haney said.

"You're out of your mind," Silva muttered.

"What's come over you, Silva? Yesterday you said you were going to tell him off if he didn't pop with the scoop."

"Shut up, you stupid idiot," Silva whispered. "He'll hear you."

Haney turned to the headquarters officer. "Captain Langer, sir?"

The captain turned to the big Navy man. "What is it, sailor?"

"Gunner's Mate Silva, here, wants to tell you something."

The captain looked at Silva. "Yes?" he said, annoyance showing on his sea-weathered face.

One of Joe Silva's attributes was his ability to improvise. "I just wanted to tell you, sir," he said, looking into the captain's eyes, and appearing very serious, "that I consider it an honor to serve the United States of America on this dangerous mission."

The captain smiled. "That's a fine attitude, sailor. You're the Portuguese we recruited, aren't you?"

"No, sir," Silva said. "I'm an American citizen. My parents came from Portugal. I was born in San Diego, there on Island Avenue down near where the railroad tracks and the waterfront come together."

"Keep up the good work, Silva," the captain said, turning back to Marlatt.

"You son of a bitch," Silva whispered, glaring at Haney. Haney, a mischievous look on his craggy face, pretended he hadn't heard.

"May I ask, sir," Lt. Marlatt asked the captain, "how long we can expect to be on hold status?"

Captain Langer shrugged his shoulders. "I can't tell you right now. I don't know. It depends upon certain developments. But at least a week. Perhaps a month."

He looked over at the enlisted men, then back at Marlatt. "I suggest you form liberty parties to Ponta Delgado for a well-earned change of pace. Three go, four remain here on watch, or vice versa.

"Since you will be here for a minimum of a week, you can give each party two or three days in Delgado, and repeat until we order the *Wasp* into action. But *always*—get this, Marlatt—always this boat must be adequately guarded. No one—I repeat, *no one*—is to be permitted aboard except the refueling and provisioning men from the Albemarle Naval Supply Base. And they must be under their officer's supervision.

"Naturally, if they ask questions about the disguising of this boat, or its purpose, you will refuse to answer."

The captain said he would fly now to the Albemarle base to refuel, stay overnight in the officers' billet, and return to Gibraltar the next morning.

Pollard and McLean paddled the dinghy, Captain Langer aboard, back to the floating blue Kingfisher, and soon the doughty headquarters officer was taxiing the little seaplane out of the cove.

"Anybody got any idea why we're getting a vacation?" Silva said. "Not that I'm complaining."

"I've got a feeling I'll be the last man in the United

112

States Navy to find out," Marlatt said, lighting up a cigarette.

"Whatever it is," Art Schilling said, "they don't want us to hit the wolfpack until somebody, for some reason, is ready. What the hell do you suppose it is?"

"Mr. Flag-Waving Silva was going to insist that Langer tell us," Haney said with a wink. "But then, as everybody noticed, he chickened out."

"Haney," Silva said, taking a cigarette from a pack in Haney's shirt pocket, "someday you're going to make me mad."

He put a match to the cigarette, and then, the cigarette between his lips, he said, "The reason we're not supposed to hit that wolfpack is no longer my main subject of interest. It had suddenly become those hot-pants little Portuguese ladies in Ponta Delgado. How are you going to divide us guys, Mr. Marlatt?"

Marlatt thought on it. "How about everybody draws a card from our poker deck? The three high-card men go on first liberty."

"For how long?"

Again the lieutenant's lips pursed while he thought on this facet of the *Wasp*'s new program. "Three days, three nights. Same for the next bunch. Then we'll draw all over again, to give everybody an equal chance, in case only one section can go on the next happy time."

There was always the chance, he explained, that Captain Langer would order the *Wasp* into action before the cycle of liberties could be repeated.

The paddlers returned with the dinghy. "Somebody shuffle and cut," Marlatt said, the *Wasp*'s deck of cards in his hand. "Remember, the three high cards go on first liberty."

Silva drew the queen of hearts. Haney drew the king of spades. Wally McLean took the ten of diamonds from the deck, which Marlatt had laid face down on the forward machine gun's ammo box.

"Don't you wish you could speak Portuguese, you ignorant foreigner," Silva said to Haney. "I'll be screwing my lady while you're saying 'Me Haney . . . you wanna bouncy-wouncy?' "

"Back where I come from," Haney said, "they pay a bounty for creeps like you."

Lt. Marlatt grinned. These rough-talking men had become the best of friends. If anyone talked to either of them as they talked to each other somebody would have to break out the battle dressings.

The reason for the headquarters hold on the *Wasp*'s impending attack on the U-Waffe's wolfpack continued to perplex the masquerading PT's crew. They weren't unhappy about it, though. It meant at least one long liberty for each of them in Ponta Delgado, the district capital of São Miguel, largest in size and population of the nine islands of the Azores group.

"Whatever the reason," Silva said happily, "I'm for it 110 percent."

"You're as fickle as a female," Haney said. "Just yesterday you were going to blow your cork if you couldn't find out what our mission was all about."

"Be nice to me, Frogface," Silva said, blowing cigarette smoke onto his friend's face. "Or I'll tell the ladies in Ponta Delgado you've got the clap."

The thoughts of the little boat's valiant crew were on the good times they anticipated in Ponta Delgado, though none had been in the lively little port city. They seldom gave thought, anymore, to the reason for the liberties. Plenty of time to think—and worry—about the attack on the wolfpack after Captain Langer gave the go.

The purpose behind the hold on these daring young Americans was of primary importance, however, to the war efforts of the United States and Britain, and it related directly to the *Wasp*'s little crew.

Technicians in seven U.S. and British universities and four U.S. government quasi-military laboratories were desperately trying to complete development of an ultrasonic impulse submarine detection apparatus.

A reliable, effective detector was nearing completion, the eleven facilities cooperating in sharing techniques and achievements. But several frustrating technical problems remained before it could be released to the two American electronics firms who would give AAA1 priority to its manufacture.

Crews were being trained to install the device, to be known as sonar, in every American and British warship, tanker, and auxiliary ship. "We will have sonar equipment on every Allied ship in three weeks from go," Rear Admiral F. E. M. McIntyre, in charge of the project, assured the two navies.

Meanwhile U-boats, able to approach Allied shipping with virtual immunity, were sinking thousands of tons, killing with these destroyed ships trained seamen and in the case of troop ships an enormous number of American, Canadian, and British soldiers.

It was particularly frustrating to Admiral McIntyre and his hard-working technicians that the Nazis had already invented, and had put to murderous use, a highly functional hydrophonic apparatus that successfully located the underwater sounds made by a ship's propellors. It enabled their U-boats to elude Allied destroyers and their deadly depth bombs after an attack on Allied ships or convoys.

"The cold facts are," Admiral McIntyre said, "if we don't get our own apparatus operable pretty damn soon we stand a chance of losing this war."

This was the truth of the situation in the first years of World War II. Not even America's enormous capacity to produce tankers and other ships could cope with the attrition of the German Navy's dreaded U-boats.

"If McIntyre's boys ever get that detector working," Captain Langer said, "we'll try to spook the Krauts by destroying one of their major U-boat wolfpacks, making sure they know they got hit by a combat boat disguised to look like a Portuguese fishing boat.

"That, we hope, will make them wary of every Portuguese fishing boat—there are ten thousand of them—and while they're trying to figure how to cope with the situation McIntyre's boys will install sonar or whatever the hell they finally decide to call it on all our ships.

"Then the days of U-boat supremacy will be history and we can go on with the business of winning this damn war."

It was a grandiose scheme, and a lot of factors had to fall into place to precise times, a chancy game at best.

Meanwhile, Joe Silva and the other men of the *Wasp* who had won first liberty privileges were thumbing their way to Ponta Delgado.

"I can't make up my mind whether to get a woman first or get drunk first," Wally McLean said happily.

"I'm going to do both first," Joe Silva said.

Chapter Seventeen

Three weeks and two days from the time Navy Captain John J. Langer, Deputy Commandant, Azores-Gibraltar Sea Frontier, appeared in Pico Cove, he came again.

This time he arrived in a gull-winged Mariner, a Martin PBM-3 patrol bomber. Its pilot landed on the sea just outside Pico Cove, then taxied the big seaplane throughout the narrow rock-wall entrance to the cove, the plane's wings barely clearing the rocks.

A half hour earlier, when the big Gibraltar-based bomber was very close to São Miguel Island, Captain Langer had radioed Lt. Marlatt of his imminent arrival.

Now the Mariner's crew was lowering a fabric dinghy to the cove's placid water. "He's bringing the troops this time," Guns Haney said to his buddy, Joe Silva. Both of them had returned from their last liberty the preceding day.

"He realizes our importance," Silva said, leaning on the rail, picking his teeth with a straw he had pulled out of the little boat's only broom.

Five men had gotten into the dinghy: Captain Langer, a commander, a lieutenant commander, and two enlisted men who wore sidearms. The enlisted men began to paddle toward the *Wasp*.

Lt. Marlatt, standing at the starboard rail aft of Silva and Haney, said, "Either of you swab jockeys want to make book on what he's here for?"

"I like to think big," Silva said, "so I'll bet five cents he's here to tell us our happy vacation just came to the end of its rope. Anybody want to call me?"

"I'll pass," Haney said.

"Likewise," Marlatt said. "You guys help them aboard. The captain first."

"We already knew that," Haney said. "They told us in boot camp a Navy captain is the same as Jesus, almost."

"Then help the commander aboard," Marlatt said.

"Then who?" Silva asked, grinning in his mischievous way.

"Get going, you clowns!" Marlatt said. "They're almost here!"

Soon the entourage from the Mariner was aboard the disguised PT. Langer performed the introductions to Lt. Marlatt. The commander was David Chilson, forty-three, deputy chief of Navy Intelligence, AG Sea Frontier. The lieutenant commander was James Harnett, fifty, liaison officer of the combined Anglo-American radar development project.

"The word is go," Langer said. "Put to sea and find, and destroy, a Nazi U-boat wolfpack. Let's hope it will be their *Amselrudel*, . . . their best, their most vicious, their most successful. Use any and every means to destroy it. Recall your liberty party, Marlatt, provision, and be on your way in twenty-four hours!"

Captain Langer, proud of the *Wasp*'s achievements, showed his colleagues about the disguised PT. "It seems to me," Lt. Cmdr. Harnett said, "that we have a hell of a lot riding on this little boat and its crew. Isn't there some other way to trick the Germans into withholding U-boat attacks while we equip our ships?"

"If there's a better way," Langer said, "tell me. We haven't been able to think of it."

Commander Chilson was even less impressed by the sloppy-appearing little boat and its ragtag crew. Marlatt, Silva, and Haney had uncut straggly hair and long-unshaven faces, and they wore the tattered garments of impoverished Portuguese fishermen.

"Don't put them down," Captain Langer said. "They're a tough bunch. They've got a great track record. And they're going on a mission whose chances of survival are like drawing to an inside straight."

"I still don't like it."

"Well, now, Chilson, maybe you'd like to go with them just to be sure everything is done the way you feel it ought to be done."

"You know very well I wouldn't go—I haven't been at sea for fifteen years."

"Then at least give them your best wishes. And maybe a prayer, Chilson. They're going to need 'em both!"

"I hope it works," Harnett said, his lips tight. "We've got millions of dollars, thousands of hours of research by the best scientific brains in England and America, and God knows how many ships and lives riding on those men."

Langer and the others went back to the bow, where Lt. Marlatt, looking more like a beach bum than the commanding officer of one of the most secret missions of World War II, was smoking a cigarette and talking with Silva and Haney and the two enlisted men from the seaplane.

"We're shoving off now, Marlatt," Langer said. "Any questions?"

"Yes, sir. Suppose we can't find a surfaced wolfpack? We've done a lot of cruising since we began this operation and we haven't even been close to one."

"God, man . . . think positive!" Langer said, his face tense. "Search for one . . . and keep searching!"

"It may take a while."

"I understand. Just keep looking."

Silva, who, with Haney, had been listening to the dialogue said, "Captain Langer, sir, may I ask a question?"

Langer and the others turned toward Silva. "Go ahead, Silva. What is it?"

"What if we see some nice juicy U-boat floating around on the surface, just asking to be sunk, while we're looking for the wolfpack?"

"Sink the son of a bitch," Langer said. "But keep its crew, if you can, from knowing their antagonist is a fishing boat that isn't a fishing boat."

"What if we can't?" Marlatt inquired.

"Sink it anyway. We're so close now to the time when the Nazis are going to find out about the masquerade that it won't make significant difference. But all factors considered, if you can destroy U-boats without revealing your identity, do so."

After the entourage was in the dinghy and on its way to the seaplane, Lt. Marlatt said, "Silva, get on your horse and ride into Ponta Delgado and tell the other guys their liberty just came to a sad, sudden end."

"Why not let us toss to see who goes?" Haney said. "Why should this little freak have to assume the responsibility when it's probably more than he can handle?"

"Because he speaks Portuguese," Marlatt said. "If he has to ask where they are he can ask."

"OK, sir. But remind him he is forbidden to drink alcoholic beverages and lay ladies while he is on official Navy business."

"You're reminded," Marlatt said, looking over at Silva with a wink.

Haney and Silva paddled the *Wasp*'s dinghy to the jungled shore on the island side of the cove. "I've got the feel, old buddy," Silva said, his face grim, "that tackling that wolfpack is not going to be all fun and joy."

"We're crazy to even try it," Haney said.

"We could go AWOL," Silva said, looking at the shore's dense foliage.

"I thought about it, paddling over here," Haney said. "But you want to know something? I won't. And you won't."

"Why won't we?"

"Because we're a couple of stupids. Now get out and bring those other idiots back here."

"When we get back," Silva said, "I'll make like a gull with a fishhook in his belly."

This was the signal of the returning liberty parties—the screech of an agonized seagull. It assured the men on the *Wasp* that they wouldn't paddle into an ambush. São Miguel was said to have more German agents than crabs on its beaches.

Silva leaped out of the boat and vanished into the foliage, and Haney paddled the dinghy toward the *Wasp*. He stopped paddling and looked back at the shore's jungled foliage and thought about his wife and children. "Goddamn this war!" he mumbled. Then he resumed paddling toward the dinghy.

Midmorning of the third day of the *Wasp*'s resumption of its deadly search-and-kill, its crew came upon a U-boat being refueled by a tanker.

"For chrissake," Lt. Marlatt said happily. "Jackpot!"

The U-boat was the *Haifisch* ("Shark"), a 1,000-ton six-tuber with the class designation U-sb41. She'd had a beat in the Channel and had recently been assigned independent free-hunt status by the U-Waffe.

Her captain was Korvettenkapitän Adolph Mischler, thirty-nine, a rising star in the U-Waffe whose most recent kill was the storeship HMS *Lloyd Richard*, a ship with extensive refrigerated space—one of the British Admiralty's legendary "beef boats"—which had been hauling 12,000 tons of beef and 9,000 tons of butter and other dairy products to beleaguered, food-rationed England.

Two 18-inch torpedoes from the *Haifisch*'s forward tubes had sunk the big storeship, the incident occurring in the green Atlantic waters between the Scilly Isles and Lizard Head near the west portal of the English Channel. The *Haifisch* had surfaced after the sinking and her platform gun crews had practiced their skills by shooting the ship's survivors.

The *Haifisch* was an *ersklassig* (first-class) submarine of the U-Waffe, and after she refueled, Mischler intended to take her into the American Sea Lane, where he would lie in wait for another Allied ship to sink for the glory of the Reich.

Refueling at sea, even in the Nazis' U-boat sanctuary, was always a hazardous operation. The tanker and the surfaced U-boat had to remain motionless, which made them a tempting target for the enemy.

It wasn't likely that an enemy would attack the *Haifisch*, Mischler was convinced. There was nothing on his hydrophone and no sign of enemy aircraft. But he would feel better when the refueling was finished. He felt trapped when refueling at sea. If he had to order a crash dive, such a dive would be impossible.

"Hurry, you *Dummkopfs!*" he bellowed to the seamen on the tanker, the *Fettmaterialwarenhandler* ("Fat Grocer"), which carried diesel fuel in large bunkers for her charges, and also ammunition, spare parts, torpedoes, and great stocks of foods. In addition, she had comfortable quarters and recreation facilities for U-boat crews.

The seamen whom the *Haifisch*'s captain had addressed were manning the line through which diesel fuel was flowing into the U-boat's tank. They glared at Mischler. These men, Karl Burch and Wilhelm Taskner, did not like Mischler, who had abused them from the moment they had begun transfer of the diesel fuel. "Let's give old high-and-mighty the snail treatment," Burch said to Taskner, who thought it a fine idea.

Burch shut off the flow of diesel fuel by turning a valve at the hose's point of connection to the metal pipe that led to the deck from the number-two bunker's pump. He sauntered to the rail and looked down at Mischler, who was standing on the U-boat's platform. "I didn't hear you, sir," he said, "on account of the noise."

"I said hurry it up, *Dummkopf!*" Mischler bellowed.

"You mean the oil? That's what you want us to hurry with?"

"What the hell else?"

"Sir, the pumps only pump at a certain speed. We can't make them pump any faster."

The veins began to protrude from Mischler's forehead. This stupid man was driving him *verrückt*. "Get back to that hose and turn it on again!"

"Yes, sir," Burch said. "Don't worry, sir. I'll go right back and turn on the oil."

He sauntered toward the turn-off valve. Midway he turned and went back to the rail. "Leutnant, sir," he said, looking down at Mischler.

"It's Korvettenkapitän, not Leutnant, you stupid donkey! Don't you know rank insignia when you see it? What do you want?"

"Don't get mad at me, sir. I'm only doing what they told me to do."

"What is it?"

"Nobody's supposed to smoke on a U-boat's platform while we're transferring diesel fuel. I'm supposed to tell you that."

The veins on Mischler's head were really protruding now. "Nobody is smoking here! If you look around you could determine that for yourself!"

"I know that, sir. That's the first thing I noticed. But that doesn't mean somebody won't be smoking later on. That's against the rules. So if anybody——"

"Listen, you idiot!" Mischler bellowed. "The men on this U-boat know that smoking on the platform during refueling is *verboten!* We're not a bunch of recruits just out of a training station! Now get back there and turn that valve on again!"

"All right, Leutnant," Burch said.

"It's Korvettenkapitän, goddammit!"

"*Jawohl,*" Burch said. "You already told me. I'm sorry I forgot. All right, Korvettenkapitän, I'll turn it on."

He thrust out his right arm and clicked his heels. "Heil Hitler!" he said.

"Heil Hitler," Mischler said, the muscles of his cheeks causing them to twitch.

While Burch sauntered to the shut-off, Mischler croaked to the *Haifisch*'s chief gunnery officer, who had been checking the deck rifles, "How do you suppose that moron ever got in the Navy?"

Burch, proceeding as though he had all day, came to the shut-off valve. His friend Taskner was waiting there. "You're getting better at it," Taskner said, grinning while he turned the valve's wheel. "I thought he was going to lose his mind."

"It gets them every time when you call them Leutnant," Burch said, a smile on his broad Teutonic face. "It really pisses them off. As big a hurry as he was in for us to turn on the juice, he took time to make sure I understood he was a Korvettenkapitän."

Taskner looked over at the Portuguese fishing boat that was trawling near the U-boat and the tanker. "I envy those guys," he said. "No war to worry about. When they get through with their work they can go home to their wives and kids. Jesus, I'd like to see my wife and kids."

"I wonder if they appreciate how lucky they are," Burch said, looking at the fishing boat, which was the masquerading PT and whose officer, Lt. Marlatt, was looking at the scenario with nonreflecting optic glasses from within the *Wasp*'s decrepit little deck house.

Marlatt sauntered out of the deck house. While he put a match to the cigarette between his lips he said, "We're going to get them both. We'll concentrate on the tender, which will be a big bust for the U-Waffe. Then if the U-boat has been able to submerge we'll straddle her and lay some Torpex eggs."

The strategy—two enemy ships in one assault—would require tactics substantially different from those the *Wasp*'s tough little crew had used on single U-boats. Marlatt and the others discussed how best to launch the attack. "We're in position right now," Marlatt said. "Everybody know what they're to do?"

Everybody knew. "Then get to your attack stations," Marlatt said, the cigarette dancing between his lips. "In exactly sixty seconds it's go!"

Sixty seconds later Pollard put a 3-inch high-explosive shell through the *Fettmaterialwarenhandler*'s skin just above her waterline, the point at which Marlatt and the other Americans had calculated one of her diesel bunkers would be.

Simultaneously Joe Silva shot off the deck valve with a burst from his Oerlikon, the terrible blast severing the diesel hose and the legs of Seamen Burch and Taskner. The continuing fusillade mangled their legless torsos, and when they fell further it tore through their heads.

Meanwhile Broughton swept the deck of the Nazi tanker with his twin .50-caliber machine gun, wiping out its men. Then he fired into the bridge. His terrible arcing fire demolished the compass, radio, chronometer, helmsman's wheel, and chart racks and disemboweled the helmsman and the tanker's captain, Kapitän Hans Westerkamp.

Chapter Eighteen

The incident with the seaman who was pumping diesel fuel from the tanker had jangled Korvettenkapitän Mischler's already taut nerves. It was driving him *verrückt* watching that *Dummkopf* and the other seamen. They had to be, he reflected, the two slowest men in the German Navy. He decided to go below and drink a cup of coffee while they filled the U-boat's tank. He would feel better if he were off the platform where he couldn't see those *Dummkopfs*.

He had just begun to descend the conning's ladder when the Americans on the masquerading fishing boat began their attack. "What the hell's that?" he croaked.

It was an enemy attack, of course. But where had it come from? This was no time to ponder that question. This was the time to get the *Haifisch* under water, and as fast as possible! The conning's hatch was immediately above Mischler's head. He slammed it shut and swung its massive locking lever. Too bad about the men on the platform. He'd write their families a nice letter sometime.

He pushed the diving horn's button and the toggle that turned on the conning tower's dim blue light, then quickly descended the ladder and darted across the deck to the speaker which hung from a toggle on the port bulkhead.

"Attack stations! Attack stations!" he bellowed above the raucous noise of the diving horn.

He pushed the button above the speaker's toggle that connected him with the navigation complex. "Dive! As fast as you can!" he screamed to Leutnant Willie Siebert, his navigation officer.

Mischler didn't take time to put the speaker back on its toggle. He ran to the sea scope. He had to know who was attacking. But the Americans had shot off the sea scope's topside apparatus. "Goddam!" Mischler cursed. Then a thought occurred to him. It was probably an aerial attack anyway. Why had he wasted time with the sea scope? He darted over to the air scope. The Americans had destroyed it, too.

Mischler turned toward Leutnant Otto Kraus, twenty-four, and the two enlisted men in the scope compartment. They hadn't done anything wrong and were as perplexed as he was, and as scared. But he had to have someone on whom to vent his rage and frustration, and these hapless men were right there. He bellowed imprecations at them, at the *Dummkopfs* on the tanker, and at the Americans or whoever it was who were attacking the German ships.

Suddenly he quit his violent, senseless rantings. "Jesus . . ." he croaked, listening to the machine gun bullets that were sweeping the U-boat's port flank, and at the steel-tearing sounds the projectiles from Joe Silva's Oerlikon made blasting into the conning.

"Who is attacking us, sir?" Lt. Kraus asked his distraught captain.

"How the hell would I know?" Mischler bellowed. "You saw where I was when they attacked!"

His face was purple. He kept biting his lips. Would that verdammt navigator ever get the *Haifisch* below the surface?

It was frustrating, and frightening, to be under attack and not know who was doing it, or with what weapons. "They certainly got us by surprise," Kraus said, thinking he ought to say something.

"Shut up!" Mischler screamed. Jesus Christ, everybody knew that they, whoever they were, had caught the *Haifisch* by surprise. He didn't need some impudent young officer telling him!

It was probably good for Mischler's nerves that he didn't know what was going on. Great quantities of diesel fuel were spilling from the tanker's ruptured waterline tank onto the sea's surface. The tanker's topside fuel pipe, shot off as though it had been hacksawed, was spurting oil in an arc that splattered onto the U-boat's platform, and the mangled dead bodies of the Nazis on the platform.

Haney had fired two more 3-inchers into the German tanker, both at her waterline, the second just aft of her bow, rupturing another fuel bunker. It was spewing its oil onto the sea.

"Keep lobbing 'em into her!" Lt. Marlatt shouted to Haney. "I want to sink the bitch!"

Haney fired another of his powerful high-explosive shells into the *Fettmaterialwarenhandler*'s flank. Then another. Then, as quickly as Pollard could reload the big rifle, he fired two more, ripping great jagged holes into her flank waterline.

The sea poured through these great rents in her hull. She began to list. Then her stern began to sink.

The German tanker was doomed. She was sinking swiftly. There were no living men on her deck, and very few inside. The explosions of the projectiles from the *Wasp*'s big gun had mangled the interior of the tanker.

Meanwhile Silva had been pummeling the swiftly diving U-boat's conning with his 20mm Oerlikon, trying to rip a sub-drowning hole in it. Schilling, who had strafed the *Haifisch*'s platform from the beginning of the attack, killing the Nazis on the platform, continued to sweep the platform, holding his .50-caliber twinned machine guns' fire for longer periods on the deck guns' trigger mechanisms, and on their watertight munitions boxes. His fusillades ripped long gashes in the munitions boxes and detonated their shells, which blew open the boxes and hurtled fragments of shell casings and lead and steel noses in all directions.

"That's enough!" Marlatt yelled to Haney, who kept lobbing his 3-inchers into the sinking tanker. "Lay onto the U-boat!"

"We gotta move our boat!" Haney shouted. "Or I can't do anything!"

The *Wasp* had drifted just enough to put the submerging submarine forward of the 3-inch rifle's deck-house aperture. There was no way Haney could bring his gun to bear on the U-boat.

"Son of a bitch!" Marlatt said, his jaw squared. By the time they jockeyed the *Wasp* into position for the 3-inch rifle's projectiles there would be nothing to shoot. The U-boat was almost under the surface now.

"Cease fire!" Marlatt shouted to Silva. He ran out onto the deck. "Cease fire!" he yelled to Schilling and Broughton. "Prepare to bomb!"

The machine gunners ran to their second battle station, the Torpex depth bomb launcher. Quickly and professionally they began to load the launcher with two of the powerful Torpexes.

Meanwhile Marlatt shouted to Steve Pollard, the *Wasp*'s helmsman, "Get right on top of that wash!"

Marlatt started engines one and three, the powerful Packard twelves that the *Wasp* never used except during attack, or a fast retreat after an attack. He swung the bow toward the *Haifisch*'s wash. Only the tip of her battered conning was above water, and it vanished before he got the *Wasp* deadlined on the U-boat's wake.

Soon the *Wasp* was directly over the diving U-boat. "Hold it!" Marlatt signaled the depth bomb men. He wanted the Torpexes to strike her fantail and, if possible, destroy her rudder. "Go!" he signaled the bomb crew, bringing his upheld right hand swiftly down.

Schilling and Broughton triggered the bomb thrower. It tossed two of the big 500-pound Torpex depth charges off the *Wasp*'s stern in an upswing arc.

"Kick her in the ass!" Marlatt yelled to Pollard.

To remain over their own DBs or even close to them would be suicidal. Pollard goosed the PT's three engines, and the little boat reared up on her tail and skitted across the sea at a breathtaking 50 knots.

Marlatt signaled Pollard to pull down to service speed and cut back toward the U-boat. He was barely into the parabola of the swing when the depth bombs exploded, sending great sprays of white-flecked water up out of the sea.

"Let's go back and see what we did," Marlatt said to his helmsman.

He looked over at the tanker while Pollard took the *Wasp* toward the site of the explosions. The tanker's bow was above the sea. The *Wasp*'s crew could hear explosions inside the drowning ship. Then great volumes of diesel fuel gushed out below her stern's waterline and bubbled up onto the surface. "If that oil starts to burn," Marlatt said to Pollard, "get us out of here!"

Then the *Wasp* was at the site of the explosions, their concussions still churning the sea. There were no bodies or debris from the U-boat. "We blew that one," Haney said.

"The hell we did!" Silva said. "We can still see their wash. Which means they can't go any deeper!"

"Get right on that beautiful wake," Marlatt said to Pollard. He looked back at Schilling and Broughton. Their launcher was loaded and ready. He raised his signal arm. Forward a little more, then they'd lay two more eggs.

And as many more, he reflected, as it would take to kill that U-boat.

The depth charges had felt like piledrivers slamming onto the *Haifisch*'s flanks. The big U-boat tremored and lurched, throwing men—including Korvettenkapitän Mischler—to their knees.

The navigation officer's chair leaped up to the overhead, breaking the electric light, and fell back onto the deck along with pieces of glass from the shattered light bulb and its glass diffuser.

"Damage control parties! Damage control parties!" Mischler bellowed, getting to his feet. "Man your stations!"

Lights went out, then came back on, went out again and came back on. But less than half of them this time. The others had been shattered in their housings.

Mischler leaned against a bulkhead of the navigation compartment. He felt relief. Those two depth bombs hadn't burst the seams and welds in the U-boat's sturdy steel skin. That was something to be thankful for, and a credit to German technology.

But the interior damage had been great. Great flakes of anti-seepage plaster on the overheads cracked and hung in swaying, breaking segments. Some fell down onto the deck. Some struck men on their heads. They created a purplish dust that was choking.

"God, I hope we're deep enough when their next bombs come so they won't hurt us so much," Mischler said to no one in particular.

It was comforting, in these moments when the *Haifisch* and its men needed any kind of comfort, to know that the big U-boat was diving as fast as it could.

Then, suddenly, Mischler realized that the *Haifisch* was no longer diving, that she was on even course. "Rudder control!" Mischler bellowed into the voice tube on the port bulkhead. "What the hell happened?"

The depth charges had made the rudder's hydraulic mechanism inoperable, Mischler was told. "We're changing to manual rudder operation!"

Operating the rudder manually required backbreaking effort, and its manipulation was agonizingly slow. "Goddam!" Mischler cursed. They wouldn't be able to dive beyond effective reach of the next depth charges—and they would come, Mischler realized, at any moment.

128

More bad news was brought to the U-boat's harried captain. "Water in the aft torpedo room!"

Then good news. "We've got the rudder positioned for maximum dive, sir!"

But this wasn't the good news it had first appeared to be, Mischler realized. A swift dive would enlarge the cracks or whatever was flooding the aft torpedo room. "Pull that rudder back up to ten degrees!" Mischler bellowed to the sweating men who were manually operating the rudder.

Then the worst news of all of it. "The enemy is directly above us, sir."

"Prepare for enemy bombs!" Mischler bellowed into the electric speaker. Impulses from the electric speaker, more effective than the voice tube, wouldn't tell the enemy anything he didn't know.

"Who the hell is it up there?" Mischler said aloud, bracing himself against the passageway bulkhead. A good place to be. Right in the middle of the U-boat.

Is it Americans? Or their cousins, the English? Or maybe a Free French destroyer. Damn stupid French! Don't they know France has been defeated just as the whole world will be one day soon?

The *Wasp* tossed two more Torpex bombs into the sea above the U-boat, then quickly sped out of range of their enormous explosions.

For the *Haifisch* and its terrified crew, the explosions of these depth charges were more violent than the first.

Electrical and tube connections were torn loose. Instruments were destroyed by the horrendous blasts. They rolled the U-boat to its starboard side so violently that men were hurled against starboard bulkheads. The *Haifisch* rolled sharply to port as she recovered, throwing men who had been hurled to starboard bulkheads against port bulkheads.

When the big U-boat ceased her terrible rolls and the men were able to get to their feet, they discovered that the bow was now 16 degrees toward the sea's surface. Walking forward was like ascending a mountain.

"Go forward!" Korvettenkapitän Mischler shouted. "Everybody go forward and carry something heavy!"

Men staggered forward, each carrying the heaviest piece of loose equipment he could find. Even Mischler carried something, a typewriter from communications.

129

The men were scared. The bow had to be made heavier, the stern—the water in the aft torpedo room had filled another compartment—had to be made level with the bow, before the U-boat began to slide backward and downward. If it began the slide would continue until the sea's pressure burst the sub's damaged plates, drowning everyone.

It didn't work. The bow's upward tilt increased. The U-boat began to slide backward. "Let's try to surface!" Chief Torpedoman Alec Eschbaugh said. "Maybe we can make it!"

"You idiot!" Mischler said. "They'll kill us the minute we stick our nose up out of the sea!"

"Maybe they won't! Maybe they'll give us a chance to surrender. God, Kapitän . . . we've got nothing to lose. We're done for this way, and pretty damn soon, too!"

"We will not surface!" Mischler said. "Germans do not surrender. We are the pure warriors. If we're not victorious, let no man go back alive!"

"You *verrückt* son of a bitch!" Eschbaugh said. He was a burly man, six feet one and 180 pounds of brute strength. "Give the order, or I'll tear you apart!"

He stepped toward Captain Mischler. Mischler whipped his 9mm Walther semi-automatic pistol from its holster and fired twice into Eschbaugh's chest.

Lt. Wolfgang Dahms, twenty-six, the U-boat's engineering officer, was standing aft and a little starboard of Mischler. He brought his right hand down on Mischler's gun-holding arm in a hard judo-type chop. The captain's arm cracked like a stick, and the Walther fell to the floor beside Eschbaugh's twitching body.

"We're going to surface!" he said, looking at the others. "Everybody at cruise station!"

"No! I will court-martial you. I will have you shot for mutiny and piracy!" Mischler shouted, supporting his broken arm with his left hand.

The others ignored their ranting captain. They were scurrying to their cruise stations. Except little glasses-wearing Klaus Aschenbrenner, the U-boat's clerk and night scope watch, who had no cruise station, the scopes having been destroyed and being of no value, anyway, in the *Haifisch*'s plight. "You stupid ass," he said to Mischler. "How the hell could you court-martial and execute dead men on the bottom of the ocean!"

He picked up the Walther pistol beside Eschbaugh's no

longer twitching body and aimed it at Mischler's face. "I despise you, you bloodeating bastard!" he said. "I have always despised you!"

"*Mein Gott!*" Mischler croaked. "Don't kill me . . . please!"

Aschenbrenner pulled the trigger. Mischler lurched up, a tiny black hole just above his nose. He kept standing there, his eyes crossed, his mouth working as though he were trying to say something. Aschenbrenner fired twice into his chest. He collapsed and sprawled beside the chief petty officer's body.

"You would have drowned all of us," the little Nazi said. He fired the Walther's two remaining bullets into Korvettenkapitän Mischler's head.

Chapter Nineteen

After the depth-charge thrower on the masquerading PT tossed its deadly eggs over the U-boat, the little ship sped from the site.

It was important to be far from the powerful Torpex depth charges when they exploded. Their seam-splitting, hull-crushing concussions would not distinguish between the Nazi submarine and the disguised PT.

Steve Pollard, at the wheel of the swift little boat, reduced its speed to zero. Then he ran out of the deck shack, joining Lt. Marlatt and the others. They were looking aft, Marlatt with binoculars.

The depth charges exploded, one immediately after the other. They churned turbulent geysers up out of the sea.

"If we didn't get them this time," Joe Silva said, putting a match to a Camel, "we dropped our eggs in the wrong basket."

"We were right on target!" Art Schilling said quickly, glaring at the garrulous little gunner. "One hundred percent!"

"Both times!" added Russ Broughton, the other member of the *Wasp*'s depth charge team, his jaw squared.

He looked around at the others. He wanted them to know that when it came to depth charges he and Schilling weren't a couple of amateurs. "If we didn't get it this time it's because the Krauts have invented some kind of bust-proof U-boat skin!"

"Cool it," Lt. Marlatt said, looking at the site of the explosions to see if debris from the U-boat was coming up. "We don't know if we got it or if we didn't. We can't tell from here."

He turned to Pollard. "Let's find out!"

Pollard put the little boat into a U-swing and headed back. The bow of the German tanker was above the surface, jutting skyward at 45 degrees. The rest of the tanker

132

was below the sea. "I wonder why it's so slow to sink," Marlatt said to Silva, who stood beside him on the *Wasp*'s bow.

"Beats the hell out of me," Silva said. "We put enough holes in that bastard to—"

His mouth gaped. "Look!" he blurted. "Over there! The U-boat's coming up!"

For a moment Lt. Marlatt and the others thought it might be the nose of a whale. But it kept rising, and then, quite clearly, everyone saw that it was a U-boat.

"I knew we'd laid our eggs right in her nest," Schilling said proudly.

"Well, if that isn't something," Silva said. "Jesus Christ, one going down and one coming up!"

It was, indeed, a most unusual sight; the sinking stern of one of the *Wasp*'s victims, the rising bow of another victim.

"Circle around that oil!" Marlatt yelled to Pollard.

Diesel fuel from the shelled tanker had spread over a great area. It was still coming up from the shell-ruptured tanks below the surface, bubbling on the sea and making little whirlpools.

The sea's drift was taking the oil from the site of the depth bombing, and the U-boat's underwater progress had moved it farther from the oil, facts which Lt. Marlatt took into studied consideration. It would be the utmost folly to put the *Wasp* in that sea of oil. If it should burst into flames from the fires which were probably still raging in the partially submerged tanker, the *Wasp* and its crew would be incinerated if the explosions of its seventeen remaining depth charges did not first atomize them.

"Want I should lay a couple heavies into that U-boat's nose?" Haney asked, his grin indicating that this was what he would like to do.

"No!" Lt. Marlatt said. "Maybe they're coming up to surrender."

"Maybe they're not," Wally McLean said, his lips tight.

"So maybe they're not," Silva said. "What can they do? We took care of their deck guns. So all they can come up with is small arms from inside. If I see just one gun, guess where there's going to suddenly be a U-boat full of hamburgered Krauts."

His 20mm Oerlikon, he said, wouldn't just kill the Nazis, it would fragment them.

The U-boat's mangled conning came out of the sea. "They're coming up at a damn funny angle," Haney said.

"You dumb jerk," Silva said, taking a cigarette from his friend's shirt pocket, "they're coming up that way because we screwed up their rudder or something."

"Like I mentioned," Schilling said, "when we lay an egg we lay an egg."

The last of the tanker's stern slid below the sea. At the same time the U-boat's platform emerged from the water. The submarine was in obvious trouble. Its bow was almost 20 degrees above its stern. This caused the aft part of its platform to be awash.

The *Wasp* was very close to the U-boat, not more than 50 yards away. Silva had his Oerlikon's sights on its conning hatch. Schilling and Broughton, the *Wasp*'s depth-charge men, were at their other battle stations—the twinned .50-caliber machine guns.

"Don't fire unless I give the word!" Lt. Marlatt said, his face tense, his eyes on the conning's hatch.

The conning's hatch opened. A white cloth, attached to a hydrophone antenna, appeared. The flag waved back and forth. "For chrissake," Lt. Marlatt mumbled.

For a U-boat to surrender was almost without precedent. In fact, Marlatt had never heard of it, at least in World War II. But maybe it was a trick of some kind. "Hold your fire," he said, "but stay on the ready. If they start anything, let 'em have it!"

The hatch opened. Slowly, as if whoever was opening it was reluctant, or afraid, to stick his head out of it.

Seaman 1/K. Johann Dochtermann raised his head above the hatch's coaming, waving the white flag of surrender with a shaking hand.

He came out onto the platform, still waving the flag, his eyes on the *Wasp*'s gunners. "They want to surrender," Marlatt said.

He turned to Pollard. "Go up closer!"

He told the gunners to stay at their weapons. He didn't trust Nazis, he said. "They have used that surrender trick before."

Pollard put the *Wasp* 20 feet from the U-boat. "Ve vant to surrender," Dochtermann, the only one of the *Haifisch*'s crew who spoke English, said shakily. At any moment, now, he reflected, they'll kill me. They've got those twinned machine guns aimed right at me.

134

"In der name uff der Navy uff der T'ird Reich, ve surrender ourselfs onto your hants in accord mit der Genefa—"

"Fuck the speech, squarehead!" said Lt. Marlatt, who was a very tough man. "Tell the rest of your outfit to come out on the platform. Mit their hants in the sky up!"

"*Ja!*" Dochtermann said, greatly relieved that he hadn't been killed. He went to the hatch, still waving the surrender flag, and shouted into it.

Thirty-six men came out of the hatch. With Dochtermann they formed into three rows on the platform, their hands above their heads except for two men, each of whom had broken an arm during the violent rolls of the bombed U-boat. These men raised their unbroken arms.

"A Portuguese fishing boat that's not a Portuguese fishing boat!" Leutnant Dahms muttered to Oberleutnant Bruno Klingenschmidt, the U-boat's executive officer. "They're Americans, I'm sure of it."

"The dirty bastards tricked us," Klingenschmidt said bitterly. "We could have sunk that boat a hundred damn times. It was right off our flank. So close I could have spit on it."

"Pretty clever," Dahms said. "We've got to admit it. It fooled us. I wonder how many other U-boats it destroyed."

"The *Schwein!*" Klingenschmidt said through teeth clenched in rage.

"They weren't doing anything we wouldn't have done," Dahms said. "It's all part of the game. Whoever can outarm, outtrick, outfight, outmaneuver—"

"If you can't say anything intelligent, shut up!" Klingenschmidt said. "This is not a time to be philosophizing!"

Joe Silva, abandoning the Oerlikon, had come out onto the deck. "We got us a little problem," he said to Marlatt. "Meaning, what are we going to do with all those Krauts?"

"I wish I knew," Marlatt said. "We couldn't put them on this yacht if we stacked them up like sardines."

Silva said he had an idea. "We could tow them to where they could be picked up by a cutter or something. We could use our dinghy, and if they've got one . . . Christ, it'll take more than one more. If they've got a couple rubber rafts or floater nets we could do it."

"Now and then, but rarely," Marlatt said, grinning at

135

the doughty little gunner, "you do show signs of an intelligence above the level of an amoeba."

"Well, you son of a bitch—! Oh, Jesus, lieutenant," Silva babbled. "I didn't mean that!"

Everyone laughed at Silva's obvious discomfort. No enlisted man in the United States Navy, or probably any other navy, addresses his commanding officer in such a manner.

Then the seriousness of Silva's impropriety came to the others. They looked at Lt. Marlatt to see how he would respond. "Silva," he said, his eyes dancing, "when we get back to the beach remind me to have you put before a firing squad."

Relief swept over Silva's face. "Thank you, sir," he said with deep sincerity and even greater gratitude. "I'm sorry . . . and I apologize. My dad always said I was born with diarrhea of the mouth."

Marlatt didn't reply. There was more important business. He turned to Schilling, who spoke German, the language of his parents. "Tell them we are the United States Navy," he said, "and that we accept their surrender and to consider themselves prisoners of war. Then ask them if they've got inflatable rafts or a dinghy or a float net or anything that will sustain them while we tow them."

Schilling translated. "We have two inflatable emergency rafts," Oberleutnant Klingenschmidt replied. "Each has capacity for twelve men. But there are thirty-seven of us. As executive officer and the highest rank of this boat's survivors, I will designate, immediately, the twenty-four men who will board the rafts."

"You barbarian!" Schilling said. "So the other thirteen guys drown! But you won't be one of them, will you, you Nazi animal! You'll be in the reserved seat section in number-one raft!"

Schilling translated Klingenschmidt's proposal. "There's an officer with real feel for his men," Marlatt said. "Tell that humanitarian creep we can put the thirteen fall guys in our dinghy!"

"I've got a better idea," Schilling said. "Why don't we put his excellency in the raft with the most people?"

"That is not a nice thought," Marlatt said, a smile cracking his tough, rugged face. "But it is just overflowing with merit. Tell him to start inflating their rafts."

The Nazis worked hastily to inflate their rafts. The

136

U-boat was sinking. Its stern was farther below the surface, which tilted the platform at an even higher angle. None of the Germans wanted to be on their boat when it sank. Its powerful vortex would surely suck them to their deaths.

"Toss one raft onto the sea," Schilling shouted to Ober-leutnant Klingenschmidt, functioning as interpreter for Lt. Marlatt, "and tell ten men to get into it."

"*Ja*, but it will hold twelve men!" the German officer replied.

"Ten men! And you are not to be one of them. Now hurry it up!"

Klingenschmidt designated ten men. "Get into the raft!" he barked.

While this had been going on, Wally McLean and Haney had removed the *Wasp*'s dinghy from its securities and dropped it onto the sea between the U-boat and the *Wasp*. "Put twelve men in that dinghy!" Schilling said, relaying Marlatt's order. "Not including you, Herr Ober-leutnant!"

"But that will mean fourteen men in the second of our rafts," the German officer replied, "which will—"

"Get going, squarehead!" Schilling said.

Soon twelve of the U-boat men were in the dinghy. "Now the rest of you supermen get into the raft!" Schilling said, leaning on the rail, a cigarette hopping between his lips.

He was enjoying this. He despised Nazis. They had embarrassed him because of his German ancestry, and name. Some Americans had even doubted his patriotism.

The remaining Nazis, except Klingenschmidt, got onto the raft, which crowded it terribly, the flimsy little fabric raft being designed for twelve men only. "You, too, superman!" Schilling said.

The big German officer looked with astonishment at Schilling, Lt. Marlatt, and the other Americans, his jaw gaping. "Ridiculous!" he said after he pulled himself together. "I, this surrendered boat's ranking officer, an Ober-leutnant of the U-Waffe of Der Deutschen Kriegsmarine, will go in your craft! According to the provisions of the Geneva Convention . . . I am entitled to the privileges of a ranking officer while a prisoner of war."

"That's quite a speech," Schilling said. "However, the only benefit you're going to get is a free ticket on that raft. Now either get onto that raft or you will soon be a dead, drowned Nazi!"

"Tell him he's got the count of three," Marlatt said.

Schilling interpreted. *"Ein . . . zwei . . ."* he counted.

"Verdammt American barbarians!" the Nazi said, getting into the raft. "You haven't heard the last of this!"

He looked at the men on the raft. "I will sit in the bow," he said, "and I want but one man on each side."

Konrad Arndt, twenty-eight, a very tough gunner's mate, said, "You'll sit here with the rest of us. You're days of ruling the roost are over. In case you haven't noticed, those Americans are now running the show!"

"I will put you on report, you disrespectful peasant! I will—"

He didn't say the rest of it. Arndt flung him out of the raft. "Put him back in!" Marlatt bellowed, Schilling saying it in German.

The Nazis pulled their gasping, choking officer into the raft, very nearly capsizing it in the doing because of its overload, and soon the rafts and the dinghy, lashed together by a line from the *Wasp*'s emergency gear—the dinghy first, then a German raft, and last the other German raft, each about 30 feet from the other—were tied to the *Wasp*'s bow, 50 feet of line extending to the dinghy.

"Crank her up and take us back a good safe sub-sinking distance," Marlatt said.

They were going to put the floundering U-boat out of its misery, he said.

"How about jockeying around so I have to fire right over those Krauts' heads?" Haney said.

"Sounds like a good idea," Marlatt said, grinning.

Moments later Haney fired the *Wasp*'s 3-inch rifle. Its projectile split the air over the Germans' heads and very nearly parted the hair of the men in the last raft because of the angle of Haney's fire, which was aimed at the U-boat's waterline.

He fired again. Then again. Both times the Nazis in the last raft, which was the one with Oberleutnant Klingenschmidt, practically banged heads trying to duck below the big rifle's trajectory.

The U-boat began to sink. "Let's get out of here!" Marlatt said, looking uneasily at the U-boat. The *Wasp* was much too close to it if its torpedoes blew.

They didn't blow, and soon the *Wasp* was towing the

dinghy and the German rafts, a ludicrous sight, the dinghy and the rafts stringing out behind the wallowing PT like baby ducks following their mother.

Schilling, the crewman of many functions, was also the *Wasp*'s radioman. He sent a cryptogram to Captain Langer at Azores-Gibraltar Sea Frontier informing him of the incidents and requesting a surface ship to retrieve the prisoners.

Captain Langer was not elated. "Those guys are supposed to be finding that wolfpack, not capturing Krauts!" he bellowed to his aide.

He ordered an LCVP (Landing Craft, Vehicles, Personnel) from the Albemarle Naval Base at São Miguel to go as far into the Nazi lake as prudent the next morning and prepare to bring the German prisoners back to Albemarle.

In the last light of dusk the *Wasp* dropped her sea anchor. "Tell our guests," Marlatt said to Schilling, "that if there's any monkey business during the night we'll machine-gun the whole outfit!"

The Germans caused no trouble, probably because swells came up that kept the dinghy and the rafts bobbing in and out of six-foot troughs throughout the night, the swells continuing until dawn.

"There's only fourteen guys in that last raft!" Silva said, looking at the prisoners through the morning mist. "There's supposed to be fifteen!"

"Cast off the stern line and we'll see what's going on," Marlatt said.

Soon he and Schilling were looking over the port rail at the last raft. "Oberleutnant Klingenschmidt fell overboard during the night," Gunner's Mate Arndt explained, shaking his head sadly.

"Well, things like that happen," Marlatt said, winking at the big German, who winked back at him.

Chapter Twenty

The *Wallowing Witch*, LCVP-311, the ship from the São Miguel naval base, met the *Wasp* and its strung-out tows 142 nautical miles east by southeast of Pico Cove.

Lt. (jg) Clarence Harper, twenty-four, the *Wallowing Witch*'s captain, looked with contemptuous disgust at the Germans, crowded like sardines on the three little floaters. He wondered why the men on the *Wasp* hadn't included them when they sank their U-boat.

He hadn't been happy with this mission. A clearly marked U.S. Navy ship was in peril in this German sanctuary. He didn't like the idea of risking his life to transport German prisoners.

"What's with the sudden humanitarianism?" he demanded of Lt. Marlatt after he boarded the masquerading PT. "Or are you phony fishermen in the Kraut-catching business?"

Marlatt bristled, but before the tough little lieutenant could tell Harper he'd gone as far as he'd better go, Joe Silva, a cigarette dancing between his lips, said, "We tried sinking their U-boat, which would have also deep-sixed those Krauts. But the sumbitch had bubbles in its butt."

Lt. Harper, a washout from a Navy flying school and at odds with the world because of it, particularly because he'd been assigned to so ignominious a command, expected enlisted men to keep their place. "I don't believe the question was directed to you," he said, glaring at Silva to show him what he thought of enlisted men.

"Well, up yours . . . sir!" Silva said.

"I want this man put on report!" Harper said, turning to Marlatt. "You heard him! I am surprised you didn't reprimand him!"

"Junior," Marlatt said, the expression on his face indicating that he'd had about all of this pipsqueak he was going to endure, "the business at hand is the transfer of our prisoners to your custody. I suggest you get on with it, and then get the hell home, because you're vulnerable in these waters. Maybe some U-boat torpedo officer is sizing you up right now!"

Lt. Harper's tongue flicked over his lips. He looked out at the sea. This ragtag lieutenant was correct, he reflected. He'd better get underway. "Hurry it up!" he bellowed to his men, who were towing the floaters toward the ladder on his ship's port flank with an inboard-engined whale-boat.

Soon the floaters were on the sea between the *Wasp* and the *Wallowing Witch*. Harper looked down at the Germans. "Some supermen!" he muttered, his lips curled.

He turned back to Marlatt. "I expect you to inform their ranking officer that, as of now, they are my wards and I shall expect them to obey my orders, and that any who does not—"

"Get off of it, for chrissake," Marlatt said. "It's only a short haul back to Albemarle. Why make a production out of it?"

"I don't like you, Marlatt!" Lt. Harper said.

"That will cause sleepless nights," Lt. Marlatt said, blowing a smoke ring toward Harper, who brushed it out of his face. "How about getting those Krauts on your dauntless vessel? I can almost feel that Nazi torpedoman zeroing us in his crosswires and telling his captain, "I'm gonna get both them boats with just one go. Heil Hitler!"

"I have been waiting for you to inform the German prisoners of their status!"

"Hell, they already know," Marlatt said drily.

Harper spun toward the prisoners, looking at them over the *Wasp*'s starboard rail. "There are certain standards of conduct—" he began.

"They don't English speak," Marlatt said. "However, since you feel impelled to make a speech, I have a man here who can interpret."

He motioned to Schilling, who came up between the officers. "Inform them," Harper said, "that they are expected to conduct themselves as prisoners of war, that I am their commander, and that the slightest breech of conduct will result in the most severe disciplines. Then tell them to climb up that ladder onto my ship!"

Schilling interpreted, but not precisely. "This chickenshit officer," he said to the Germans, "will take you to an

American naval base about ten hours from here. In the meantime don't do anything to upset him. He's mean and he would probably shoot anybody who gets out of line. Understand?"

"Ja! Danke!" Gunner's Mate Arndt said.

"What did that German say?" Harper demanded.

"He said they stand in awe."

Harper glared at Schilling. "I never saw such impudent men!"

"We're a bunch a sumbitches," Silva said, grinning.

Harper's lips were tight. He opened his mouth to tell Silva that if he were in his command he would, at this moment, be in the brig. But what's the use, he reflected. He looked back at Schilling. "The Germans are not climbing the ladder! I specifically told them to climb the ladder, and I expected you to have interpreted everything I said, precisely as I said it!"

"I forgot that part," Schilling said. He looked over at the Germans. *"Klimmen der laufmasche!"* he said, jerking a thumb toward the *Wallowing Witch*'s ladder.

It would not be necessary for the *Wasp* to return to Pico Cove for provisioning or refueling. It cast off as quickly as Harper returned to the LCVP.

Lt. Marlatt was anxious to put distance between the *Wasp* and the LCVP. He hadn't been just making conversation when he'd told Harper that a U-boat might be lurking nearby. He didn't want a U-boat commander to associate the phony fishing boat with any kind of business with an American ship and radio this information to U-Waffe command.

"What did you really tell those Krauts?" Marlatt asked Schilling after the *Wasp* got underway.

Schilling explained.

"I figured it wasn't just what the admiral had said," Marlatt said, grinning. "I made out a couple words that didn't sound like anything in that clown's little speech."

Marlatt and Schilling were leaning on the port rail. "You know something?" Schilling said. "It bugged me, seeing those Germans and talking to them. Christ, they're just like us. Some of them might even be my cousins."

"They're like us, no question of it," Marlatt said. "A bunch of guys who got rooted from their jobs, families, girl friends, college. They're just like us in another aspect, too, Schilling—and don't you forget it. They'll kill us if they can. That bunch back there would have killed us if they'd had the opportunity just like we tried to kill them by sinking their sub."

"War's a crazy, stupid thing, isn't it?" Schilling said, his brow furrowed.

"It's mankind's ultimate madness. But you know what will happen to us, Schilling, if we brood on its abstracts? I'll tell you what will happen to us! We'll go home in a box. Or the ocean's fish will eat us. We've got to forget we're human beings. We've got to be animals. Then maybe we'll go home someday."

"You're dead right, if you'll excuse the pun," Schilling said. "Are we going to find that wolfpack before we have to go home for gas and groceries?"

"I hope so . . . I think," Marlatt said, his face suddenly grim.

"It's going to be rough, isn't it?"

"That's today's understatement," Marlatt said, flicking his cigarette into the sea and looking at it, his lips very tight.

Four days later the *Wasp*, searching for a surfaced wolfpack, was in the Atlantic east of the midway point between Madeira and the northernmost of the Canary Islands. "We are hitting zero," Silva said, looking out over the sea. "All we've seen since we left the *Wallowing Witch* is a million legit fishing boats."

"If we don't ring the bell tomorrow," Lt. Marlatt said, "we're going to have to go home for refills."

While this dialogue was going on the captain of U-343, an S/K. 790-ton U-boat operating under free-hunt orders, was watching the *Wasp* through the big submarine's sea scope.

This U-boat, the *Orca*, crew of thirty-nine, was returning to the U-Waffe's Atlantic Submarine Basin, 2 miles up the Loire River, for provisioning after a long and futile search for Allied shipping along the west flank of Africa, the sea route for materiel from factories in South Africa.

The *Orca* hadn't come upon so much as an Allied dinghy. "There are hundreds of thousands of tons of Allied shipping in this sea lane," the *Orca*'s commanding officer, Kapitän Rudi Gerhardt, twenty-nine, complained to the other officers of his little command. "How the hell did it happen we didn't see even one ship?"

"The law of averages works for us, and against us," Damage Control Officer Werner Baetz said. "This time it was against us. Every time we up-scoped, nothing was in sight. If we had done it a little earlier, or a little later, we might have seen something. It was just a run of bad luck."

"*Ja*, that happens now and then," Navigation Officer Heinrich Dittenberger said. "I was on a Murmansk patrol one time. We didn't see anything though we were right in the path of American ships hauling materiel to the Russians. We go back to Achziger, there on the Baltic, for refueling and the admiral screams. We weren't watching, he said. You idiot, I said to myself, we can't have that stupid periscope up all the time. It's suicide. So this run we're on now is just another one of those dry runs that nobody can do anything about."

Kapitän Gerhardt said he understood all that. "If we weren't supposed to try out at least one of those new torpedoes, I wouldn't be so concerned. But it's going to look like we're a bunch of incompetents, not finding even one target when that sea lane has more traffic than the Wilhelmstrasse in Berlin."

The torpedoes were the newly developed and untried *Hupfentorpedieren*, an 18-inch oxygen-propelled torpedo that skipped up out of the water, going airborne for about 40 meters, then on the surface for 40 meters, then airborne again. It was 60 percent faster than a conventional torpedo, the airborne parts of its deadly journey being without speed-retarding water friction. It would, of course, be seen more readily than ordinary torpedoes, but its superior speed was supposed to more than compensate for this disadvantage.

Now Kapitän Gerhardt, who had green eyes, sandy cropped hair, a waxed mustache, and a saber scar on his left cheek—the hallmark of a German aristocrat—was looking at the *Wasp* through the *Orca*'s attack scope.

He had decided to try a torpedo on her. It was an extravagance to waste one of the costly new torpedoes on such an insignificant target as a Portuguese fishing boat, whose sinking would be of no value whatever to the Reich, but it would give Gerhardt an opportunity to watch the functioning of one of the skip torpedoes, and to make a report on its performance.

Too bad for the fishing boat's crew, who were neutrals and not enemies of the Reich. But it was important to demonstrate a *Hupfentorpedieren*. If he didn't, if he returned to the Loire Basin with no more knowledge of a skip torpedo's performance than when he had begun this frustrating mission, the situation would not be favorable to his standing as a seagoing Kapitän of the U-Waffe.

He swung the attack scope 360 degrees, hoping that an Allied tanker or destroyer or storeship might have showed up. Nothing!

He swung the attack scope back to the Portuguese fishing boat. *Ligia Mondego* had been painted on her port bow. Faded letters. He could hardly make them out. Probably on the starboard bow, too. The boat's name, obviously. What an unkempt boat. Fishing accouterments all over the deck. No orderly arrangement.

A baleful Eye of God on the boat's prow. Superstitious peasants, Gerhardt reflected. That medieval religiosity is supposed to assure them of God's protection. Well, they'll soon know that God can't stop a Nazi *Hupfentorpedieren*.

Gerhardt went to his air scope. He swung it 360 degrees clockwise, then 360 counterclockwise. Nothing. But it paid to be sure. It would be the utmost folly to fire a skip torpedo and thereby pinpoint the location of its source to some Allied fighter or bomber plane that might be in the vicinity.

Gerhardt wasn't about to make such a blunder. He hadn't become one of the U-Waffe's youngest captains by being impetuous or failing to calculate every possible contingency.

He depressed the toggle on the attack scope's speaker. "Stand by to fire tube three," he said to Torpedo Officer Karl Hasselmeier.

"Tube three ready," Hasselmeier said. "Are you sure you only want to fire number three, sir? One torpedo is always a gamble. Might I suggest the usual two and four followed, after you have corrected the target if necessary, by one and three?"

"Don't be so damn efficient," Gerhardt said. "It's only a Portuguese fishing boat. One *Hupfentorpedieren* is a hundred times too much for such a bunch of junk."

Gerhardt focused the attack scope's crosswires on the *Wasp*'s port flank, right under her decrepit little deck shack. "Fire tube three!" he said to Lt. Hasselmeier.

Hasselmeier fired the *Hupfentorpedieren* in tube three.

145

Then he picked up his speaker. "Can I take a peek through the scope?" he asked Gerhardt.

"*Ja*, why not?" Gerhardt said, his eye on the scope, a smile on his broad Teutonic face. "But you'd better hurry!"

If Hasselmeier didn't get to the scope right away he would miss the show, Gerhardt reflected, watching the torpedo's strange performance.

Steve Pollard was at the helm of the masquerading fishing boat. He was idling along on the usual single engine. He glanced out the port window of the deck shack, which functioned as the little boat's bridge. Not a sign of the wolfpack they were supposed to attack. Not even a single surfaced U-boat. He looked out the starboard window. Then forward. He wished they'd find something. It was boring, wallowing around, fishing all the damn time.

He again glanced out the port window, which, like the deck shack's other window, was actually a gun aperture. Nothing here, he reflected, reaching for a cigarette, but that flying fish.

He looked back. That flying fish was no fish! It was some kind of torpedo! It was leaping in and out of the water and coming toward the *Wasp* with incredible speed.

Pollard shoved the go on the *Wasp*'s two other Packard twelves and accelerated all three of the powerful engines to their maximum. The *Wasp*, up on her tail, leaped out of the *Hupfentorpedieren*'s deadly path, but just barely, the big torpedo practically dusting the camouflaged depth charge apparatus on the *Wasp*'s stern.

Lt. Marlatt had been on the starboard deck. He had seen none of it, being thrown to the deck by the *Wasp*'s sudden acceleration. Getting up, but still on his hands and knees, he saw the Nazi torpedo skip-dive past the *Wasp*.

Then it all came together. A U-boat had fired that weird torpedo at the *Wasp*. Pollard had seen it and juiced the *Wasp* out of its path, and now, Pollard's arc indicated, he was zooming to the site of the torpedo's origin.

"Prepare to depth-charge!" Marlatt bellowed above the roar of the three speeding engines.

Schilling and Broughton darted to the depth charge thrower, both of them falling, getting up, and falling again, because Pollard had put the *Wasp* into a 30-degree bank.

146

"Where is it?" Marlatt said, lurching into the deck shack.

Pollard had taken a fix on the source of the torpedo in relation to the sun's position. "Two o'clock true, the best I could tell," he said without taking his eyes from the portion of the sea toward which he was speeding.

"Say when!" Marlatt said.

"Right about here!" Pollard said a moment later, reducing his speed to one engine at trawl pace.

"Roll her in a circle," Marlatt said. "Then go out 100 feet and make another circle."

The *Wasp* had twenty-one 500-pound Torpex depth charges. Lt. Marlatt intended to build a fence around that U-boat.

He didn't wait for Pollard's confirmation of his orders. He ran out to the depth charge men. "Fire one! Then every 60 feet!"

Broughton and Schilling triggered the apparatus that tossed a powerful Torpex depth bomb into the sea. Then, quickly reloading and calculating 60 feet of travel, they tossed another, repeating this action as Pollard continued the *Wasp* in a starboard circle.

A faint smile came to Marlatt's tense face. The depth chargers were laying their terrible eggs in a pattern that would destroy a U-boat no matter which way it went, unless it was fortunate enough to glide at absolute equidistance between two of the Torpexes.

Chapter Twenty-One

Kapitän Rudi Gerhardt was looking through his attack scope's powerful lens at the *Hupfentorpedieren* which was speeding toward the Portuguese fishing boat.

His aim had been perfect. The torpedo would make its hit exactly in the middle of the wallowing fishing boat's port flank. This pleased Gerhardt. Without being immodest, just thinking of a fact, he reflected that he was one of the best target men in the German Navy. When I put my scope's crosswires on an Allied ship it is the same as a dead ship.

The sinking of this squalid little Portuguese fishing boat wouldn't be much of an accomplishment. Those boats could be sunk all the time if he surfaced and lobbed 30mm deck gun projectiles at them. But the sinking wasn't the primary purpose of the attack on that squalid little boat out there. It was important to witness a *Hupfentorpedieren*'s performance.

Torpedo Officer Karl Hasselmeier, another rising young German U-boat officer, had come running to the scope compartment because Gerhardt had said that if he hurried he could watch the *Hupfentorpedieren*'s strange leaps while it sped toward its target.

"Take a quick look," Gerhardt said, stepping back from the attack scope, "because I want to see it make the hit."

Hasselmeier looked into the attack scope. *"Wunderbar!"* he said excitedly.

He stepped aside so that Gerhardt could watch the contact and the horrendous explosion. "There won't be anything remaining of that boat but a few toothpick-size splinters," he said, adding that the men of its crew would be vaporized.

Gerhardt, looking into the scope, didn't reply. *"Gott im Himmel!"* he croaked.

The Portuguese fishing boat had leaped forward so fast

that only its stern and rudder were in the water. The rest of it was above the surface like the skimmers at the pre-war regattas on the Baltic inlet near Gerhardt's boyhood home.

Gerhardt was astounded. A Portuguese fishing boat is a sluggish craft, but, *Gott*, not this one! Then it came to Gerhardt that the fishing boat was a masquerading enemy boat, most likely an American PT. Nothing else that he knew of, or had read about, was so incredibly agile.

The *Hupfentorpedieren*, as fast as it was, had missed its target. The fishing boat just wasn't where it had been. It wasn't fleeing, either, it was speeding toward the U-boat in an arc so fast that it was tilting 30 degrees to the sea's surface.

Gerhardt, his face ashen, realized that he had better do something about this incredible situation, and that he didn't have very much time to do it.

He pushed the diving horn's button. Then he activated the electronic speaker. The electronic system amplified his voice and, *Gott*, it had better be heard by everyone in the U-boat! "Dive!" he bellowed, calling for emergency speed.

"All hands at service stations!"

Lt. Hasselmeier, wondering what was going on, looked into the attack scope. Too late. It was awash from the *Orca*'s dive.

"What happened?" he said, pulling the scope's tube down and securing it.

"That fishing boat is some kind of combat ship!" Gerhardt quaked. "It leaped out of the torpedo's path, and it's coming toward us!"

No doubt of it, he said, wiping his brow, on which beads of sweat had suddenly appeared. It would drop depth charges onto the *Orca*.

"We've got a tough boat," Hasselmeier said. "It's plated with that new steel alloy."

This did little to solace Kapitän Gerhardt. The *Orca* was, in truth, a tough boat, one of the final flowers of U-boat development. Its class, the designers had assured U-Waffe, had no vices at all. But no submarine could be absolutely sure of withstanding depth charges, Gerhardt realized, most especially if they were the newly invented American Navy Torpexes.

"If that masquerading bastard up there is an American, and if they've got those new Torpex depth bombs, we're done for," Gerhardt said, staring glassily at his torpedo officer.

This is the most fearful, most frustrating period of a submarine crew's experience—the waiting for a "safe" depth, knowing that their boat is diving as fast as it can and realizing that at any moment in this agony of vulnerability the enemy may destroy them with depth charges.

"Jesus Christ, I could dive faster than we're going down," Gerhardt croaked.

"We're going faster than it seems," Hasselmeier said. "It always seems to take forever."

"*Ja*, but we've never had an enemy practically on top of us," Gerhardt said. "The other times we've been under attack we had time to get the hell out of range."

"Range" for a submarine is generally 30 fathoms (180 feet). If the *Orca* could get to this depth, at which depth charges are impotent because of the sea's pressure, she would survive the attack.

But if the *Orca* couldn't reach this refuge before the bombs started dropping, she was in grave peril. "All glory is fleeting," Gerhardt said.

"Don't go getting melodramatic," Hasselmeier said. "We're not dead yet!"

A depth charge exploded off the *Orca*'s bow. Almost immediately another depth charge exploded off her port bow. Both did nothing more than rock the U-boat.

"They're laying their eggs in a circle," Gerhardt said. "We went between those two. But they'll lay them in expanding concentrics."

"Maybe we will be lucky enough to go between two of the next circle," Hasselmeier said. "And maybe they don't have enough depth charges to make more than one circle. It wasn't any bigger than a Portuguese fishing boat, you said."

More depth bombs exploded, port and starboard, both aft of the *Orca*, and at increasing distances. "That's the rest of the circle," Gerhardt said, his face taut and grim. "God . . . if our luck just holds out!"

"We could expedite our dive," Hasselmeier said, "if I fired the torpedoes in the aft tubes. They would give us a push, much like the jet rockets Ordnance is experimenting with. Further, it might be a good idea to empty those tubes in case a depth charge explodes on our tail."

150

The torpedoes in the bow should be kept in their tubes, he added. "Their weight up in front is helping our dive."

"We will not jettison any torpedoes," Gerhardt said. "If we are to die I hope it is in a blaze of glory."

"I never particularly wanted to be barbecued," Hasselmeier said drily. "Somehow I don't attach much glory to it."

Gerhardt opened his mouth to tell Hasselmeier that what he had just said had unpatriotic overtones, but before he got any of it said, Radio Apprentice Luther Schultz, eighteen, ran up to him. "Sir, we have reported our situation to U-Waffe Command. They replied that our message was garbled. They ask for clarification. Must we repeat in *geheimmittel*"—secret—"transmission or may we use straight German?"

"Geheimmittel!" Gerhardt said.

"Yes, sir!" Schultz replied. Then he ran back to the code room.

"You're not thinking it through," Hasselmeier said. "The enemy quite obviously already knows where we are. Before another message can be coded a bomb might knock out our transmitter. Why not send it straight? Headquarters ought to know we're under attack by a masquerading fishing boat."

"I thought you were so damn sure we wouldn't be harmed!"

"I am. But I also realize that anything can happen anytime in this business. Rudi, headquarters ought to know about that masquerader up there. That's damn important!"

"I'd say what happens to us in the next five minutes is a damn sight more important!"

"You're the Kapitän," Hasselmeier said, shrugging his shoulders.

A depth charge exploded off the *Orca*'s starboard bow. The U-boat rocked violently. "I was hoping," Gerhardt said, "that they wouldn't have enough eggs for another circle."

"Maybe we'll be lucky enough to go between those in front of us," Hasselmeier said. "We've already made it with the starboard one. If the one to port—"

He didn't finish. A Torpex struck the U-boat's platform. The men in the boat could hear the *click-click-click* of its detonator. "Oh, my God," Gerhardt babbled. "It's staying on the platform!"

"We dived right under the son of a bitch," Hasselmeier said, his lips tight. "But maybe we'll hold."

The depth charge exploded. The U-boat rolled like a bottle. Its lights went out. "Switch to emergency lights!" Kapitän Gerhardt shouted into the electronic speaker after he got up off the deck.

"Fire in the forward torpedo compartment!" the damage control officer reported.

Hasselmeier swooped up the speaker's mouthpiece. "Forward torpedo room!" he shouted. "This is Leutnant Hasselmeier. Salvo all tubes! Salvo all tubes!"

"No!" Gerhardt screamed, reaching for the speaker. "It will impede our dive. We need the weight!"

Hasselmeier kept gripping the speaker. "It may prevent us from going up in that blaze of glory you mentioned! God, man, didn't you hear damage control? There's fire in the forward torpedo room! Don't you realize how sensitive torpedoes are to fire?"

Another depth bomb exploded. It was very close to the *Orca*'s port midsection. It rocked the big U-boat. "How many charges have those people up there got, for God's sake?" Gerhardt croaked. "This is the third pattern those *verdammt Schwein*—"

He didn't finish. He had been incinerated. The *Hupfentorpedierens* in the *Orca*'s bow had exploded. The U-boat had suddenly become a great ball of fire. Its incredible heat, more than 2,000 degrees, instantly transformed living men into ashes.

Command Headquarters of U-boat Operations of Der Deutschen Kriegsmarine were in a camouflaged one-story reinforced concrete building with two stories underground. It was near Eckenforde, a small city in Schleswig-Holstein on Kiel Bay, just south of Germany's point of connection to conquered Denmark.

Officials in Operations, where the current locations of each of the German Navy's more than 500 U-boats were indicated with miniature movable submarines on chart tables, became alarmed after their orders to *Orca* to clarify its garbled message went unanswered.

"Try *Orca* once more!" Deputy U-boat Director Kapitän Franz von Heisler ordered operatives in the code department.

There was no response. The *Orca*'s crew had become ashes when its torpedoes exploded while it was 160 feet below the ocean's surface, sending a great ball of fire, contained by the submarine's steel skin and the sea's pressure, throughout the interior of the U-boat, instantly incinerating its men.

"We have lost another U-boat," Kapitän Heisler, fifty-two, a Prussian aristocrat with an upswept mustache, reported to Admiral Karl Doenitz, Chief of German U-boat Operations. "Like the others, it was lost in waters we believed to be secure. And like the others, we have no description of its assailant. The only report we have that might correlate to the lost boats is the one from the *Grossdeutschland*, and that doesn't tell us anything specific."

The U-boat *Grossdeutschland*, crippled by the explosion of gasoline poured down her conning by the sea guerrillas of the disguised American PT, had been able to make her way to Port Risner with only eleven able men. The big U-boat was scarcely navigable. The Americans' attack had virtually destroyed the once-mighty *untersee* killer.

The fourteen injured survivors of the attack, whom Kapitän Wassermann had confined to a single compartment because their moans were demoralizing the others, were barely alive. They'd had no medical attention. The *Grossdeutschland*'s medical technician had died in the attack and his medicaments had been destroyed. "All we can do for you men," Kapitän Wassermann had said, "is keep your burns covered with oil from the deck guns' hydraulic mechanism."

After the *Grossdeutschland* wallowed to Port Risner, Wassermann lost no time making contact with U-boat Command at Eckenforde. "We were attacked by a boarding party from an American submarine or surface ship of which we had not the slightest warning on our hydrophone system."

Admiral Doenitz was deeply concerned by the mysterious attacks on his U-boats. It was a personal affront as well as a disaster to U-Waffe. Doenitz had organized, developed, and orchestrated the U-boats' devastating campaign. His U-boats had achieved substantial victories. All big ship convoys on world routes to the port of London

153

had been forced to avoid the Channel, and all coastal convoys had been ended.

Doenitz's U-boats had very nearly won the battle of the Atlantic. They had even had the audacity, and the ability, to engage in *Paukenschlag* off New York.

"We have become complacent," Doenitz said, "because everything has been going our way. But an American submarine has gotten into our sanctuary and is destroying our U-boats."

He did not believe it was an American surface ship. "We have continuous reports on every surface ship in the area, each requiring identification which is then verified. So it has to be an American submarine. It is equipped with some kind of apparatus that neutralizes impulses from hydrophone equipment. This permits their undetected approach to our surfaced U-boats.

"This American submarine must be found and destroyed!"

Doenitz said he would order, Priority One, fighter and bomber planes and surface ships to the area.

Two twin-engined Heinkel landplane bombers borrowed from Reich Marshal Hermann Goering's vaunted Luftwaffe. three scout bombers from Navy Air Group Stuppe, and four Henniger single-engine observer seaplanes from Kleinmeerbusen Field began dawn-to-dusk air patrol of the Nazis' east Atlantic sanctuary. Simultaneously, two 600-ton lighters from Africa Naval Command at Port Risner and the submarine rescue vessel *Dauffenbach* from Navy Group Center began twenty-four-hour surveillance of the sanctuary.

"No longer," Admiral Doenitz assured his colleagues at U-Waffe Command, "will that American destroyer of our U-boats elude our detection and destruction!"

It would be impossible, he explained, with all that air and surface cover in such a relatively small area.

"Those American submarines will soon learn that the U-Waffe cannot long be tricked."

Chapter Twenty-Two

German Navy Aviation Leutnant 2/K. Otto Feltz, twenty-three, was flying a Henniger observer seaplane 1,000 feet above the placid sea in the U-Waffe's sanctuary. "Nothing but two surfaced U-boats and those Portuguese fishing boats," Feltz, bored with this monotonous duty, said to his navigator, Chief Petty Officer Bruno Oppenheimer, twenty-seven.

It was the fifth day of their patrol. They had seen no sign of the American submarine that Admiral Karl Doenitz, chief of U-Waffe Operations, believed to be ambushing and destroying his U-boats.

"Old Doenitz has got a corncob up his ass," Feltz said, "if he thinks there is an American U-boat around here any-place. I wonder how much longer we've got to stay on this stupid mission?"

"Hey, Otto . . . look!" Oppenheimer said, pointing to the sea's surface about 20 degrees off the little seaplane's bow.

Feltz circled lower. "It's a bunch of dead guys," he said, smiling because he had at last found something.

Oppenheimer had been looking at them with binoculars. "They're U-boat men, I think. Jesus, some of them are swollen up like pigs."

Feltz landed on the placid sea and taxied over to the bodies. "Jesus Christ, they stink!" Oppenheimer said. "They must have been dead a long time, to stink like that."

They were bodies of men from the *Ich Dien*, the U-boat the men of the *Wasp* thought they had failed to destroy because no debris surfaced. The *Ich Dien* had continued its ghostly course, 20 fathoms below the sea's surface, but her fissured batteries soon had become exhausted and the *Ich Dien* had sunk to the ocean's floor 30 fathoms (180 feet) under its rolling surface.

The bodies of the crew had quickly begun to decompose, their bellies inflating grotesquely, then bursting, their horrid effluvium blending with the chlorine gas from the ruptured batteries.

The combined gases had exerted a pressure on the sunken U-boat's already weakened welds that exceeded the ocean's pressure. A seam in a forward compartment had burst, and the compartment's bodies and its gases had been ejected through the rent in the U-boat's plating.

A body hurtled up out of the sea while the Germans in the seaplane were looking at the other rotted corpses. "That's the spookiest thing I ever saw," Lt. Feltz said shakily to Chief Petty Officer Oppenheimer. "A dead body just suddenly coming up out of the ocean. Jesus, look at his face!"

"You can hardly tell it's a face, the way his head's swollen," Oppenheimer said, holding a kerchief over his nose.

"We're supposed to bring back identifications from any bodies we find," Feltz said. "I don't know how we can do it with these, the way they stink. I don't think I could even touch one of them."

"I've got a sudden idea, Otto," Oppenheimer said. "Why don't we get out of here and tell HQ we found some bodies but the sea was too rough to land on."

"*Ja*," Feltz said, gunning the seaplane's engine. "That's what we'll do."

Their report, relayed by the commandant at Kleinmeerbusen Field to Command Headquarters, U-boat Operations, did little to soothe Admiral Doenitz's frayed nerves. "Those bodies only confirm the obvious fact that an American submarine is out there!

"I want it found and destroyed!"

The *Wasp* was wallowing in the German U-boat sanctuary, searching for the wolfpack the sea guerrillas intended to attack, meanwhile dragging its fishing seines to authenticate its masquerade.

"There sure is a hell of a bunch of Kraut planes flying around here all at once," Joe Silva said, waving to a Nazi fighter pilot who had been flying very low, searching for the shadowy outline of a barely submerged American submarine. "I wonder what they're looking for?"

"I'd say they're looking for the rascals who've been deep-sixing their U-boats," Lt. Marlatt said, taking a cigarette from the pack in his shirt pocket. "They think it's either a surface ship or a submarine. I'd lay odds on the submarine."

"They would be real pissed off if they knew this friendly Portuguese fishing boat they've been waving at is not a friendly Portuguese fishing boat," Silva said.

Haney had come out of the deck shack, where he had poured himself a cup of coffee. "We ever going to find that fucking wolfpack?" he said.

"Don't hurry the day, you gung-ho freak," Silva said, taking a cigarette from the pack Haney held in his hand.

"I thought you were utterly fearless," Haney said, striking a match and putting it to his friend's cigarette.

"I am," Silva said, blowing smoke through his nose. "But I also realize one disguised PT against a wolfpack of Kraut U-boats is not the kind of odds the smart money likes to bet on."

"Maybe the war will end before we find them," Lt. Marlatt said, leaning on the bow rail.

"You bet," Haney said.

"It could," Silva said.

"Christ," Haney said.

He went back into the deck shack. "He's a sensitive soul," Silva said.

"You two idiots are making me a mental case," Marlatt said, a grin on his unshaven face.

The *Wasp* dropped its hook in the last light of dusk. About 0100, Art Schilling, who was standing second watch, saw a red flare in the dark Atlantic sky. He awakened the others. "Something's going on 60 degrees starboard. . . . I figure it's about 2 miles from here."

Marlatt put his night optics on the sea 60 degrees starboard of the anchored boat. "I can make out something," he said, "but I can't tell what it is. Let's move in a little closer."

Marlatt kept looking with the optic glasses. "It's two . . . no . . . three surfaced U-boats," he said a little later. "Two parked. One coming in aft of the port boat."

He gave the glasses to Silva, who gave them to Haney after he had looked at the U-boats, and so on until each man had seen the surfaced Nazi submarines.

"Well, here we go," Broughton said, his lips tight.

"That's not the wolfpack we're looking for," Marlatt said. "At least not all of it. Besides, what could we do at

157

night to three of them? One we could handle, maybe. Negative on three. When we hit the wolfpack it's got to be when we can see who we're hitting and who to get the hell away from."

"In other words," Silva said, "we're not going to do anything to those U-boats out there?"

"There's nothing we can do without blowing our mission, if not killing ourselves," Lt. Marlatt said.

"The hell there isn't!" Silva said. "We can fire a star shell over them! That'll scare the living soup out of them! They'll bust their ass trying to outdive each other."

A smile creased Marlatt's unshaven face. He turned to Pollard. "Take us closer. Real slow and easy so we don't spook them. I want that shell to go right over them."

Soon Marlatt decided the *Wasp* was as close to the surfaced U-boats as it could go without alarming them, because Portuguese fishing crews seldom worked at night.

Broughton said he'd had experience with star shells. "You have to know the angle to fire them. Otherwise they don't go where you want them to go."

"OK, you're the *Wasp*'s official star shell man," Marlatt said.

"Are they going to suspect us?" Wally McLean, the *Wasp*'s worrier, asked the others. "Christ, if they do you know what they can do with their deck guns. We won't have any more chance than a snowball in hell if all three of them open up on us."

"They won't think it's us," Silva said. "Why would a fishing boat fire a star shell? Besides, who ever heard of a fishing boat with a military parachute-type phosphorus star shell?"

McLean said he hoped he was wrong. "But like I said, if they start firing at us we've got our balls on the barb wire."

"Hell, we've got them on the barb wire twenty-four hours a day in the sea guerrilla business," Schilling said.

"We're going to proceed," Marlatt said. "It's not a subject for debate. Everybody understand?"

"*Ja. Wir verstehen*," Schilling said, reaching for a cigarette.

"No butts!" Haney said quickly. "We want them to think we're sound asleep. Also, what's that *verstehen* shit?"

"It means 'understand.' What I said in the language of the Krauts, meathead, was 'Yes. We understand.' "

158

"Quiet, everybody," Broughton said, aiming the star shell projector. "It's been quite a while since I fired one of these buggers. You're making me nervous."

His aim was perfect. The phosphorus shell exploded squarely over the middle of the three surfaced U-boats, which had formed into a triangle. The shell, emitting its bright white light, slowly floated seaward, suspended by its parachute.

The Nazis panicked. The officers on their platforms dived into their conning towers, slammed their hatches, and pushed their diving horn buttons. The hell with the men still on the platforms. An enemy ship was illuminating them . . . probably that American phantom killer. It was important to dive immediately.

The Americans, leaning on the *Wasp*'s starboard rail, watched the U-boats' frantic dives. They could see them clearly in the star shell's bright light. "We succeeded in scaring the piss out of them," Silva said.

"Those guys in the water sure got the shaft," McLean said.

"That is what's known as tough luck," Silva said.

"It's a hell of a thing to do to your own men," McLean said. "Jesus Christ, slamming the hatch and diving and just leaving those guys on those platforms. Even for Nazis, that's chickenshit."

"You saying I shouldn't have mentioned the star shell caper?" Silva said. "Let me tell you something, bubblehead. I hate Nazis. They screwed up everything for me. Every goddam thing I had . . . all my plans. I just wish we could have zombied those U-boats and killed every Kraut on every damn one of them!"

The Americans kept looking at the Germans in the water, the unlucky men who had been on the U-boats' platforms and who had been unable to get to the connings before their hatches were closed. They had dived off the platforms and now were trying, desperately, to swim from the rapidly increasing vortexes of the submerging submarines.

"You're getting your lumps watching those guys, aren't you?" McLean said. "You know something, Silva? You're basically a sadistic—"

"Knock it off, McLean!" Lt. Marlatt said.

"Yes, sir!" McLean said. "I won't say another word. I

just don't particularly like to watch people drown, is all I was saying in the first place."

"Nobody's drowned yet!" Silva said. "They're all still swimming. Besides, who's making you watch?"

"Both of you, button it up!" Marlatt barked.

No one said anything for several moments. "What good will it do them if they do make it?" Haney said. "They don't have life jackets and they're a hell of a long way from land."

"Maybe they think we'll pick them up," Schilling said. "They can't help but see our boat."

He turned to Marlatt. "What about it? Are we going to let them drown? Or are we going to be the great American humanitarians?"

"We couldn't get to them in time even if we wanted to," Silva said.

"You were clearly told to keep your mouth shut," McLean said.

"Both of you were clearly told!" Marlatt said.

The men kept watching the Nazi swimmers. The vortexes of the rapidly diving U-boats were swirling the sea's surface in downward spirals. The swimmers were being drawn toward these murderous whirlpools. It was like the wind blowing a flying bird backward.

"There goes number one," Haney said.

The German, on the edge of a vortex, was flailing his arms, trying frantically to swim from its inexorable suction. He began to vanish. The Americans could hear him scream.

"I wonder how far down they get sucked," Haney said.

"I also wonder," Schilling said, "how long before they actually drown."

"Can I say something?" Silva said, turning to Lt. Marlatt.

Marlatt didn't reply. Two Germans were drawn into a vortex. Their shrieks, heard on the *Wasp*, were haunting.

Then, quickly, the remaining Nazis, still trying desperately to escape the vortexes, were sucked into their swirling whirlpools.

"Well, that's that," Haney said after the last German had vanished.

"Can I say what I was going to say?" Silva said.

"Go ahead," the lieutenant said.

"What I was going to say is, they'll float up in a couple

160

minutes. I personally saw it happen. We're off Baja California with our tuna fleet and this rich Mexican dude on a big fancy yacht thinks he can go where we went, not thinking about the difference in our drafts. He tears the keel off his boat on one of those underwater reefs. He goes down like you wouldn't believe in the deep drink on the seaward side of those reefs.

"These four dudes who are on the deck try to swim toward my boat, the closest one. They don't make it. They get sucked down like those Nazis we just saw.

"A minute later they pop up out of the water like a porpoise. One guy went totally up out of the water. You could see daylight under his head."

"I would have supposed," Schilling said, "they would come up head first."

"Not necessarily," Silva said. "Two of them came up feet first. The guy I mentioned and another one."

Schilling looked back at the sight of the U-boats' vortexes. The star shell had parachuted into the sea. He could not see the bodies of the Germans.

Lt. Marlatt pulled a cigarette from the pack in his tattered denim pants. "The smoking lamp is lit," he said.

The others began to light up. "You had a case of big mouth for a while, there," McLean said, glaring at Silva while he put a match to his cigarette.

"I'd rather have a case of big mouth than a case of stupids, stupid," Silva said.

McLean flung his cigarette out into the sea and lunged toward Silva. "You're asking, stupid," Silva said, clenching his fists.

Neither man struck the other. Suddenly a ship's powerful floodlight illuminated the *Wasp* almost as brightly as their star shell had illuminated the U-boats. "Everybody play it cool!" Marlatt said quickly. "If they turn out the light, stay right where you are!"

The light went out. After about five seconds it came back on. "If we'd been gone from here they would have been suspicious," Marlatt said. "They might have started shelling us."

He turned to Silva. "If they come alongside, it's up to you."

The ship, keeping its flood on the *Wasp* as it approached, was the lighter *Seehund* from Africa Naval Command, one of the ships Admiral Doenitz had ordered on twenty-four-hour patrol of the U-Waffe's sanctuary. "Did you see where that star shell came from?" someone on the lighter's dark deck shouted in Portuguese through a megaphone.

"We saw the star shell, naturally," Silva replied, introducing himself as the fishing boat's captain. "But we have no idea where it came from. We have been here on the deck watching to see if we see anything."

"Leave the area!" the German said. "If we find whoever fired that shell there is going to be shooting. You might get mixed up in it if you're too close."

"Well, we don't want to get mixed up in it," Silva said.

The *Seehund* turned out its floodlight, and Silva translated the dialogue. "Get underway!" Marlatt said to Pollard.

Silva and McLean did not resume their hostilities. They and everyone else on the *Wasp* had a greater concern.

Had the Nazi ship's floodlight revealed anything on the *Wasp*'s deck that would make it suspect? If so, at any moment the light would come on again, and with it, deck-sweeping gunfire that would chop the sea guerrillas to little fragments.

Chapter Twenty-Three

Kapitän Gerhard von Seggern, Hauptsächlich (chief) of the nine U-boats of the U-Waffe's vaunted *Amselrudel*, was elated.

His wolfpack was about to make the biggest score of its bloody history. It was going to attack a twenty-four-ship U.S. convoy transporting military supplies, American soldiers, foods, and high-test gasoline from Boston Harbor to the port of Liverpool.

For the unsuspecting Americans, already well on their way across the choppy Atlantic, a disaster was calculably inevitable. The Allies were still unaware that Nazi cryptologists had broken the British convoy cipher, a variation of which was also used by the Americans.

The convoy would wallow into an ambush of the most savage U-boat wolfpack of the Nazi *untersee* fleet, and there would be nothing the convoy could do to prevent this disaster. Sonar had not yet been perfected. The Americans would not know of the U-boats' proximity until the Germans unleashed their deadly torpedoes.

Kapitän von Seggern's U-boat, *Tippelhehrt* (U-579), was the *Rudel*'s flag. She was a Deutschkreiger ("German Warrior") Class—a faster, better-armored, better-armed submarine than the finest of the U.S. and Royal Navies. She was a veteran of more than 110,000 Allied tons, a killer commanded by one of the U-Waffe's aces.

Now that von Seggern had received word of the convoy's route from U-Waffe Command he could hardly wait to lead his wolfpack to the lair in which the *Rudel* would lurk while it awaited the convoy's arrival.

"It will be our greatest victory," he assured his officers. "For this we will surely be awarded the Kriegsmarine Cross First Class."

Kapitän von Seggern, forty-three, was the second of five

sons of wealthy Berlin industrialist Wolfgang von Seggern, owner of the Mannlicher Ordnance Industries in Berlin, Hamburg, Munich, and Frankfurt.

He was six feet four. His eyes were piercing and deep-set in a craggy Teutonic face. His hair was sandy and cropped. He had the inevitable saber scar on a cheek, his left.

He was intelligent, cautious, and calculating. He had been graduated from the Gruenenberg Technical University and the Hohenhochst Naval Academy. He had married Ilse von Warnecke, daughter of the famed Baden-Württemberg medical scientist Dr. Karl M. L. von Warnecke. He was the father of two teenage sons, Kurt and Adolph, both leaders in the Hitler Jugendstreitkrafte ("Youth Military Force").

His brothers Johann, Heinrich, and Wilhelm managed the family's factories. Another brother, Konrad, oldest of haughty old Wolfgang's sons, was *Oberschaarfuehrer* at the Auschwitz concentration camp. His work: to supervise the tidy gassings of 1,100 Jews per day, the cremation of their bodies, and the sacking of their ashes for use as field fertilizer by the German Ministry of Agriculture.

"All of us von Seggern brothers," Kapitän von Seggern liked to say, "are in the service of the Reich. Together we manufacture the rifles, artillery, and tanks that will win this war against international Jewry, we sink their ships, and we exterminate Jews, the scourge of the earth."

The American ships, zigzagging toward disaster, were Convoy 711, code name Pilgrim's Progress. Fourteen of its vessels were EC-2 Liberty cargo ships carrying 100 self-propelled 105mm guns, 100 31-ton M4 Sherman tanks, 200 jeeps, 32 Grumman Wildcats, 87 small landing craft, 400 wooden cartons of .50-caliber machine gun ammunition, cases of spare parts for jeeps, 2,000 tires for jeeps and other vehicles, and miscellaneous ordnance items.

Two storeships were loaded with frozen beef, butter, condensed milk, whole eggs, and hundreds of sacks of flour from U.S. mills. There were also two P-2 transports, 600-foot troop ships, each with 2,400 American troops aboard.

One four-bunker AOG gasoline tanker carried high-test airplane fuel. It was the last of the cargo ships. If it was torpedoed, the convoy's planners had decided, the other ships would not proceed into the sea of flames its burning gasoline would create.

The convoy was guarded by the U.S. destroyer *Linne* at the head of the zigzagging column, two destroyers, *Garner* and *Robert Witmer*, at the column's rear aft of the gasoline tanker, and a destroyer-escort on each flank armed with forward and aft 3-inch rifles, 50s, 20s, and 40s.

The destroyers were armed with twin 5-inch rifles in fore and aft turrets, twinned 40s in sponsons, 20mm rifles, and twinned .50-caliber machine guns. Additionally, the destroyers and DEs were fitted with fantail depth charge throwers. The armaments on both the DDs and DEs had been modified for the ships' transfer to the United Kingdom.

The convoy would be a major prize for Kapitän von Seggern's wolfpack even if only half its ships were destroyed.

"We will hit them in daylight," von Seggern had informed the captains of the other eight U-boats in his dreaded wolfpack. "We can see better in daylight, and there is little they can do to harm us."

It would be great sport as well as a service to the Reich to sink the American ships, he said. He despised the Americans. They had interfered in the war, causing difficulties for the Reich. For this they would be punished after Germany won the war.

In the meantime, the torpedoing of Convoy 711 would be an important step toward Germany's victory. "I hope we kill every American soldier on those two troop ships!" he said to his executive officer.

The wolfpack came to its lair, the Atlantic 30 miles southwest of the southernmost coast of Ireland, and when night came the wolfpack surfaced. Von Seggern wanted to give its men an opportunity for exercise and fresh air on the U-boats' platforms. Meanwhile the U-boats' deck gunners checked their weapons to be sure nothing would impair the shelling and strafing of the convoy's ships—and their survivors—after the torpedoings.

While these activities were going on the U-boat captains assembled on the *Tippelhehrt;* von Seggern did not want to risk radio communications with them so close to Allied tracking stations on the Irish coast.

Each U-boat was assigned primary and corollary targets. "I want a minimum of two torpedoes in each American," von Seggern said. "Then we will surface and complete our attack."

Kapitän Heinrich Baechler's U-boat, *Unartigjungfrau* ("Naughty Virgin"), would attack the gasoline tanker as its primary target. "I want the sea a mass of flames. This will terrify and confuse the others."

Korvettenkapitä Franz Schnabelhaus, CO of *Fliegendstern* ("Flying Star"), and Oberleutnant Kurt Mueller, CO of *Dunkelhengst* ("Black Stallion"), would attack the troopships, then tankers with the self-propelled guns and Sherman tanks on their weather decks.

The other U-boat commandants were assigned the remaining ships of the hapless convoy, whose captains did not know that their cryptograms were being monitored around the clock by code men in the wolfpack. "The convoy will be in attack position one hour after dawn," von Seggern said happily. "We could not want a better time. The morning mists will have lifted. Our meteorologists predict a clear day and gentle seas."

Morning came. A light haze hung over the Irish coast. The sea and sky were brilliant shades of blue. The seas were rolling smoothly. The convoy was cutting wispy wakes as its ships zigzagged in a constantly changed interspersed pattern, which required the utmost wheelhouse vigilance and skill.

Kapitän von Seggern, watching the convoy's approach through the *Tippelhehrt*'s attack scope, pushed the voice tube's toggle. "Torpedo room! Is everything ready?"

"All tubes loaded and ready," Torpedo Officer Karl Krutzmeier said.

"Action stations!" von Seggern said through the voice tube's speaker. "All hands at action stations!"

The men were tense and eager. At any moment the attack would begin. Most of the men were smiling. They liked to sink American ships. The more they sank the quicker the war would end, and then they could return to their wives and jobs and schools.

The tanker *Woodard*, its weather deck carrying German F4F rigid-wing Wildcat fighter planes and self-propelled 105mm heavy artillery rifles, was in von Seggern's crosswires. The other U-boats were also targeting their victims.

166

A radio signal from the *Tippelhehrt* would alert them. Von Seggern wanted the first torpedoes to strike simultaneously, to seriously cripple the convoy at the beginning of the attack.

Von Seggern pushed the voice tube toggle to communications. "Send the alert!" he said.

The alert was the single German word *Angreifen*, meaning "attack."

"*Angreifen!*" Communications Officer Fehreinger spoke into his transmitter.

Kapitän von Seggern began to count. "*Ein . . . zwei . . . drei . . .*" This would afford time for *Angreifen* to be received by the other U-boats and for their captains, their targets selected and in their scopes' crosswires, to order firing of the first torpedoes.

"Fire one. . . . Fire three. . . . Fire two. . . . Fire four!" von Seggern said over the scope speaker to Torpedo Officer Krutzmeier.

The powerful torpedoes hurtled out of the *Tippelhehrt's* forward tubes in the sequence von Seggern had ordered, a pattern designed to cause the least turbulence to the submerged U-boat.

At almost exactly the same moment, torpedoes sped from the forward tubes of the *Amselrudel's* other U-boats.

The *Tippelhehrt's* torpedoes tore into the tanker *Woodard's* port flank below her waterline. Their terrible explosions, deep inside the doomed ship, demolished her engine room and its crew, shattered bulkheads and compartments, killed more than half her crew, and set off horrendous fires.

The *Woodard*, flooding, rolled to port. "Abandon ship!" her captain, Merchant Marine Lieutenant Commander John L. Sundholm, shouted into the bridge speaker.

He turned to the other men in the bridge. "Son of a bitch!" he said bitterly. "We were almost there!"

He and the others ran out onto the deck, now tilting 20 degrees to port, into scenes of incredible confusion and horror. The torpedoes' explosions had blown great, gaping, jagged-edged holes in the deck plating. Flames shot up out of two of them.

Several men on the deck had been killed by the torpedoes' shrapnel or impaled by jagged steel slivers from the deck's punctures. Other men had been injured in varying degrees. Some had escaped injury. To these men Sundholm, a megaphone in his hands, bellowed, "Lower the starboard boats and rafts! Starboard! Not port!"

The ship was tilting even more. The Grummans and the 105mms were coming loose from their moorings. They began to slide off the deck. Two men who were lowering a port raft were crushed when the undercarriage of one of the big artillery pieces, sliding toward the sea, rolled over them.

The other men on the deck, including the helmsman and navigator who had been in the bridge with Sundholm, tried to lower the starboard rafts and boats. It was too late. The *Woodard* was now 35 degrees to port. The last of its Grummans and 105mm rifles had torn loose from their moorings and hurtled into the sea, sweeping off wounded men and several men who were trying to scramble up the sharply inclined deck.

Fires were raging in the tanker's mangled interior. The men on the deck could hear their crackling flames and the screams of men trapped below. "Let's get out of here!" Sundholm shouted to the men who had made it to the starboard rail and were gripping the rail to prevent a slide down the deck into the sea on its port side, where they would be in grave peril if the ship rolled over on them. "Jump out as far as you can," Sundholm said, looking at the sea, which seemed dangerously far below the upthrust starboard rail. "And then swim . . ."

He didn't say the rest of it. Gasoline from the tanker, whose bunkers had been filled with high-test aviation fuel, had spread around the ship, surrounding it, and had burst into flames.

"Oh, God," Sundholm said. It would be certain and agonizing death to leap into those flames. It would be death to remain on the sinking ship.

Sundholm, twenty-nine, a former mathematics teacher at Cincinnati's Alan Jason High School, gripped the starboard rail and looked out at the rest of the convoy. Seven ships had been torpedoed, maybe more. The troopship *Billy Clark* was sinking. It was east of the flaming gasoline's perimeter. The soldiers and men of its crew who had survived their ship's torpedoes were leaping into the sea. A destroyer-escort was speeding toward them and laying a smokescreen.

"Those damn Nazis were waiting for us," Helmsman Artie Sanders said, gripping the starboard rail, tears streaming down his cheeks, because he knew he would never again see his wife or his little daughter. He closed his eyes. "Goodbye, Karen," he said. "When our little girl is old enough to understand, tell her how much her daddy loved her."

He began to cry. Sundholm looked at him. Then he looked out over the carnage. "Goddam you Nazi murderers!" he screamed.

Something inside the doomed ship exploded. It blew a great gaping hole where Sanders and Sundholm and the others had been. Moments later the *Woodard's* battered, burning hulk sank into the rolling morning sea.

Similar tragedies were being enacted on the other torpedoed ships. Then the U-boats fired their reloaded torpedo tubes. The damage to the convoy's ships was almost beyond belief. "Surface!" Kapitän von Seggern said to his helmsman, and the message was relayed by the *Tippelhehrt's* radio to the other U-boats of the wolfpack.

The *Tippelhehrt's* conning came up out of the sea, awash with frothing water. Moments later the platform was above the sea. The conning's hatch opened and its deck gunners ran to their weapons followed by twelve Germans with MP38s (*Machinen Pistole* Model 38), murderous rapid-fire weapons called burp guns by Americans.

The *Tippelhehrt's* 6.5mm and 2cm Vierling gunners began to shell the deck of a tanker that had escaped the torpedoes. They shot off its bridge and its starboard AA rifles, annihilating the men in the bridge, the gun crews, and other men on the weather deck.

Meanwhile the *Tippelhehrt's* machine gunners and the twelve men with MP38s were firing at the Americans who had leaped into the sea, directing most of their fire at the soldiers who had abandoned the torpedoed troop ship and who were floating on the sea's rolling surface sustained by life jackets and pneumatic belts.

It was bestial and a violation of the Geneva Convention to shoot these helpless men, but Kapitän von Seggern had told his gunners, "Kill those *verdammt* Jew-lovers!"

While this bestiality was going on, von Seggern stood on his U-boat's platform, his arms folded, a smile on his craggy Teutonic face. *"Wunderbar!"* he said, his smile broadening.

169

The situation for the convoy was chaotic. Three ships were afire—a cargo ship and a troop transport. Two cargo ships were sinking. So was the destroyer *Robert Witmer*. Lt. Cmdr. Sundholm's ship had vanished. Also the gasoline tanker and the other troop transport. Both storeships were listing.

Many survivors were in overloaded lifeboats. The tumultuous wash of the destroyer *Linne*, speeding to lay a smokescreen between the U-boats and the crippled ships and the men in the water, capsized two lifeboats, flinging their occupants into the bloodied water.

Soldiers, Navy gunners, and merchant marine men in other boats, on rafts, and in the water died in great gory swaths as the Nazis' machine gun and MP38 bullets swept them.

Suddenly the *Linne* and the other destroyer turned toward the surfaced U-boats and sped toward them. "Go below!" von Seggern shouted to the men on the *Tippelhehrt*'s platform.

Quickly the *Tippelhehrt* and the other U-boats disappeared into the sea, then snaked out in all directions at their maximum underwater speeds of 16 knots.

Moments later the *Tippelhehrt*'s sound room reported, "Enemy ship starboard 10 degrees . . . 7 . . . 5 . . ."

"Stop engines!" von Seggern bellowed into the voice tube. "Shut off all electrical devices!"

The men in the *Tippelhehrt* could hear the destroyer's propellors. "Intensity of propellor sound is three," sound room reported. "Intensity two . . . intensity one . . . he's directly over us!"

"Stand by for depth charges!" von Seggern said. "Damage control parties man your stations!"

The propellor sounds faded. "That was a close one," von Seggern said, relief in his harsh Prussian voice. "Resume dive to 20 fathoms, then true toward our rendezvous!"

An hour later the *Tippelhehrt*, now 7 fathoms below the surface and many miles from the ambush, radioed the wolfpack's other U-boats. "*Naughty Virgin,* report! *Flying Star*, report! *Black Stallion*, report!"

This continued until requests for reports had been made to all of the *Rudel*'s boats.

Each of the U-boats reported that it was underway and on course. None reported damage or casualties.

170

"Wunderbar!" von Seggern said happily.

For the American convoy it had been a disaster. For the Nazi wolfpack, a tremendously successful attack.

A great victory for Germany!

Chapter Twenty-Four

After the savage attack on the American convoy the U-boat wolfpack fled to the "Nazi lake," the U-boat sanctuary between the Azores and the northwest shores of Morocco.

Here, in waters that Allied ships feared to enter, the *Tippelhehrt* and the other eight ships of Kapitän von Seggern's dreaded *Amselrudel* surfaced on a placid Atlantic sea.

The German service submarine *Ostertag* arrived a little later with diesel oil in a stern bunker, provisions of food and medicaments, torpedoes, ammunition for platform weapons, and parts for engine and gun repairs.

The *Ostertag* was an enormous, bulbous submarine, originally a troop and supply transport. In addition to her crew of thirty-four officers and men she had been designed to carry 120 troops and 70 tons of equipment. The space for the troops had been refitted into a recreation area for the benefit of crews of attack U-boats who had endured the emotional and physical stresses of long unrelieved periods of sea duty.

The Americans on the *Wasp*, dragging a beam trawl off the masquerading fishing boat's stern, came upon the wolfpack and the *Ostertag* the third day after a cryptogram from Captain Langer had told them of the wolfpack's bloody attack on Convoy 711, and that the wolfpack would probably appear in the Nazi sanctuary for provisioning, particularly of its torpedoes. "That's the wolfpack we want," Langer had concluded.

"Well, there's the Katzenjammer kids," Lt. Marlatt said to the other Americans, all of them pretending to be involved with the duties of a fishing crew.

"I can't say that I'm the happiest guy in the U.S. Navy," Joe Silva said.

"This is no time to run out of guts," Guns Haney said,

looking at the U-boats while he pretended to be mending a trawl.

"Nobody said they were running out of guts," Silva said. "What I meant was, that's a hell of a lot of U-boats for one PT to tackle."

"It sure is," Marlatt said. "But we're going to tackle them. And then we're going back to Pico."

"That's the old team spirit, coach," Silva said.

Since the arrival of the cryptogram from Langer the sea guerrillas had rehearsed their attack strategy, each man at attack station and pretending to be firing his weapon.

Pollard, the *Wasp*'s helmsman, hadn't rehearsed his part, though, which would be full-throttle speeding around and between the U-boats while the others fired their weapons.

Such a performance would have aroused the curiosity of legitimate fishing boats and, more important, the German aircraft and surface ships that Nazi Admiral Karl Doenitz had ordered into surveillance of the sanctuary with instructions to find and destroy the phantom American submarine that was destroying U-boats.

No German had suspected that the phantom U-boat killer was the masquerading fishing boat that was, at this moment, wallowing within attack range of the wolfpack.

Kapitän von Seggern, alerted to the hazard of the phantom American submarine, had ordered deck watches on all boats of the surfaced *Rudel* and constant vigilance by their hydrophone officers. "I want to be informed of the slightest suggestion of the approach of any submerged craft!" he said to these men.

Von Seggern, standing on the *Tippelhehrt*'s platform, a long black cigar between his teeth, looked out at the surrounding seas. Nothing but that fishing boat. He looked at it with binoculars. He wondered if they had women aboard. Sometimes they did. Once he had watched a shapely young Portuguese woman bathing from a bucket on the bow, not caring that he was looking at her.

It had been interesting. She had bathed in a most provocative way. Von Seggern lowered the binoculars. No women on the miserable little boat. Just its crew.

Oh, well, he reflected, he'd do more than just look at a woman when they went back to St. Nazaire. He'd find that curvaceous little French girl again. Yvonne her name was. She was really something. She knew all the tricks.

Von Seggern was smiling. Everything was going his way. The attack on the convoy had been successful beyond his most optimistic projections. The weather here in the sanctuary was delightful. The crisp sea air smelled good. Soon he'd go over to the *Ostertag* with the other captains and play ball in its recreation area, then feast on a fresh meat and vegetable dinner in the transient officers' wardroom with bottles of cold beer to wash it down.

The *Wasp* was in attack position. Lt. Marlatt, a cigarette dangling between his lips, sauntered into his decrepit-appearing little deck house. Pollard was at the wheel. Silva stood behind his Oerlikon 20mm rifle. Haney was looking through the 3-inch rifle's aperture. McLean, who would be Haney's loader, stood beside two open boxes of 3-inch shells.

"Everybody ready?" Marlatt said, the cigarette bobbling.

"Everybody ready," Silva said.

The deck was ready, too, except for Lt. Marlatt, who would man the forward .50-caliber twinned machine guns. Schilling and Broughton were on the stern, their depth charge apparatus loaded, a seine thrown over it to conceal it from the Germans.

Broughton was near the depth charge launcher's trigger. Schilling was beside the aft .50s. He would hose the U-boats' decks in the first phase of the attack, and after Broughton tossed the depth charges he would help him reload, then return to his machine guns, repeating this procedure.

Each man was tense, realizing that this might be the last day of his life, that even in minutes he could be dead. Each man had his second station if another was killed or severely wounded. "If it comes down to just three of us who can still function," Lt. Marlatt had said, "get the hell out!" Three men could do little to the remaining U-boats, and if they attempted further attrition they would be annihilated, and for no real good to their cause.

"The go is five seconds," Marlatt said to the men in the deck shack. Five seconds would give him time to get to the forward machine gun and jerk away the phony wooden bait box that covered it.

He went out to the bait box and very quickly lifted it off the twinned .50-caliber machine guns and swung the gun's sights toward the wolfpack. A fraction of a moment later Haney pulled the 3-inch rifle's lanyard, Silva began

174

to fire his 20mm Oerlikon, and Marlatt and Schilling opened fire with their twinned .50s.

Haney's first projectile, aimed squarely at the open hatch of the *Seeteufel*, exploded on contact with the conning's plating opposite the hatch. Shrapnel from the powerful high-explosive shell mangled bodies, scopes, phones, and voice tubes in the compartment below the conning, including the conning's aluminum ladder. At the same time the steel nose of Haney's shell tore a gaping, jagged-edged hole in the conning.

Meanwhile a bow-to-stern swath of Lt. Marlatt's .50-caliber bullets swept the Germans off the *Seeteufel*'s platform, including its commandant, Kapitän Oskar Kresge.

The *Seeteufel*'s Executive Officer Willie Onstadt, thirty-four, who was in the U-boat's head, came running into the demolished compartment accompanied by Navigation Officer Hans Wittenauer, who had been shaving.

"Jesus Christ . . ." Onstadt babbled, looking at the destruction and the mangled bodies while he buttoned his pants. He had been sustaining his pants with his left hand because he hadn't taken time to do more than hurriedly use toilet paper back there in the officers' head.

"What the hell happened?" Wittenauer said.

"We're under air attack! Christ, can't you hear it? Get the two tallest men you can find, and have one of them stand on the shoulders of the other and close that hatch!"

"I'm going to order emergency dive!"

Ensign Max Fischbach and Seaman 1/K. Kurt Lehmann were the *Seeteufel*'s tallest men, both six feet three. "I'll stand on your shoulders," Ensign Fischbach said, thinking it would be inappropriate for an enlisted man to stand on his shoulders.

Soon the ensign's head was even with the lower part of the conning's hatch. *"Mein Gott!"* he croaked, staring at the hole in the plating opposite the hatch.

He looked down at Lehmann. "We can't dive!" he said excitely. "They shot a hole in the conning! Right across from the hatch!"

"Jesus! We've already started the dive!" Lehmann croaked, his eyes wild. In another moment the conning would be below the surface, and if that stupid ensign up there didn't at least close the hatch, water would pour into the *Seeteufel* from two big openings.

"Close that hatch!" he bellowed, looking up at the ensign. "We've got to warn—"

He didn't finish. The ensign's head had suddenly vanished. Joe Silva had seen the big German peeking out the conning. He had swung his Oerlikon toward him. Its 20mm bullets reduced the ensign's head to a hideous pinkish-gray mist which sprayed on out the hole in the conning opposite the hatch.

"Mein Gott!" Lehmann babbled, staring up at the decapitated ensign. Then blood gushed up from the ensign's neck, his knees buckled, and he fell down onto the seaman who had been sustaining him and who had been too shocked by it all to step aside and let the corpse fall onto the deck.

"Jesus Christ . . ." Lehmann croaked, staring at the ensign's headless corpse while he wiped the dead man's blood from his face. He had never seen anything like it. It was almost unbelievable. Here was a man with whom he had been talking just a couple seconds ago and now, all at once, he didn't have his head.

Water poured down onto the stunned seaman. It brought him to the realities of the situation. "I've got to find somebody and tell them to stop diving!" he babbled.

Lehmann, his eyes wide, terror on his broad peasant face, wallowed through the bloodied seawater, already lapping over the hatch's coaming, toward navigation. He had to tell Lt. Onstadt or somebody to surface before it was too late.

It was already too late. The *Seeteufel* could no longer surface. She could only continue to fill with water and sink, drowning her men like rats in a trap.

Kapitän von Seggern, the wolfpack's Hauptsächlich was more fortunate than the *Seeteufel's* machine-gunned CO. He had been leaning against the conning, on its shady side, smoking a big black cigar, when the attack began. He darted around the conning and dived through its open hatch, escaping by a fraction of an inch the sweep of .50-caliber machine gun bullets that shot everyone else off the *Tippelhehrt's* platform and damaged its guns.

"It's that goddam fishing boat!" he squeaked, picking himself up off the deck below the conning's hatch.

"Get up there and close that hatch!" he bellowed to the chief petty officer at the chart bench.

The chief petty officer climbed the conning's ladder. He

fell back, the top of his head removed by machine gun fire.

"You get up there and close that hatch!" von Seggern bellowed to the enlisted man, Klaus Schneider, nineteen, who had been polishing the air scope's lenses.

"No, sir!" Schneider said, staring, his mouth hanging open, at the chief petty officer's half head. It was making him sick, looking at the chief's brains, but he couldn't keep from looking.

"That is a direct order!" von Seggern screamed.

"No, sir . . . they'll kill me, too!"

Von Seggern jerked the Walther 9mm pistol from the holster on his hip. He shot the recalcitrant seaman twice in his young scared face. Then he darted over to the sea scope. He looked into it. "Thirty degrees port! Emergency speed!" he shouted into the electronic speaker.

He switched the speaker's toggle to torpedo room. "Stand by to fire forward tubes!" he bellowed.

A torpedo in that phony fishing boat's belly would damn quick end its attack, he reflected, his jaw squared.

He looked back into the sea scope. "Damn!" he said, his teeth clenched. It had been shot off somewhere topside. He could see nothing. He cursed bitterly. The *Tippelhehrt* was blind! He couldn't destroy an enemy he couldn't see. He couldn't dive, either, with the hatch open.

"I'll get it closed!" he muttered.

He would keep sending men up that ladder to close it, no matter how many got their heads shot off. One of them, at the end of a burst, would be able to close it.

Pollard had fired a 3-inch high-explosive shell into each of the U-boat's connings. This had been Priority One of his part of the attack. "Make it impossible for the bastards to dive," Lt. Marlatt had said.

He had completed this duty and now was lobbing HEs into the *Ostertag*, the big supply submarine.

There were no living Nazis on any of the U-boats' platforms. The *Wasp*'s machine gunners had shot them off with their opening bursts, going from one U-boat to another without breaking fire.

Meanwhile Silva had destroyed the U-boats' scopes, immediately transferring his Oerlikon's fire to the destruction of deck rifles and machine guns and blowing up the ammunition in its platform watertights.

The *Wasp* hadn't escaped injury. A *Naughty Virgin*

twin 2cm Vierling gunner had fired a short burst into her in the instant before Silva fragmented him with a sweep from the Oerlikon. None of the Americans had been killed, or even wounded.

The sudden, ferocious attack had caught the Germans in total surprise. The *Wasp*, zigzagging among the U-boats at great speed, had been a frustrating target for Nazi gunners in the few moments before they were wiped off their platforms.

Each of the U-boats attempted emergency dives. The three that succeeded were peppered with Torpex depth charges. They blew up in geysers of fragmented men and metal.

The *Fliegendstern*, unable to dive because her rudder had been mangled by one of Haney's 3-inchers, was destroyed by depth charges hurled against her flank. They blew enormous rents in her plating. She sank quickly.

The *Dunkelhengst* rammed another U-boat, the *Unerschrocken* ("Dauntless"), while both were 3 fathoms below the surface. The *Unerschrocken*, her starboard flank pierced, sank immediately. The *Dunkelhengst* surfaced stern first and listing to port, her water-filled bow below the surface. The *Wasp* flung a Torpex depth charge against her keel. She exploded in a horrendous burst of orange-and-black flames.

The big fat supply submarine, *Ostertag*, was listing to port, her bow 30 degrees toward the sky, diesel oil spurting from her ruptured bunker. No point in wasting more shells on that one, Haney decided.

Suddenly the forty replacement torpedoes in the racks on the *Ostertag*'s bulkheads exploded. The big U-boat and the men of its crew who had survived the *Wasp*'s attack were blown skyward in minute fragments of flesh and metal.

A great wave, created by the holocaustic explosion, rolled toward the *Wasp*. "Jesus!" Pollard croaked. The wave was twice the height of the *Wasp*. He accelerated the little boat's three powerful engines to their maximum and spun the wheel to port.

He outran the wave, the *Wasp* up on its tail like a scared rabbit, the men on the deck hanging onto their gun mounts to keep from sliding off the sharply tilted deck.

Chapter Twenty-Five

Only one U-boat was still on the sea's bloodied surface. It was the *Tippelhehrt*. Her 6.5cm deck gun tilted skyward at a useless angle. Her twin four-barrel Vierlings, fore and aft on the platform, had been blasted off their mounts and shot out into the sea by Silva's 20mm Oerlikon.

The big U-boat was unable to dive. She would flood. Haney had shot a hole in her conning too jagged for her damage control men to repair even with an emergency plate and welding equipment.

The great wave created by the explosion of the supply submarine's torpedoes, followed by waves of diminishing heights, had tossed the *Tippelhehrt* like an empty bottle. Kapitän von Seggern and the men of his command had been thrown from one bulkhead to another. The *Tippelhehrt* became a shambles of loose gear. Gauges broke, petcocks spurted, cork flew from overhead. Two men were injured by flying objects, and Leutnant Hans Kretschmer, twenty-four, was killed.

He had been thrown violently from port to starboard in communication. A sharp steel filing toggle on the starboard bulkhead impaled him between his shoulders. He hung there, his eyes crossed, blood dribbling from the corners of his gaping mouth, his hands fluttering.

With each roll of the big U-boat, seawater had poured through the conning's perforation and open hatch. Von Seggern and the others were terrified. It was a situation about which they could do nothing, and they would drown if it continued.

But soon the *Tippelhehrt* no longer rolled and tossed. The waves launched by the supply boat's explosion had run their course. "Climb up that ladder and tell me what you see!" von Seggern barked to burly Seaman 1/K. Hasso Schleiger.

Schleiger climbed the conning's ladder. He peeked out

the hatch, only his eyes above its coaming, and then he looked out the jagged hole Haney's 3-inch rifle had blasted through the conning's wall.

"We're the only U-boat!" he yelled down to von Seggern. "That damn fishing boat is still there, though. About 600 meters off our port stern at 20 degrees."

"How do the deck guns look?" von Seggern demanded.

"The Vierlings are gone. The 6.5 is sticking up like a wedding prick, but it looks to me like it can be fixed."

"Pull your head down but stay up there," von Seggern said.

He looked at the deck. He was standing in a horrid mixture of seawater and blood from the man he had killed and from the three decapitated bodies of men he had ordered up the ladder before the exploding torpedoes' waves hit the big U-boat. Their bodies, barely covered by the water, were sliding back and forth with the U-boat's roll.

"Pump this water out of here!" he bellowed to an officer who had been watching Schleiger climb the ladder. "And rack these bodies over in the corner, there!"

He looked up at Schleiger. "Where's that fishing boat now?"

Schleiger peeked out the hatch. "It looks to me like it's right where it was. I can see men walking around on its deck."

"What are they doing?"

"Nothing. They're just looking at us."

Von Seggern's brow furrowed while he thought about the options that were available to him. He couldn't dive. He couldn't outrun that masquerading American Navy PT boat. He couldn't destroy it with gunfire because his deck rifle had been damaged. There was just one thing he could do . . . he could torpedo that damn American boat!

He went to the bulkhead's speaker. "Prepare to fire forward tubes!" he said to his torpedo officer.

Then he ordered his executive officer, Korvettenkapitän Karl Schultz, thirty-seven, to report immediately. After Schultz, who came running, arrived in the compartment below the conning tower von Seggern said, "I'm going to torpedo that tricky American! I'll climb the ladder and give you directions to relay to the helmsman—our scopes are *gebrochen* so we can't use them. When I've got the bow in the direction of the Americans I'll tell you. You will immediately order forward torpedo room to fire a

180

four-tube salvo. Then tell them to reload just as fast as they can for another salvo!"

The Americans on the *Wasp* had been elated that only the *Tippelhehrt* remained on the surface after their attack on the Nazi wolfpack.

"Let's get up a little closer and kill that Kraut and then go home," Lt. Marlatt said.

It would be like shooting a duck in a rain barrel, he said. "They can't dive. They can't shoot back. They can't outrun us."

"I've got some bad news," Haney said. "We're out of 3-inch ammo. I don't have even one shell left."

Marlatt's lips became tight. He looked over at the *Tippelhehrt*. "Here's what we'll do. We'll run up fast and toss Torpexes against her flank."

Those depth charges, he said, would blow the surfaced U-boat out of the water.

"There's just one thing the matter with that idea," Schilling said, lighting a cigarette. "We don't have any more depth charges."

"Christ . . ." Marlatt said. It was a unique opportunity to sink a Nazi U-boat and they had nothing to sink it with.

"Well, then," Marlatt said, "we'll go home. The Krauts can't follow us."

He turned to Haney. "You got their screw and rudder, didn't you?"

"I can't be sure," Haney said. "We were doing figure-eights and I was shooting at all those Kraut boats just as fast as possible. I don't know for positive if I got that specific one. As fast as we were laying it onto them and zooming around all the time there's just no way to tell."

Marlatt said the situation was nothing to worry about. "We'll sucker them with a feint toward the northeast. Toward Gibraltar. We'll soon break contact with speed. There's no way they can keep up with us."

He ordered Pollard to get underway on the feint course at maximum 50 knots for ten minutes, then zigzag at service speed for twenty minutes. "By then we'll be over the horizon, after which we'll head for home."

"I've got some more damn lousy news," Pollard said. "Which I just found out. One of their slugs punctured our fuel tank. We lost everything down to the hole. We've just

181

barely got enough juice to make it home with one engine. And at no more than 12 knots."

"Goddam!" Marlatt muttered, biting his lips.

Joe Silva had been watching the U-boat. "They're swinging their bow toward us!" he yelled. "They're going to torpedo us!"

Everyone looked over at the *Tippelhehrt*. "Take us forward!" Marlatt said quickly, turning to Pollard. "And kick it!"

Pollard ran into the deck shack, and a moment later the *Wasp* was 40 degrees off the U-boat's bow, which caused Kapitän von Seggern, standing on his conning's ladder, to curse bitterly. "If the bastards hadn't moved I'd have had them in just 2 more degrees!"

Pollard swung the wheel toward Pico Cove, and a minute later Silva said, "They're following us, Mr. Marlatt!"

Marlatt ran into the deck house. "Keep watching them!" he said to Pollard. "Zig and zag so we're never in line with their bow!"

"I don't think we've got gas enough for all the way back if I've got to zigzag."

"We'll have to take the chance! If we don't, if they line us up and fire a spread, we're a bunch of dead heroes in small pieces."

Marlatt went back onto the deck. He looked at the U-boat again. It was still following the *Wasp*. "There goes our secret hideout," Haney said.

"That's not our immediate problem," Marlatt said, his face very grim. "After nightfall they'll try to fix that big deck gun. If they can do it they can wipe us out. So hope for a moonlit night. If we get one, Silva, here, can keep them from working on that damn gun."

"The first Kraut comes out on that platform," Silva said, "gets the old Oerlikon treatment."

He had plenty of ammunition, he added. "So that's one thing we don't have to worry about."

Kapitän von Seggern climbed down from the conning's ladder. His face was livid. Those tricky Americans were driving him *verrückt*. "Get up on that ladder, Langemeier," he said to a boatswain's mate, "and keep us on their tail!"

If he couldn't do anything else to that disguised boat up

there, he said, he could at least find its lair and radio the location to U-Waffe Command.

He decided he would radio U-Waffe Command right now with another message. He strode aft toward the code room. He was raging. Nothing had gone right since the Americans had attacked. Not one damn thing!

He stepped over the code room's coaming. "Connect me with those incompetent idiots at U-Waffe Command!" he bellowed.

A moment later a radioman held up a transmitter's microphone. Von Seggern snatched it out of his hand. "This U-Waffe Command?" he bellowed.

"Yes, sir," a communications officer said. "Please transmit with appropriate cryptograph!"

"Fuck it!" von Seggern shouted. "Who told us to watch for a phantom American submarine? It was an American Navy PT disguised like a Portuguese fishing boat, you *Dummkopfs*. It destroyed my wolfpack! Every boat except mine!"

He slammed the speaker into its cradle. "If those morons call me back," he said to the radioman, a Leutnant 3/K., "tell them, even if it's Doenitz himself, to stick it up their ass!"

"Yes, sir," the Leutnant squeaked.

He would tell Admiral Doenitz no such thing. He didn't know what he would tell him, or whoever responded to von Seggern's intemperate outburst. He would try to think of something, though. A tremor snaked down his spine. He had never seen von Seggern in such a rage. He was mean even when he was nice, but now he was practically a slavering beast.

Night came. The moon was bright. There were few clouds. "Don't let them repair that gun, for chrissake," Marlatt said. "Don't let them even get close to it."

"Don't worry about it, Mr. Marlatt," Silva said. "I'll hamburger the bastards if they even think about crawling out on that platform."

Marlatt has certainly got a case of nerves, Silva reflected, his eyes on the U-boat's platform, his Oerlikon ready to fire. He keeps looking at the sky all the time, worrying that a German plane will give us the bananas. And he keeps measuring our gasoline, trying to figure if we've got enough to make it to Pico Cove.

About an hour after the last light of dusk, two Germans

183

crawled out of the conning's hatch and slithered toward the 6.5 rifle. "That's a no-no, you dumb Krauts," Silva said.

He pulled the Oerlikon's trigger. The Germans' suddenly fragmented bodies were swept off the platform by his aft-to-stern sweep with the Oerlikon's 20mm bullets.

Twice more during the night, von Seggern tried to sneak gun repair crews out to the deck rifle. Both times Silva annihilated them with sweeps of his fast-firing Oerlikon.

The U-boat kept following the *Wasp*. "They won't come into the cove," Marlatt said, "but they'll try to keep us trapped in there until their bombers show up."

"What about those dudes at our airstrip on São Miguel giving that U-boat the one-two before we get there?" Silva asked. "Or aren't we on the same team?"

"We're still officially on secret detached duty," Marlatt explained. "Which means we're strictly on our own."

"Well, hell, they came out and got those Kraut prisoners we were towing."

"Don't try to figure it," Marlatt said. "I don't understand it either. Anyway, it will make no difference if we run out of juice before we get home. Those Krauts will dance around us until they repair that deck gun, then blow us to wherever brave American Navy men go."

"I wish there was a filling station out here someplace," Silva said.

"So do I," Lt. Marlatt said, his lips tight.

The *Wasp* glided into the cove an hour before dawn. The *Tippelhehrt* didn't follow the *Wasp* into it but stopped just outside the volcanic overhangs which framed its narrow entrance.

The Nazis, no longer in peril of the *Wasp*'s Oerlikon, began to repair their powerful platform rifle, finishing soon after the sun came up. They fired into the cove, then angled the gun's muzzle to port and fired again, then starboard of dead center.

"Do it again," Kapitän von Seggern said to his gunners. "But fire three each way from center, and spread them so we cannot possibly miss that damn American boat!"

Their fire did not even scratch the *Wasp*. It had turned sharply starboard from the cove's entrance, then starboard again, the cove bulging seaward for several yards at this point. No gunfire from outside the cove's narrow mouth could reach a boat in this little refuge.

"We'll make them think they got us," Lt. Marlatt said. "We'll make some smoke and explode something. And then, if they fall for it . . ."

He explained what they would do if they succeeded in suckering the *Tippelhehrt* into the cove.

The *Wasp* had been fitted with a smokescreen generator. The crew had not had occasion to use it, but each man had been taught how it worked, because any of them might sometime have to put it into operation.

Soon it was emitting thick black smoke. Silva fired erratic bursts from his Oerlikon onto the cove's rocky walls which echoed and re-echoed, creating the effect of uncontrolled explosions.

"We got them!" von Seggern said excitedly. "Those tricky Americans weren't so damn clever after all!"

He decided to take the *Tippelhehrt* into the cove. It would be a sheltered place to hide while his damage control men torched off the jagged edges Haney's shell had made in the conning and welded a steel plate over it. Then the *Tippelhehrt* would be able to cruise under the sea's surface.

The *Tippelhehrt* began to glide into the cove. Six men were on its platform with MP38s. If any of the Americans were still alive they would stitch them with murderous bursts from these fast-firing machine pistols.

"Let them get in just a little bit more," Lt. Marlatt said to Silva, both of them lurking in the *Wasp*'s deck shack.

Soon the *Tippelhehrt* was totally in the cove. "Go!" Marlatt said to his tough little Oerlikon gunner.

Silva swept the U-boat's platform. The six Germans, chopped across their chests, died before they realized the Americans had ambushed them.

Immediately the other five men of the *Wasp*'s little crew leaped onto the *Tippelhehrt*'s sea deck from the rock ledge on the island flank of the cove's entrance. They tossed cans and bottles of gasoline—all that had been left in the *Wasp*'s tank—down the U-boat's conning. Then Haney fired a magnesium flare into it.

Instantly a great whooosh of yellow and silvery flames shot out from the conning.

The Americans didn't take time to admire this colorful pyrotechnic. They jumped back onto the ledge, scrambled over the rock wall's summit, and dived down its opposite side.

Silva and Lt. Marlatt were already there. "Hang onto your front teeth," Silva said, hugging the rock wall. "That baby's going to blow like Gabriel blew his horn."

The Americans could hear the screams of Kapitän von Seggern and the other trapped Nazis for several tense moments before the *Tippelhehrt*'s torpedoes exploded with a detonation that fragmented the big U-boat.

After the cove's geysered water no longer rained down on the Americans, they peered over the crest of the rock wall. There was no trace of the *Tippelhehrt* or her crew.

The last U-boat of the mighty wolfpack was now kaput.

Epilogue

After the seven young Americans on the masquerading PT destroyed the German U-boat fleet's vaunted blackbird wolfpack, Admiral Karl Doenitz ordered his *Unterseeboots* to stay out of the Atlantic between the Azores and the coasts of Morocco and the Iberian Peninsula, the U-Waffe's former lake.

This removed U-boats from their most effective sanctuary, the place from which devastating attacks against Allied shipping had been launched. For the Nazis it was a costly situation; Allied material and troops would now be able to proceed with insignificant interference.

Something clearly had to be done. The Germans ordered the Portuguese government, though neutral and not subject to German orders, to withdraw the more than 10,-000 Portuguese fishing boats from Atlantic and Mediterranean waters.

The Portuguese refused. An important segment of their economy depended upon their fishing fleets.

The Germans tried to intimidate Dr. Antonio Salazar, Portugal's dictator-president. Withdraw those boats or we will shell every one on sight, they told Salazar.

If you sink even one of our unarmed fishing boats, Dr. Salazar replied, you will force us into the war on the Allied side.

This presented the Nazis with a dilemma of great significance. Allied airfields in Portugal would end the U-boats' forays. Best to keep Portugal neutral.

It was a humiliating situation for the Nazis. One disguised little American Navy boat was keeping their mighty U-boat fleet virtually immobilized. Find that *verdammt* boat and destroy it, they ordered the Luftwaffe.

German fighters and bombers, badly needed elsewhere, searched for the *Wasp*. They were searching for a phantom. The *Wasp* had been so severely damaged by the ex-

187

plosion of the *Tippelhehrt*'s torpedoes in Pico Cove that it was towed out to sea and sunk by gunfire from the destroyer-escort *Marsh*.

Unaware of this development, Nazi airmen kept searching for the *Wasp* in the former U-boat sanctuary. It was frustrating. There were hundreds of Portuguese fishing boats and they looked alike. Further frustrating the German airmen, they had strict orders not to shell or bomb a bonafide Portuguese fishing boat.

While German diplomats tried to coerce, intimidate, persuade, or cajole the Portuguese government, and while German airmen continued to search for a masquerading PT that no longer existed, American and British technicians worked hurriedly on the final development of sonar. It was, at last, an effective submarine warning system—its ultrasonic detectors could pick up meaningful rebounds of impulses sent out from its apparatus.

While the Nazis were still squabbling with Dr. Salazar's government, American and British ships were quickly and secretly equipped with sonar devices and assigned trained men to operate them.

By the time the Germans got around to sending their U-boats out again, American and British ships were no longer the rabbits of the sea.

The era of the wolfpack had ended.